MW01133538

The Granny Witch Apprentice

By

R.R. Roberts

The Granny Witch Apprentice
Author R.R. Roberts
ISBN-13: 978-1724655233
ISBN-10: 172465523X

This is a work of fiction. Names, characters, and their interactions with the places expressed in this story are the products of the author's imagination or are used fictitiously. Any resemblance to actual persons, living or dead, is entirely coincidental.

For my grandmother, and the times spent picking blackberries at the cemetery.

Buy, sell or trade
2 for 1 trade

CINDY'S OPEN BOOK

Shipshewana booth 438   260-993-2401

Introduction

Growing up, I loved going to visit my great grandmother on her farm in Eastern Kentucky. Summer afternoons were spent wandering though fields of tall grasses, and stumbling across deer that were hardly visible through the man sized rushes and sedges. Snowy winters meant rolling down the steep hill sides and running my fingers through the horses' thick winter coats to combat the cold.

The stories my great grandmother related about her childhood were guaranteed to be one part hilarity and one part catastrophe. She grew up in the cabin her father built near the edge of a spring fed cliff face, and described climbing down the cliff using an old rope ladder to collect water. If you ask any one of the old folks about Ice Cave, they've all explored the cavern at some point or another in their youth and insist it's filled with solid ice all year long. Of course, as it goes with all legends, the only ones who still know how to find it are either passed on or too old to make the trek. I grew up hearing lots of stories and legends like this, including ones about water witches. Sitting around the table playing rummy, or watching song birds from the front porch were the best times to catch a glimpse into the little known memories of my great grandmother's life.

While parts of this story are tales I grew up hearing, the majority of this narrative is modeled after historical events. This novel is an episodic journey into a year of one young woman's life in 1805. While the characters themselves are fictional, their relationships and the events that connect each chapter are very much a part of history.

The greatest technical challenge of writing this book proved to be the nature of spoken word. A person's cadence offers a level of complexity from a person's community and culture that is not easily captured in a way that honors the voice on paper. English speaking European immigrants spoke differently than their American born children. Indigenous peoples learning English as a second language interacted with European immigrants also learning English as a second language. The inhabitants of eastern Kentucky maintain unique colloquialisms from their neighbors to the west. African American Vernacular English, and Smokey Mountain English utilize distinct syntax from General American English.

How can each community represented in this story be honored without causing detriment by way of linguistics? To write a spoken accent is to forsake written Standard English. To exclude a spoken accent is to erase someone's voice. I addressed the challenge through compromise: No word is spelled the way it might sound, because ultimately I will never know with certainty how someone in 1805 in any given social circumstance may have spoken. However, measurable grammar rules identify standard conjugations of Smokey Mountain English, African American Vernacular English, and General American English. By following these rules, distinct communities can each be represented more richly within the context of *The Granny Witch Apprentice.*

Grammar aside, it was difficult to quiet my 21st century feminism in the narrative. Ona's relationship to Enda Cambor could not flourish without experiences that reshape her biases. At first, I was slow to plug in those growing pains; but to ignore them would be to minimize the experiences of people navigating relationships during the period of anti-miscegenation laws. It took more than one try to strike the balance in Ona's character development that allowed for growth from prejudices, without creating a tale of the savior complex.

The history of Kentucky's formative years is both beautiful and tragic. Why bother telling a story that takes place in such a difficult time? The land was transformed in a very short amount of time from grassland and forest, to sprawling cities with a prosperous Southern market. I wanted to share a small piece of Kentucky's story that connects readers to a time and place that continues to impact the commonwealth as we know it today.

There is no such thing as being blessed, we simply reap from the hard work and sacrifices of those who came before us.

Acknowledgments

I have been afforded such meaningful people in my life that the word 'friend' hardly scrapes the surface. They are music chasing, bourbon sipping, dumpster diving, contra dancers. The conversations that occur over the chaos of too many dogs wrestling at our feet are irreplaceable.

Together with our trusty pups, we have navigated damp caves beneath a mile of bedrock. Our spirits stirred with goose bumps on the hallowed ground at Cane Ridge. We hiked steep hills in search of forgotten cemeteries and old tavern ruins along abandoned turnpikes, using the words "book research" as an opportunity to gain new life experiences.

Thank you for offering advice, reassurance, and editing expertise leading up to moment when it was time to take a breath and jump. This story would never have come to fruition without the love and support from such fine ladies, and without the plot altering wisdom of one man well versed in the words of Stokely Carmichael.

Thank you to Anna Wiker-Piecynzski, Laura Murphy, Megan Martin, Clare Wiker, and Ben Staton for all of your patience, encouragement, and hard work in helping bring this story to life.

Table of Contents

Chapter 1 1

Chapter 2 11

Chapter 3 19

Chapter 4 58

Chapter 5 76

Chapter 6 106

Chapter 7 132

Chapter 8 142

Chapter 9 165

Chapter 10 179

Chapter 11 190

Chapter 12 206

Chapter 13 223

Chapter 14 253

Chapter 15 281

Chapter 16 300

Chapter 17 307

Chapter 1.

August 1805

Ona America Christie stirred at the clamor of voices outside the cabin. She stumbled out of her pallet bed up in the loft to investigate the peculiar commotion. Light flashed between the loose chinking of the roughhewn cabin. It bobbed up and down in a strange dance that left her with an uneasy feeling. Her thin summer quilt and empty pallet invited Ona to crawl into bed and fall back asleep. At fourteen, she was nearly grown and ought to have some sense. Ona wiped her messy red hair out of her face, bunched up her chemise, and descended down the ladder from the cabin loft.

Ona held her breath at the groaning ladder for fear of waking her godmother. She didn't have to worry about her steps on the bottom level; it was a dirt floor. She waited silently, listening for Fannie's loud snoring over in the corner before slipping out the door. Ona darted behind the cabin barefoot into the night. The grass was damp, the air being heavy with moisture so that a thick fog crept low upon the earth.

A great wilderness cradled the small cabin where Ona lived with her godmother, Fannie. Tonight, the property was lit by a small yellow fire gliding through the air. Through the darkness Ona could just make out the silhouette of an enormous dog. It stumbled in and out of the forest, crashing through shrubs growing in its path. It moved slowly as if it were injured. Ona's eyes grew wide in amazement as the animal slowly made its way back toward the forest, taking the dancing search light with it. The glowing fire of a lantern swayed curiously above, briefly illuminating the thick, wrinkled face of a big hound dog, and a gruff looking man chasing after it.

The man stopped in the middle of the yard, heaving himself up on a solitary headstone, reaching for his rifle. He carelessly plopped his lantern in the grass, illuminating words in the roughly carved marker that set where her head rested underground: *Abigail Grace Christie (1775-1792)*.

The man worked at jamming powder into his rifle before he reached into his weathered coat, revealing several round lead bullets weighing down his pockets. Shaking hands scattered lead rounds across the grave. He swore, launching himself off the headstone and unknowingly smearing mud with his feet across the name of Ona's mother. He scoured the grass for a single shot, eagerly scrambling upright once triumphant. The man fiddled with his lantern until the light blinked out and there was nothing but darkness.

Ona's feet started moving when she recognized the man. He was Jeremiah Sunday. According to Ona's father, Jeremiah Sunday was hit with an arrow in his chest during an Indian raid. His whole family was slaughtered and everyone thought old Sunday had been taken up to heaven with the rest of them. He was trapped in the woods unable to move, with his family lying dead around him for three days before a fur trader brought him back to town. Reverend Johnson said Jeremiah Sunday was blessed as anyone to be so lucky he survived. Fannie said he was the poorest man she ever saw.

Goose bumps bristled on Ona's arms. Jeremiah Sunday had no business tromping through people's property with no respect for the living or dead. Ona scanned the dim shapes of the yard, searching for Jeremiah Sunday's lamp light. She heard rustling from the earth cellar and men shouting. A short burst of light and a shot fired, ending with shattering pots, smashed jars and loud cries coming from inside. Ona's breath caught in her chest, and she hid behind a tree not knowing who the second voice belonged to.

The hound dog darted out from inside the dilapidated cellar, with a belt of small, colorful beads tied to its tail dragging the ground behind it. Jeremiah Sunday was quick to scramble after it. A young man Ona had never seen before crawled to the entrance of the cellar. Ona started in shock. His movements were tender, and pain played across his face in a deep frown. She moved toward the

3

injured man, stopping in her tracks when she realized he was Indian.

The man's stony gaze did not waver. Ona's stomach knotted up when she saw that he was staring at *her*. She swallowed her nerves and did not look away as she approached him. His fingertips were painted in fresh crimson liquid.

"You alright?" She ventured.

His lack of reaction made Ona feel braver. She bent to ease him off the ground into a sitting position, but when she touched his skin he jerked away, as if he had been touched by a hot iron. Ona examined him cautiously, wondering if he was dangerous. He wore a plain white shirt tucked into long pants and his hair was cropped short like any of the young men in Calico. He seemed nothing like the stories she heard from the Halstead kids who lived even farther out past Ona in the wilderness. Ona saw nothing immediately threatening about him, so she knelt gingerly beside the man, finding the source of blood pooling around him.

"Shot in the stomach. What a cruel way to die," Ona said softly.

Ona's words stirred something in him. He tried to stand up, but could not. Ona caught him before he hit the dirt floor. She draped his arm over her shoulder and guided him toward the cabin. He was a heavy burden. Fannie was brilliant with medicine plants and would be able to help. Although Fannie was training Ona in the same path of granny witching, Ona had never seen a person shot in the stomach before. They made their way slowly to the cabin.

"Fannie!" Ona whispered fervently. She lightly kicked the door, trying to make enough noise to wake up Fannie, keeping quiet enough in case Jeremiah Sunday was still around. The man weighed on Ona, his head slumping near her face. She could feel his strained breaths warm the side of her neck. Ona managed to wiggle the door open, grating against the dirt floor loud enough to finally disturb Fannie.

"Good gracious, Cricket!" Fannie cried. Her voice was gruff from years of smoking pipe and she spoke with a fading Scots-Irish accent.

"He's been shot, Fannie!"

"Obviously, girl. Get him on his back. He can't be upright like that!"

Fannie made quick work of herself, and Ona gathered tools to cauterize the wound. Fannie cast the end of her knife into the fire for several minutes before pressing it on the wound. The man didn't make a sound, but he passed out in Fannie's pallet. The old woman's blankets were soaked in blood and ash from the white hot blade. Ona dabbed his face with a wet rag.

"Is he gone make it, Fannie?"

Fannie stood with bloodied hands crossed over her thick arms and sighed. Her wispy, white hair was in complete disarray and her lips parted into a frown exaggerated by innumerable wrinkles.

"No."

"Where does he come from?"

"Hard telling, Cricket. Folks live out here in they own towns, separated from Calico by the ridge or the valley or the creek."

"But he's Indian, Fannie."

Fannie did not respond, but she cleaned her knife up with a rag. Ona heard lots of things from lots of different people about the Cherokee rumored to live near Calico mountain. Folks in Calico said they lived in secret communities and attacked the people in towns. Fannie said the Cherokee were benevolent people and would be good neighbors if the people of Calico stopped trespassing left and right and acting like murderous cowards. Fannie would know, she had lived with the Cherokee after all.

"Is he a good neighbor?" Ona's gray eyes fell on the man's chest moving up and down erratically.

"Your father gone to fight them over building that road through here. They don't want to quit their use of it after they promised to give it up." The Federal Road was to connect one end of the country to the other, and it needed to cut right down Indian lands to do it. Fannie rinsed her hands in the bowl of water at her bedside and wiped them on her apron. Ona examined the man more closely. His injuries made him seem smaller and less intimidating than the stories she'd heard.

"We at least made him more comfortable for his final hours. I'm too old for this kind of excitement. Wears me out," Fannie paused, watching the dying man breathe laboriously in her bed.

"Watch over him," she directed. The old woman ascended the ladder up to the loft. Creaky knees or not, Fannie was quick moving when she felt like it. Another shot fired outside the cabin. It sounded like the remains of the cellar collapsed.

"Don't go out there, Cricket," Fannie called. She was not worried by the activity; she seemed mostly agitated that her sleep was disturbed. The man began twitching, restless in his sleep. Ona touched her hand softly to his forehead.

"I'll be right back," Ona slipped out the door, venturing out into the night. The sight of the cellar was heartbreaking. Little wooden sticks and logs lay strewn about the yard in brittle pieces from where the cellar built into the hillside caved in. It was so much more than a cellar. Before the cabin was built, it was a half-face cabin where Ona took her first breath and where Abigail Christie breathed her last. She tried to swallow the knot in her throat. Most importantly, all of their food was in that cellar.

The hound dog sniffed around the debris, moving on unsteady legs with a gunshot wound on its neck. She took a step closer toward it, but the dog lifted its head and growled at her. Ona tried to keep calm. After all, it wasn't some monster that destroyed their cellar; it was just old Jeremiah Sunday.

"You alright, Mr. Sunday?" Ona's voice shook, calling out into the darkness.

Her whole body was in tremors. She didn't know if she should be on the watch for Jeremiah Sunday in the shadows, or the dog dragging the beaded belt in front of her. Ona sank to the ground in a crouch. She sat small and nonthreatening, watching the dog from the corner of her eye, before calling out again.

"Mr. Sunday? Are you there?"

The hound dog was much larger up close. The green glow of round eyes twinkling just out of reach became locked on her. Ona became electric, her pulse flooding her brain like a drum. The piercing gaze of the creature was calling out to her. The dog's paws were as big as Ona's own hands, and as they took steps nearer to her, the air became thick with a damp, soured odor that caught in Ona's throat.

Its long muzzle reached out to touch her with its wet nose. Was that a whimper? Ona could feel hot breaths panting on her skin with red saliva stringing down from the animal's mouth.

The eyes that followed her stirred within Ona's spirit, drawing upon the connection between people and dogs since times when humans were ancient and wild. She reached out with one hand mesmerized by the misery and sanctity of this creature when a final shot fired past her and into the forehead of the dog. As it dropped, Ona fell backwards to the ground, shrieking.

The first thing Ona noticed were his shaking hands. Jeremiah Sunday was mostly uninjured, though his face and hands were cut from broken rock and shattered jars that were waiting to be filled with the garden's bounty over the coming weeks.

"You messing with that ole hound dog, girl? You wasn't gone touch him was you?" Jeremiah's voice was rough. He sounded accusing.

"No, sir," Ona stammered, heart hammering through her chest.

"That beast is a-working for the Cherokee. A monster like that is liable to kill a young lady. Better to shoot straight, sweetheart." Sunday swayed on his feet and stunk like bitter corn whiskey.

"Yes sir, Mr. Sunday." Ona stared at her bare toes, and wriggled them against the moss on the ground. Her muscles strained with apprehension, waiting for him to answer for the destruction he brought upon the Christie house that night. Sunday had left Ona and Fannie to clean up the dying man, and left them not a bite to eat for the winter either.

"You best be moving along back to bed. Shit. You and that old witch probably got church in the morning."

Ona stood up slowly, taking steps backward to the house.

"That man. Why'd you do that to him?"

Jeremiah Sunday spat by his feet. "That Indian stole some slaves and went to selling them for his own profit. Now they loose I guess, but at least the dirty thief is caught. It was a public service." He slung his gun around his shoulder and started off toward the woods.

Ona called after him. "What about our food? It's all gone!" She balled her fists together, trying to steady her anger.

Jeremiah Sunday turned around to face her, eyes bloodshot under the starlit sky.

"Makes no difference to me, sweetheart." He disappeared into the trees, following no particular path, and whistling a cheerful tune.

Ona made sure she could no longer see Jeremiah Sunday's shadow before returning inside. Under the light of the moon shining through the cabin's loose chinked walls, she examined the dying man's face. His lips were dry and cracking. She sloshed red water out in the yard, filling up the bowl again with the last contents of the water pitcher. She soaked the still pink rag, wringing out droplets of water on the man's mouth. He stirred and she parted his lips to allow his parched tongue water.

Ona jumped when the man reached up suddenly, grabbing her arm. His fingers brushed over the back of her hand, and in an instant fell away as he succumbed to a fit of coughs. Ona eased to the opposite side of the room, curling up on the cool floor. Ona was certain her father would know what to do, but Rowland Christie was dispatched into the Western territory, where he had been fighting south through Tennessee for the past several months. Ona watched the man for a long while, but eventually the sound of the man's wheezing subsided and sleep overtook them both. Ona did not wake for the death rattle.

Chapter 2.

When Ona woke up that morning, the man was dead. She covered him with a sheet, waiting for Fannie to decide how to bury him. Ona sat on the cool cabin floor with a sweet drink in hand. Her muscles were coiled tight against the damp morning air. Her thick, unruly hair was jammed haphazardly inside her cotton cap, with wild red coils springing out around her face. Most folks were dutifully on their way to the Baptist Church, but not Ona or Fannie. Today they would bury the Cherokee man.

Ona inhaled the spicy, sour aroma of her drink: a combination of corn whiskey, ginger, sorghum, and vinegar. It was a favorite drink during late summer, to help keep farmers upright while they worked the end of harvest. Ona and Fannie didn't grow any crops besides the garden, but Fannie liked to make it this time of year anyway. Fannie said it reminded her of the hemp farm she worked with her late husband down in the fertile fields of the Bluegrass.

Fannie knew the name of each plant and animal in the mountains and she tutored Ona in the same way. The people of Calico called them granny witches. Fannie was well regarded around Calico for her profession as a midwife. She possessed skilled hands at producing remedies that cured most maladies. Fannie guarded her herb lore from most everyone, only revealing her craft to Ona little by little over the years.

Lessons with Fannie were different than lessons at school. A few times each month, Ona attended a makeshift Bible school at Calico Mission Church. Fannie was quite publicly on bad terms with the headmaster after he attempted to force Ona, along with several other children who lived far from town, to live at the church year-round instead of trekking the long commute into town each week.

When the Methodist church established three years ago and opened its doors as a school, Ona's father insisted she attend. Being fourteen, there were not many other students Ona's age. By this time, most of Ona's peers had dropped out to become apprentices or help around the farm or, as in the case of Nelly Mahoney, to get engaged.

Fannie used her own books to teach Ona, mostly ones she illustrated herself, about the plants of Eastern Kentucky. These books had no words though, since Fannie could not read or write. Fannie kept these books hidden to keep her profession safe, although periodically Ona was permitted to look through them.

Fannie entered the cabin from the outdoors, hiking up her stockings from under her soft blue dress. Strands of her wispy white hair were coming loose from thin braids hanging down the side of her face. Her skin was flush from work. Fannie was petite, plump, and aging, but still had all her strength. She seemed to be the opposite of Ona, whose thick red hair jutted out in every direction at her shoulders, refusing to be tamed. Like Fannie, Ona's body was strong after working around the cabin. She chopped wood, fetched the water, scrubbed the clothes, worked the garden and gathered up wild plants. Ona turned the garden by hand with a hoe, for they had no horse to plow, and spent her free time climbing trees.

"It's bad outside. Everything in the cellar is gone. We've got no crocks left unbroken. If I write, perhaps Rowland will send us something so we can put up what's left of the summer. We'll need to put out some fall potatoes, and if we get the turnips and cole crop going we can make it through the winter."

Ona mulled over this information in dreary silence. Fannie carried on sounding smug, "You never know, Mrs. Miller might catch her another cold and we always do make a fortune off them insufferable canker sores." Fannie winked, and her voice cackled in delight. She lived to barter. Fannie spoke with a faintly remembered Scots-Irish accent, a mark of time from the land where she was born. After spending so much time with the old woman, Ona barely even recognized it. Fannie lit a tobacco pipe and puffed silently. Her gnarled figure relaxed into the creaking rocking chair, which over time had worn smooth from use.

"I got started some on picking up the mess from last night." Fannie took another puff from her pipe and exhaled slowly.

Ona witnessed other kids from Calico lose their crop for one reason or another. People would give them what they could; but when winter settled in people could not afford to give any more. Fannie took care of the little ones in families like that when their skin became hot to the touch with fever and stretched tight across their bones. Families that lost their crop usually could make it if they had a gun. Ona's father was using their gun in the fighting for the Federal Road.

Rowland Christie arranged for Fannie to watch over Ona during periods of deployment long before he was dispatched to fight in the current conflict. Fannie had lived with the Christies for as long as Ona could remember. They shared a close bond. She was a kind, yet superstitious old woman who was quick witted and possessed great talent for both gardening and bickering.

Fannie made remedies for the sick and helped deliver the healthiest babies. She grew an impressive garden and knew where to find all the useful plants in the forest. She could cross sticks a certain way and find water underground; people called it water witching. That's why everyone in town called Fannie a granny witch. For all of Fannie's cleverness and all of Ona's resourcefulness, surely, they would not starve this winter. Ona swatted a fly on her arm, remembering the task at hand.

"We got to bury the dead man, Fannie."

"Oh?" Fannie blew out circles of smoke, frowning. "How do you suppose we do that?"

"What else can be done? We can't waste time, Fannie. Flies aside, what if old man Sunday comes back? You never saw him last night. He was mad."

"Tell us what you saw, Cricket." Cricket was what Fannie had called Ona from the day they first met, when Ona was barely three.

Ona related her encounters, from the altercation with Jeremiah Sunday down to the hound dog he killed. Fannie sat back in her rocking chair, eyes closed, considering Ona's information before speaking lightly.

"Well you know what they say: What is, will be, unless we set our minds for things to shake out differently." Sometimes Fannie was impossible. Fannie nearly always spoke in riddles and it could be exceptionally irritating when trying to get a straight answer from her. It was one requirement of being ancient. She was in for a long one this time.

"We fix our own truths, Ona. What if the man Sunday chasing was dangerous? It sounds like he was a thief. Say Jeremiah wasn't drunk or crazy, and you already said you smelled the stuff on him, but say it was just Sunday trying to right a wrong? What would be your choices now? Bury them and forget it? Confront Sunday? Tell the people in town about the missing slaves?" Fannie listed off each option on her knobby fingers.

"I don't know what we should do," Ona shook her head.

"Cricket, you found the Indian man. He's your burden and you got to see it through."

Ona did not know the man who died. She didn't know if he was a criminal or an innocent person. He was a trespasser, but so was Jeremiah Sunday. Ona shared Fannie's thoughts that it might be possible to live peacefully with their Cherokee neighbors, but the old folks of Calico described endless conflicts years before so that there was hardly any Cherokee left to be neighbors with.

Jeremiah Sunday didn't need any more trouble. He was a miserable, unhappy man who lived at the edge of Calico all by himself. He would make an easy target for ill meaning people; and who knows, maybe he was provoked into doing what he did.

"I'll get the shovel," Ona decided slowly.

Ona spent most of the morning digging a grave. Two, actually. She collected the beaded belt from the dog's tail and tied it around her waist, but it was too big and fell cross ways over her hip. The colorful arrangement of beads was completely unfamiliar to Ona. Upon closer examination, the beads appeared to be painted and made mostly of clay or small animal bones. Ona admired the rattle of the belt while she toiled in digging the shallow graves.

Not even noon, and the sleeves of Ona's dark blue dress were rolled as high as they would go, with her skirts tied up at her knees.

She wondered what her father would say when he found out she put a Cherokee man on one side of Ona's mother and a hound dog on the other. It just seemed natural to give her mother company.

Ona stopped to listen to the birds and jar flies, the last vestiges of summer, when her eyes fell on the wreckage of the cellar. When Ona was very small, it was just a half-face cabin with a blanket over the front to keep out the winter wind. When Rowland Christie built the house, they used flat creek rocks to block in the old thing for storage. With the cellar's collapse, they had lost their stored food and any extra clay crocks intended to put food by before winter.

It would take months for money to arrive from her father. She imagined the fall harvest and nowhere to put it. She pictured flies swarming rotting cabbages in late September and empty bellies by January. Turnips would keep in the ground, however, and they could dig clay up from the creek to mold more crocks.

Fannie helped Ona carry the bodies to their graves and Fannie leaned over the graves for a long while just whispering to them. Ona helped Fannie move bodies plenty of times. Fannie was the closest thing to a doctor in Calico. Ona did not like watching Fannie perform her eerie ritual for the dead. Instead, Ona took to cleaning up the yard, collecting the pieces of the cellar rubble into a pile.

"Working outside is the perfect time to think about all life's problems," Fannie once told Ona. "Work relieves stress on the body, and it's simple enough that you can think on what's weighing down

your heart while still being productive instead of moping around
like some kind of poet."

Chapter 3.

The earth shook in little vibrations with each running step Ona took toward the garden. They were too slight for Fannie to notice, but obvious enough to give the silent mole a pause while tunneling deep in the cool, dark earth and for foraging robins across the yard to flee skyward into the safety of the dense, green canopy. The garden fell silent as Ona approached barefoot through the thickly planted tiger lilies that framed the vegetable patch. She plucked four flowers and laid one on each grave. She tucked the last one out from under her cap.

It was a sin to work on the Sabbath, but Fannie said God would understand there was a lot of cleaning up to do. So this week, Ona would miss church to clean up their property from the fracas of the night before. Ona hoped there would be enough work to stay home from the Bible School on Monday, too. She stacked broken clay in one pile and wood planks in another. She carried armfuls of crumbled rock to the cliff edge across the field and chucked them into the creek below. The wood they could use throughout winter for cooking and heating.

By the time Ona finished cleaning up the yard Fannie had laid down for a nap. Ona sat on a large rock in the garden, studying the path Jeremiah Sunday had taken. She deliberated only for a moment before following in the direction that Jeremiah Sunday disappeared the night before.

The woods were a place both mysterious and comforting for Ona. There was the part of the trees where she could still see the berry patch, the field and the cabin with smoke rising above the canopy. This was the part of the forest where Ona once made slug kingdoms, maintained her childhood fort, and more recently, drew pictures of all the birds she saw after climbing the gnarled oak tree to her favorite vantage point.

Beyond this familiar place was the creek Ona often fished with her father. They spent many sunny afternoons collecting lucky quartz, watching crawdads battle and darters school. Past the creek, the trees grew thick and the ground disappeared into ferns and bramble. This was where Rowland Christie went to hunt deer and turkey, where wolf howls sang on quiet nights, and where Fannie said the fey folk lived. Ona had never been beyond the creek. Where did the Indian man come from? And where did Jeremiah Sunday sneak off to? She imagined well-worn paths guiding the feet of total strangers so close the Christie cabin, never leaving the shelter of forest, but moving silently to unknown destinations.

Ona approached the creek at the edge of her familiar woods, dipping her toes into the cool spring fed water, watching tiny fish scatter and the disturbed creek bed cloud her steps. She held her breath, stepping up from the shallow water and onto solid ground. The trees were thick and light filtered through the leaves in small clusters that lit up the forest like fine jewels scattered in every direction. Ona walked slowly through the ferns, searching for a trail to follow.

Ona closed her eyes against the late summer breeze and inhaled the damp, dark soil and decaying leaves. She breathed in the citrus aroma of spicebush and freshly fallen pine needles. It was as if the forest opened up. A wide path emerged through a small clearing in the distance. It was probably a logging road. Ona's father harvested black cherry trees and tulip poplars, selling the lumber off to the people in the Bluegrass. Everyone in these parts cut their own trees to make their homes, but the people in the cities paid others to do it for them.

The path of golden-brown needles laid out before her was cleared through a stand of cedar and pine. It followed a ridge top that had logging strips branching out off the main path. Ona was cast into the shade of the forest canopy the deeper she wandered along the logging road, leaving sight of the creek. She began to count the birds, giving up after a while as they became too many to number. Every so often, deer flitted in and out of green briers beside the trail before disappearing into the trees once more.

In the dimming evening light, Ona turned around to head back to the cabin. Only, the pine trail had split a few times, and she couldn't quite recall every fork she had turned at. Ona came to her first fork and veered left, but the trail quickly thinned, disappearing altogether after several yards, so she turned around to try a different path. The road weaved and turned several times during the day.

As the sky changed from orange to pale purple, Ona began looking for a place to make camp. She was thirsty, and her stomach was growling. The dried pine needles were a soft bed under her bare toes, and she slowed to a halt before sinking to the ground to rest against a tree. Once still, Ona became acutely aware of the twilight noises surrounding her.

Birds shifted on their roosts above her and nervous turkeys murmured quietly among themselves. Insects tickled at her legs, and arms, and neck, crawling across her with dozens of tiny legs. A whip-poor-will shrieked incessantly, jarring Ona wide awake each time her eyelids drooped. It seemed that underneath every leaf there was something rustling, hooting, squeaking, and scratching. Far off in the distance, Ona heard howling.

The purple sky fell into blackness and the moonless night consumed everything around her, including Ona herself. Her heart quickened. Where had the path gone? In a panic, Ona tried standing up, but she stumbled over massive roots sticking out of the ground. She felt along the ground, finding the tree she had decided to sleep under.

Ona sat small and curled against the tree, having no defense against panther cats or wolves. She knew that she was some place behind the Christie and Halstead properties, not too awful far from home. So long as there were logging roads, she was near enough to friendly neighbors. Thus, she resigned herself to watching the stars.

"Enda already done said it ain't much longer to the split now," a young girl's voice wavered with some uncertainty.

Ona jerked her head up and the girl stopped suddenly in her tracks, eyes wide and let out a shriek. If Ona had not looked up, the party would have marched on top of her. The girl, a little younger than Ona, was guiding a man and woman without lamplight through forest. The man had a small boy sitting high up on his shoulders. They were not walking the ridge top path that Ona followed; they were trekking up the steep mountainside through uncut land.

The girl in front of her had dark skin with black pig-tail braids that curled up just above her shoulder. She wore a plain cotton dress and ran barefoot, just like Ona.

"What in the Sam Hill," Ona scrambled to her feet, guffawing.

"Well, what a surprise! You by yourself all the way out here in the wild? What your name, honey?" The woman was tall and lean, with short black hair cropped close to her head. The man beside her was so tall he had to bend over, hanging on to the child's feet dangling off his shoulders, whispering quickly into the woman's ear.

"My name's Ona." She spoke with caution. Ona narrowed her eyes, wondering what would cause a negro family to run amuck in the woods. What were they hiding from? The woman smiled sweetly, taking the man's hand in hers. They did not appear the way Ona imagined criminals to be; rather, they seemed like a family.

"Miss Ona, you sure up awful late. They ain't no houses back in these hills; where you going?"

"I live up Calico Ridge and come looking for wolves with Jeremiah Sunday. He's here close. He just found tracks and went to look at them, that's all." Ona attempted to cover her suspicion in a lie. The couple tensed at her words, but the young girl snorted and shook her head.

"Don't worry. That ole man Sunday so full of corn whiskey he can't find his hat from his head. You live up Calico Ridge? That's a long walk south of here." The girl let out a heavy sigh, clicking her tongue.

"Listen, my cousin following behind us. Just walk down that hill where we come and you run into him about a mile off. It about time for me to turn back anyhow. He take you home." The young girl waved the family on, who continued up the mountainside scanning along the ground in search of the trail split.

Ona smiled, forgetting about wolves and Jeremiah Sunday. "That's kind of you. You sure he'd do that for me?"

The girl nodded. "Yes, Ma'am."

"Thank you! Hey— Where y'all headed in the middle of the night?" Ona asked, curiosity peaking.

"No place for me. They trying to get out from under some Indian who done them wrong," the girl shrugged her shoulders.

"Really," The image of the dying man flashed across Ona's memory. "How did they get away from the Indian?"

"I don't know. I only meet them yesterday through my cousin, Enda; he been the one helping them. Mama didn't want no part in them. She tell me stay home, but I sneak out when she gone to sleep. Enda promise to take me up the mountain if I help. He tell me to walk the family up the hill to the trail split before I turn around. Enda be hanging back to cover the tracks all night. If you start now, you find him down the hill, surely."

"Thank you! What's your name?"

"Adelaide. And you keep that dry!" Adelaide held a finger up to her lips before marching up the hill after the family. Ona spun around, beginning her descent down the mountainside.

Ona followed a small path she found after stumbling across a modest sized cairn just off the base of the mountain. It felt backwards to be going downhill, when she had walked the ridge all this way, but she wanted to find the girl's cousin and get home sometime before daylight. She grimaced at the thought of school in the morning with the Bible teacher at the Methodist church, Mr. Wexler. Ona did not even attend the Methodist church. Fannie and Ona went to the Baptist church in Calico.

Fannie thought schooling past reading and writing was pointless. Ona, who managed both, heartily agreed. Rowland Christie was adamant Ona go to school as long as possible; because if she were educated, she wouldn't have to work so hard, so Ona walked to the Calico Mission Church every Monday for Bible school. Reverend Johnson of the Calico Baptist Church would not teach Bible school because it was a sin to work on the Sabbath and he was busy with ministerial duties through the week.

Ona walked slowly through the forest, which appeared much more amiable once the moon revealed itself through the cloudy night. She walked softly along the narrow path, listening for footsteps that might belong to Adelaide's cousin, but instead of footsteps she could only hear her own stomach growling.

The night air was growing cooler, and her bare feet began to ache with cold as dew settled on the chilled earth. She kicked up leaf litter and chestnuts, hungry and frustrated. The creatures of the forest fell silent, listening to her complaints. Ona squinted out of one eye and saw the same endless stretch of trees above her and brown beneath her. She trudged through the woods, watching the sun peek over the horizon. Great. She was definitely not going to be on time for school today.

"Are we playing hide and seek? You're never going to win if you keep on crashing through these woods like a one-man parade." A mess of leaves and mud shaped like a boy laughed impishly, swinging down from a large beech tree and dropping right in Ona's way.

"Tell you what. I'll teach you how to play. I'm the best there is." He winked an icy blue eye at her. Ona was so shocked she stumbled backwards and hit her head on the tree behind her. She rubbed the bump furiously.

"Who are you?" She demanded. The boy stood up, offering a hand to Ona, who was still nursing the knot on her head and sitting on the ground. He wore patched green trousers that were rolled up at the knee with no shirt to speak of. His skin was a deep, warm shade of brown. He was absolutely filthy, covered in grime and dirt. Ona couldn't tell if his hair was supposed to be a muddy shade or if it might be a different color after several baths. She ignored his hand and stood up, brushing herself off. He was a head taller than her and maybe a year older.

The boy pointed at himself with his thumb saying, "My name's Enda. Enda Cambor!"

Ona knew she had an accent like this. At her school, they were taught how to hide it away and speak like educated people. The main job of the Methodists at Calico Mission Church was to educate the poor children of Calico Ridge. They brought the Word of God and the tools to interpret it.

Before the Methodists came, Ona didn't know anyone around the ridge was poor or uneducated. Turns out, everyone was. And accents, their teacher Horace Wexler told them, were a sign of laziness and poor education. Fannie said it was nonsense and that accents didn't mean anything except for a mark on where one's people came from, and people came from all over God's earth, so she thought accents made people and places pretty special.

"Well Enda Cambor, nice to meet you. I'm Ona. Ona America Christie. Do you have a cousin called Adelaide? She was accompanying a negro family, and they was walking up the hill for some time."

"That negro family is my business, not hers. What do you want with Adelaide?" Enda's smiled faltered, and he tilted his head sideways.

"She said you could help me get home. Is that true?"

"Oh sure, Adelaide mentioned some lost girl a-wandering back in these hills," Enda winked. "But first I seen my baby cousin home safe, of course."

"Of course."

"Where is home for Little America?" Enda slowed his pace to match Ona's.

"Calico. Ain't you never been there?" Ona put space between herself and the boy, suddenly aware of how close he was beside her.

Enda Cambor raised his eyebrows and his light blue eyes crinkled with laughter. "Ona, would you believe that you're standing smack in the middle of Calico Mountain? Congratulations, you found it!"

Ona balled her fists up, breathed deeply, and relaxed her fingers. Looking up at the sky, rather than his stupid twinkling eyes, she spoke more clearly.

"Enda Cambor, do you know the way cross the creek toward the edge of Calico Ridge Road?"

"Ona, seem like you could stand some breakfast." The boy smiled, shaking his head. A few paces ahead Enda shook a small tree until its lumpy green fruit fell. He picked it up and tossed it to her, taking another for himself. Splitting it open with a small knife from his pocket, he traded the halved one for hers and cut the other one open for himself.

"They call it a pawpaw."

Ona, not shy about food, took a bite of the mushy fruit and spat out seeds the size of coins. The sweet fruit helped steady Ona's shaking fingers. Enda finished his first fruit and walked back for another.

"And sure," he said between mouthfuls of pawpaw, "I'll get you back up the creek. You live out with that ole water witch?" He sounded impressed.

"Mostly. Fannie is just a midwife, though. We're not witches, we're Baptists." Ona dropped her gaze to the ground. Accent tucked safely away.

The boy shrugged his shoulders, shaking off Ona's comment.

"Suit yourself! Can you keep up, Little America? " He stretched each arm behind his head, smiling mischievously.

"Of course!" Ona eyed him, standing tall. She refused to be bested by someone so obnoxious.

Enda darted ahead of her calling back, "Good! I don't got much time for favors."

Ona inhaled the rest of her pawpaw fruit while chasing after him, spitting out the seeds as she went. They ran until Ona's sides ached and her lungs screamed for a break, but she kept going so not to lose the boy who remained infuriatingly just barely ahead of her. He was faster than anybody she had ever seen before. Enda skidded to a halt when he reached the creek that cut through the Christie property. Ona smiled broadly; the well-worn dirt path on the other side of the bubbling, spring fed creek was a welcome sight.

"The path across this here creek will take us yonder to the cabin." She pointed through the trees, breathless. Ona wanted to pay him for his help somehow. "If you come on home with me Fannie can fix you up with a hot breakfast before you turn back."

Enda twisted his hands together behind his head and his eyebrows furrowed underneath beads of sweat. He was also breathing hard.

"I ain't so sure about that. It wouldn't be fit for all that. We ought to leave the old lady out of this." He grinned at Ona. She shrugged her shoulders before bidding him farewell.

Ona splashed through the creek, squishing through the mud as she climbed up the bank to her side of the creek. She ran the familiar path home, tearing through the garden and into the house. Fannie was not home, but glowing embers were still smoldering in the stone pit and there was a large piece of bread and hunk of cheese on the table beside it. Fannie may have gone to deliver an infant. Mrs. Lafayette had called Fannie out to her property many times over the past few weeks, she was fixing to have a baby any day now.

If that was the case, Fannie would probably be holed up three days with that family. Mr. Lafayette was nice enough in Ona's opinion, but his wife Marie acted like she was in the room with something ugly and smelly whenever she saw the Scots-Irish kids from outside of town. Mrs. Lafayette was often sick for an opium tea that Fannie refused point blank to cook up. She and Ona were there several times a year for Mrs. Lafayette's bouts of incurable lethargy. Fannie said that Mrs. Lafayette's sickness could be cured if she left the house more, but Mrs. Lafayette was rarely seen outdoors.

The girls at church all whispered about the beauty of Marie Lafayette. They idolized her porcelain skin that rarely saw the sun. Fannie said that the fragile skin of Marie Lafayette is what made her dead useless. The Lafayettes were one of three families in Calico wealthy enough to afford slaves. Mr. Lafayette was a lawyer and owned most of the businesses in downtown Calico, along with Mr. Cambor the mayor, and the Beaudin family. Ona went to Bible school with the Beaudin girl; her father was a well-known judge.

Ona hurried to the edge of the field beside the cabin. She strung a bucket around her shoulder and took hold of a rope ladder staked into the ground. Ona steadily climbed down the forty-foot cliff face using the familiar worn rope rungs that lay against slick rock. Slow trickles of water leached from the rock face, sliding into a pool at the bottom of the cliff. She climbed all the way down the ladder and crouched on a boulder worn smooth from innumerable years of steady water drips splashing against the surface.

Ona dipped her bucket in the pool of water and carefully made her way back up the ladder before using some of the water to rinse the mud and muck off of her legs, feet and hands. Ona felt around to fix her hair, gasping in surprise. Her cap had fallen off some time in the night and her hair lay wild and unkempt around her shoulders. It was her only cap. She decided to make the journey to school regardless, fixing her hair back in a tight braid that wrapped against her head. Ona draped a light shawl around her shoulders, stuffing her worn out copy of the Bible in a simple cloth purse with her cheese and bread before heading out the door to school.

Fannie did not have any clocks in the home, but Ona kept a small pocket watch stashed in her purse. She knew that school would begin in ten minutes, but it took forty minutes to walk there. Ona examined the watch, reflecting how it was given to her by the headmaster for being late so often.

"Since punishment has no obvious effect on your punctuality, perhaps this will help you be timelier, Miss Christie." The headmaster's dark eyes were stern as he held the switch in his hand and Ona left school that day with tears staining her cheeks, welts on her legs and pocket watch in hand.

Horace Wexler thought little of the youth who used the services of the Mission Bible school, but attended Sunday service elsewhere. Perhaps it was rude, but it was the first school the average child of Calico could attend. Prior to the building of Calico Mission Church just three years before, only the wealthiest sons could afford an education at boarding academies in cities like Lexington and Frankfort. Thanks to the Methodist initiative, more children had a chance to learn how to read and write, if only to better learn the Word of God.

Ona stole through the doors of her school house twenty minutes late. Maybe if she ran like this all the time if she could outrun Enda someday. Pine needles poked out from her braid which threatened to unpin from the top of her head. As Ona found her seat, she realized she forgot to wash the mud off her face earlier at the spring. Her desk mate Blanche Beaudin was visibly appalled.

Blanche had golden hair that she tied into curls each night and wore, in Ona's opinion, an unnecessary number of pleats in her dresses. Her grandfather settled Calico Ridge and her father currently presided as the only legal judge in three counties. Today Blanche was sporting quite the ruffled getup, a real vision in pink, complete with white stockings and a massive, pale pink ribbon drooping across her over-sized capote bonnet. Something told Ona that she and Blanche were wearing the same repulsed expression.

Blanche's brother was one of the lucky boys who made it into an academy. He was a couple of years older than Blanche and Ona, and no doubt headed to a university after his time at the academy ended. Blanche was privately tutored at home for a number of years, in addition to attending the Bible school on Mondays.

Some folks speculated the only reason Mr. Beaudin put Blanche in the Bible school served as a political move to mingle with voters during her father's reelection year. For the first time since Judge Beaudin's election more than decade prior, he had someone running against him. Either way, Blanche's prior education led her to excel in reading, writing, and memorization where all the other students desperately struggled.

The headmaster, Horace Wexler, rose from his seat at the front of the room, peering down at Ona over her desk. He sighed heavily and lifted his arm, striking Ona across the face with his ruler. She could feel the stinging sensation begin to welt. Her eyes watered, but she did not cry, and she did not look at him. She stared straight ahead of her. Across the room, thirty other students ranging from five to fifteen shifted in their seats uncomfortably. They kept their eyes forward, knowing better than to watch the scene playing out in front of them.

"Miss Christie! You are late! *Again!* And you're filthy, not to mention brazenly immodest! Girl, pray tell—where have you been?" Horace Wexler was a tall man with a hooked nose. He was a retired minister from Maryland and was among those who swarmed from the north, rallying to help educate the morally depraved children of the hills lacking in propriety. His nostrils flared and his thick side-burns framed his face in a threatening angle.

"Sir," Ona began, her heart beat racing. She wanted to cry from the stinging on her face, but she did not. She could not give him the satisfaction of weakness. She was too big for him to be treating her this way, and the whole class knew it. Mr. Wexler was already of the opinion girls should not be educated.

"I—I gone to the woods this morning for a walk. I must have lost track of time. I was a-rushing to get here and I felled. Lost my cap, too. I am truly sorry for disrupting class." It was a miracle she was not thrown out of class for arriving late and dressed inappropriately.

"You were late to your education because you were too busy frolicking these godless lands?" The headmaster leered over her. He was a foul force to reckon with on a regular day, but the old man was particularly nasty with Ona. He had heard the whispers about Fannie. Some called her a water witch, or a granny witch. Fannie called it healing. But the headmaster only saw an old sinner relying on the devil's hand tricks.

"Where did you find such an unholy thing?" The headmaster accused. He pointed at Ona's beaded belt, arranged in abstract shapes that Ona found interesting.

"It's mine. That's all that counts," Ona said stiffly.

The headmaster clicked his tongue in disgust, muttering something about Irish filth. "Miss Beaudin, will you please recite to us the verse from Acts?" Blanche obediently stood up and curtsied in the aisle before sounding off her scripture.

Ona kept her eyes fixed on the globe in front of the room for the rest of the class, only speaking when spoken to. The globe was positioned over Western Europe, and Ona wondered if she would ever visit there. She would like to see large, bustling cities or gentle country sides dotted with flocks of sheep and their shepherds the way her father described. The noon church bell signaled an end to their time and Ona flew out of the school room before the headmaster decided to rethink her enrollment at the school.

Blanche's care taker arrived in a carriage, as she was picked up every week from school and transported back to downtown Calico. Ona began the long walk home, but at least she spent most of it with other kids who lived out her way. They were teasing her about her run in with the headmaster.

"Oh, don't worry about that old coot," Zelma McDaniel waved dismissively. She was sweet girl with wild, curly brown hair that trailed from under her cap down her yellow flowery dress. The McDaniels and the Christies were longtime friends, all the way back to Ulster.

"She's right," a tall boy, Talmadge Halstead agreed. "He's been madder than a wet hen all day! Tried to write me up for telling my brother to sit up straight!" Talmadge was the oldest in the class, and Ona was second after him.

They were walking with Talmadge's three younger brothers who also went to school with them, but they were playing tag, racing ahead of the group. Ona kicked up dust on the road with her bare feet, cursing the headmaster. One of the Talmadge's brothers giggled, looking back at Ona. There were actually eleven children in the Halstead family, but the two girls old enough to be in school stayed home to help raise the five who weren't.

"Really, Ona. Where did you find that belt? It looks Indian!" Zelma examined it closely.

Talmadge patted Ona on the back in mock pride. "She finally take up after her daddy." He motioned shooting a pistol.

"No, I went and found it in the woods, on the other side of the creek." Ona shrugged off Talmadge's arm.

"Do you think there could really be Indians in Calico?" Zelma's eyes widened.

"Nah, it's got to be some old forgotten belt. No Indian could get through Calico anymore without us knowing about it." Talmadge frowned. Ona did not comment one way or the other. She rolled the beads silently between her fingers, listening to their musical clinking. The Indian was dead, and it would only bring Jeremiah Sunday trouble to mention the altercation and the negro family that ran away.

Ona was not the last stop at the end of the road on Calico Ridge. Talmadge and his brothers still had another mile or more when Ona waved goodbye, turning down the small dirt path to her cabin. It was only a quarter mile or so from the main road to the cabin, but her cheese and bread from lunch had worn off and she was exhausted. Ona dropped her Bible on the little table and went to work. She swung out the iron arm which held the cooking kettle away from the ashes of this morning's fire, bending to build a small fire and setting water to boil.

Ona had to be extra careful building a fire. Their cabin had no chimney. Rowland Christie built the cabin in haste to get his daughter out of the half-face cabin, intending to add one later. The only trouble being, he was never home long enough to get the job done. Instead, there was a little triangle shaped gap between the pitched roof and the highest log of the cabin. They built the fires in a stone ring near the back of the cabin to let the smoke blow out the opening. There used to be an identical opening above the front door, but Ona and Fannie chinked that in years ago to help cut down on rain and snow from blowing inside.

Ona wandered into the garden tracing her fingers along the bright orange tiger lilies that outlined the garden. They were a decorative fence; but in a pinch, you could also eat their root tubers like a potato. She walked up and down the rows of vegetables methodically until she found a delicious surprise: ripened sweet corn. She picked four ears before returning to the cabin. With nights cooling off, she planned to make soup.

Ona returned to the garden and found a nice head of cabbage, some wild onions near the forest, and snatched rosemary and sage from the cabin's rafters. Ona combined the ingredients with water, letting the soup simmer in the kettle into the evening while snacking on apples.

Ona withdrew to the forest while the soup stewed, carefully and quietly turning over rocks and looking inside of tree cavities searching for signs of Indians, like the one she saw two nights ago. She had always heard stories about them, but had never seen one before the other night. Ona meddled for over an hour when finally she saw the soft green orb of a lightning bug shoot out of a rotting log and flee deeper into the forest.

Ona looked up at the sinking sky, waiting for the thumbnail moon to peek out among the stars. She wondered if the family taking strange course from the woods were nearly to their destination. Ona bit her lip, glancing back toward the safety of the cabin where warmth, food and a soft pallet of blankets awaited her. Only she didn't go back. Ona bounded into the darkening forest after the lightning bug.

The lightning bug appeared and disappeared like a small flame ignites, only to suddenly burn out and rekindle nearby. She pulled her shawl tightly around her and crouched behind a hemlock tree just inside the forest edge, peering through the branches waiting for the lightning bug to make its move. Two more glowing lights appeared near the ground in front of her, rising high above her head.

Ona tiptoed out from behind the hemlock, walking softly through the trees. She smiled at the three hovering orbs before they took off, zooming ahead of Ona toward the creek. It was this simple pleasure that helped her forget red stained sheets on Fannie's empty bed. Tomorrow they would need Ona's attention. Ona chased after the lightning bugs, growing closer with her arm outstretched, and fingers closing just before she lost her footing over a gnarled root near the creek bank. She toppled to her knees at the edge of the water, which flowed black and shiny under the moon.

"OW!" Ona hit the ground hard. Her hands and knees were scraped and stinging. She pulled herself together, sitting down cross legged in the dark leaf litter on the cabin's creek bank, staring out across from her to where the insects disappeared. Ona's disturbance seemed to shake the forest alive in the budding night. The carpet of ferns across the creek were illuminated by a magnificent show of lights slowly rising from the low-lying forbs.

Ona sat very still, watching the scene unfold in awe. The glowing lights twinkled, moving to and fro from the forest bottom into tree canopies. Each luminescent lightning bug seemed to be its own being, but all of the entities interacted with each other.

A handsome, albeit dirt smeared face appeared in the green light cast off the orbs. It was Enda Cambor. He did not seem at all taken by the luminescent creatures; in fact, he swatted them out of his way. Enda looked on at Ona from across the creek and she sat frozen in amazement. How was he just walking among them like that? Why were they not afraid of him?

Enda Cambor plodded through the forest floor flushing out even more lightning bugs in his path before splashing through the small creek and climbing up the bank to reach Ona's side. He sat down next to her, long legs stretched out in front of him.

"Wiley little critters. I'm surprised you seen them all like that. They don't shine for all folks."

"Do they come out a lot?" Ona picked at blades of grass, staring at the show of lights dancing gracefully before her. Of course she had seen lightning bugs before, though never so many in such a spectacle.

"Every night." Enda stretched out and lay on his back, staring up at the little moon. He chewed on a long piece of grass.

"You should see them all when it rains. Their light shining on all the wet earth lights up these hills just like stars in the night sky."

Ona spent a lot of time in the woods and she had never seen anything like that before. Enda must have been outside nearly all the time.

"Enda?" Ona looked at him. "How did you know the negro family you helped cross the mountain?"

"The man I live with is an Indian hunter. He track this one man all through the hillside. The Indian seem like he was taking them slaves some place, but when the fighting broke out they slipped off. They were scared. Didn't know these hills, or which was way up. So

I asked them where they headed, they tell me Canada, so I walk them as far as I can. Adelaide kept on with them, too. She wanted to get out and see Calico, but I bet she paid the price this morning when her daddy woke up." Enda shook his head.

"Who's the Indian hunter?" Ona asked. She had a feeling who it was.

Enda kept his eyes on the sky. "Jeremiah Sunday."

Ona paused. Everybody knew old man Sunday. Ona always thought Sunday lived alone at the edge of town; but the story was that he owned a shop in town and everyone loved his wife and two girls. But after his family was killed in a Cherokee raid, he never opened the doors to his shop again. Nowadays, he was all the time being thrown out of the tippling house downtown for getting too drunk.

"No one ever said Sunday had a boy!" Ona said, surprised.

"That's because he ain't got a boy." Enda spat out his blade of grass, standing up. Ona was confused.

"I said I live with Sunday, not that he was my old man." Enda was stiff and defensive. Ona didn't know what to say. Enda Cambor was like a feral cat with a rotten attitude, but she felt very sad for him all of the sudden.

"Sunday ain't got any slaves, do he?" Ona asked, confused.

Enda clicked his tongue in disgust, standing up and brushing off his pants. He stalked back towards the creek and deliberated for a moment, his voice dripping with venom.

"That old man ain't got a pot to piss in. Nobody owns me, Ona. I keep myself and abide the laws of God and earth alike, on account of my choosing to. Not any reason else." Enda was breathing hard. He reached into his pockets and pulled out Ona's thin, white cotton cap, tossing it at her.

"You found it!" Ona fiddled with the strings of her cap between her fingers. "You come all this way just to return my cap." The small act of kindness brought feelings of gratitude to the rims of her eyes. "Thank you."

Enda turned around, lifting his hand in farewell and began his descent to the hills beyond the creek. His leaving stirred a strange sense of urgency that flooded through her stomach, bringing Ona to her feet. "Enda, are you hungry? I got supper going."

Enda paused, kicking a walnut through the leaf litter. "Yeah, I could eat."

Ona and Enda spent the evening gorging on soup, and drawing pictures of the ferocious monsters of Calico Mountain, like wolves, and panthers, and legendary catfish. Enda constantly glanced up at the closed cabin door, anxious. All night he was very careful not to touch anything hanging on the walls or sitting out on the tables. Ona erased the oversized catfish from her school slate board.

"Where do you get something like that?" Enda gestured to the board and chalk.

"It's for school. Papa brought them here to me. They come all the way from Virginia to help you learn letters and the Scripture."

Enda shook his head slowly.

"Letters, like your name," Ona clarified. "E-N-D-A. Here," She traced each letter out on the board. "See?"

Enda's eyes widened, tracing his finger over top of Ona's lettering. "Can I try?"

He sat directly opposite of Ona, never once getting close enough to accidentally brush shoulders. He moved softly, as if he was afraid somebody would find him out. Despite successfully spelling out his name, then Ona's name, when Ona tried to get him to write out his last name 'Cambor', Enda became noticeably uncomfortable. He tossed aside the chalk and wiped the board clean, glancing around the cabin.

"You want to be gone from here," Ona observed.

Enda looked on at the front door, "I don't like mucking up the house of some ole water witch."

"Then don't." She opened the door, leading the way outside. They stopped at the graves Ona had dug and Enda's eyes dropped to the muddied headstone of Abigail Christie.

Ona picked at a piece of dirt over her mother's name and went into the house, returning with a bowl and pitcher. Enda followed Ona across the field and watched in amazement as Ona climbed down the precarious rope ladder in near total darkness to the spring fed pool. She filled her pitcher with water and made her way back to the headstone. Ona knelt on her knees and cleaned away the muck covering her mother's name.

"Who done something as disrespectful as this?" Enda asked. He knelt beside Ona, watching her clean meticulously in all the cracks.

"Jeremiah Sunday."

Enda picked up the end of Ona's beaded belt, trailing in the dirt and looked at the fresh graves beside Abigail Christie's marker.

"He done this?" Enda's voice was quiet, like a small boy instead of a young man.

"I shouldn't of worn this. It ain't mine to begin with." Ona quietly untied the beaded belt and folded it at the head of the Indian man.

"This looks Cherokee. If you and that witch buried him, y'all should keep a hold of it to honor his memory." Enda picked it up, studying the colors and designs between his fingers. He handed it back to Ona, who kept a protective hold over it. The belt held a certain power over Ona that carried the weight of the dead man with it.

Ona opened her mouth to speak, but Enda was already moving. He stood up silently and took off toward the creek. He was gone a little while before he returned with two large stones, one under each arm. Ona helped Enda position them beside Abigail Christie's headstone. Enda took off once more and came back with muddied hands cupping root bulb clusters of familiar greenery.

"Daffodils?"

Enda shrugged, "It's what we planted when my parents died."

"You and Jeremiah Sunday?"

"No, me and my granny,"

"Where is your parents buried at?"

"A negro cemetery on outside town." Enda padded the ground down gently around the flowers where the Cherokee man was buried. He sat down against Abigail's grave, brushing the dirt from his hands off.

"How'd they die?" Ona whispered. Some small part of her hoped Enda had killed his parents the way Ona had killed her own mother. Abigail Christie's grave outside the cabin was a constant reminder of Ona's first sin: murder. She had committed the crime of existing at the expense of another.

"My mother run off with an Indian. It took a long time before they seen her; but when they did, her own daddy, the Mayor Cambor, killed them both for their sin."

"How'd he find her if she run off?" Ona was confused. Mayor Cambor was white. Enda spoke slowly, tracing the story through his memories.

"He never knew nothing about me. Not for ten whole years. Then one day, he found us all. We lived with my father's family nearby some caves not too far off from Calico. That creek actually flows out a cave right near where I grown up." Enda pointed back towards the forest where they caught fireflies.

"Ever since soldiers came to lay stake on the land, we been fighting. Some of us made ready to flee south, using the caves that go all the way through Tennessee and into Carolina. Most of them were killed in the fighting. Some of our neighbors," Enda gestured

46

toward the grave, "moved deep into the mountainside and completely disappeared."

"Is that when the Mayor seen you?"

"My father took my mama and I into hiding. Then, late one night they took me to meet my granny. We was leaving to go south the next morning, and mama wanted to say goodbye to her family. We was all there: me, granny, mama and my father. When the mayor seen them, he shot them both and turned me out."

Ona didn't know what to say, but he seemed a lot smaller sitting beside her telling the story, so she wrapped her arm around his shoulder. He startled, but did not move away.

"I'm truly sorry." Ona paused for a moment. "Why would the mayor do a thing like that?"

Enda's blue eyes pierced straight through her. "She was just a slave, Ona."

"Did you meet Jeremiah Sunday after?"

"It weren't long after that before he found my rabbit snares and followed them straight to where I was staying. He's a hard man to get on with, but if it weren't for Sunday, I'd be dead."

"Don't he know who your father is?"

"He can never know that."

Ona was right. Enda had committed the same crime of existing. But Ona was also wrong. He was different from her. His sin did not make him unworthy of love. Enda Cambor did not murder his mother in the way she had taken her own mother's life. They

47

watched the thumbnail moon rise high into the sky before drifting off to sleep, still resting against the grave of Abigail Christie.

Ona stirred from her slumber when she heard a knock at the cabin door. She sat up quickly, shivering with cold from the night air. Enda stirred beside her and she signaled him to keep quiet.

"That's the only door to the cabin." Ona whispered a string of curses in the safety of the dark night, thankful it wasn't a bigger moon out.

"So? You ain't allowed out after dark?" Enda shot back quietly.

"Stay here. Something ain't right."

Ona crept to the opposite side of the cabin before standing upright. Sure, it might look funny to be outside so late at night, but Fannie always did stuff like that and the people seemed to expect her peculiar behaviors. It'd be only natural for Ona to inherit those mannerisms too. Less natural would it be for Ona to be caught out late with a boy who most of Calico did not know existed.

"Who's there?" she called from across the yard.

"It's just your man, Wash McDaniel. I brought my girl Zelma with me, I know y'all are friends."

A burly man swung his lantern to face Ona's voice, squinting into the darkness. He seemed surprised to find Ona outside, but said nothing. Ona liked Mr. McDaniel. He was a warm spirit with a thick red beard, and a long friendship spanning oceans with her father Rowland Christie. His wife, Anna was plump with beautiful dark curly hair, just like Zelma. The McDaniels were good friends of Ona's father.

Ona was used to seeing Mr. McDaniel around town; he owned the general store where all the mail and goods came through. It was strange to see them so late at night, however. Ona and Fannie almost never had company, only Ona's father when he was home on leave.

"That is, err— we might could come inside, Cricket?" Mr. McDaniel took off his hat and held it tightly between his hands. He carried a long instrument wrapped in cloths under his arm. Ona didn't understand why he was so uneasy. Zelma's eyes were red, like she had been crying and her small hands curled around her father's arm. Somehow, her yellow flowery dress didn't seem as cheerful as earlier. She would not look at Ona.

Ona opened the door and hoped they didn't notice the second bowl of soup and extra cup lying around the abandoned slate board. She cast the belt aside on Fannie's bed before lighting a candle to brighten the cabin.

"Come here, you poor child. Cursed by God seems like to wander this earth an orphan." Wash wrapped his thick arms around Ona, squeezing her tight for a long moment. Tears splashed from Zelma's face and Ona offered her friend a handkerchief.

"Excuse me?" Her stomach hardened into lead and she was having trouble remembering where she was. In the cabin? Wasn't Enda here just a moment ago? Chills shot down her back and Ona tightened her plaid flannel shawl. It had belonged to her mother and her father liked to see her wear it.

Mr. McDaniel spoke in a strained voice, choking out every word as if it were hollow and he was not the one speaking them.

"Your father was an honest soldier who dedicated his life for our country. He was a fine man. Come up from Ulster with your Ma before you was even a thought in the stars. All by their selves they made a life here. We all did. They was with us through the worst of it. A finer couple, a nicer baby girl, you can't of found nowhere." Mr. McDaniel broke down into sobs, placing his large, warm hand on Ona's shoulder. Zelma wrapped her arms around Ona and sniffled softly, petting Ona's fiery orange hair, still springing freely around her shoulders with her forgotten cap on the cabin floor.

"They quit the fighting back in January if you can believe. There was one last stand after the battles over the road. Sounds like them Indians is ready to make peace. They're agreed to let us build the road. Seem like they shipped your father and all them other Kentucky boys to Tennessee where they finally defeated them damn Indians. Your father, he was a courageous fighter. He died a hero, Ona! They'll put a treaty in place thanks to the likes of fighters like Rowland Christie. He did Calico proud down there. All them Kentucky boys did."

Ona stood frozen, her limbs transformed into weights that she could not rouse even if she had tried. Mr. McDaniel reached into his pockets and pulled out a letter and a small drawstring purse laden fat with coins. He sniffed loudly, before reading aloud.

"We only just received word today of his passing back in February. President Thomas Jefferson mailed this just for you, girl! 'To honor the hero, Lieutenant Colonel Rowland Christie for his acts of valor in service to God and country.' To honor Rowland's service– This is his pension, Ona. Do you understand what I'm saying?"

Zelma placed her hand softly on Ona's shoulder just as the word 'orphan' began to register in Ona's mind. Mr. McDaniel unwrapped the long, skinny package from its cloths revealing a flint lock long rifle and a sword with a bronze eagle head on the hilt. Ona looked closely at the eagle and wondered whose blood stained its brass feathers. "These was your father's. They can be yours now. Ona, look at me, girl."

Ona wasn't listening to Mr. McDaniel anymore. She shut him out, no longer acknowledging his words. Ona instead focused her attention on Zelma, "Come here now Zelma, honestly, cheer up with them crocodile tears." Zelma hiccupped through her tears, trying to pull herself together.

Ona began picking up the clay dishes from dinner. Mr. McDaniel and Zelma stood in the doorway, concerned for Ona's strange behavior.

"Do you want some soup?" Ona gestured with the empty soup bowls in her hand, but her knees gave way unexpectedly and she fell to the ground, sending broken pieces of the clay bowls flying in every direction, jarring Ona from the fog of Mr. McDaniel's news. She was up and slipped past her guests quicker than lighting, taking to her only haven: the woods. Near the forest edge, Enda grabbed her arm and pulled her close.

"Hey, wait! What's happened?" His voice was filled with concern and his blue eyes searched her face for answers. Ona didn't hear him. She only felt something holding her back from the animal drive to escape.

"Let me go!" She wrestled out of his grasp and took cover in the trees.

Ona heard people calling after her, but she couldn't remember who they were, and it didn't matter. She couldn't hear them, and she didn't want to talk to them. She was faster than them. She could run away. Ona's body was filled with the sensation that she had to keep moving. The cabin lights quickly faded behind her and she was lost to the darkness.

Ona ran without any sort of awareness. She did not feel around in front of her for branches or brambles, nor did she watch for hills or holes. She crashed through the forest running at full speed and slid down the muddy bank, stumbling across the stream. The creek flowed slow and black, like oil. Only a few hours before, the water seemed so inviting; but now it seemed like an obstacle jumping out to trip her.

There was nothing tangible chasing Ona, save for her own hysteria. It licked at the heels of her shadow and bubbled under the surface of her lips. She tried to choke it back, to run from it, to put it far behind her, but the dark monster slipped its black tendrils around her ankles and dragged her to the earth. Ona crawled on her hands and knees fleeing her own nightmares, but her misery seemed to be just as fast as she was. She collapsed to the ground, defeated by the monster.

Flashes appeared before Ona, dreams interrupted by memories. Last winter, when her father came home for just a few days to be with her over Christmas. Their cabin was crowded, and everyone sat either piled on the floor, in the two wooden chairs, or on the beds. They invited all their friends over for a feast. There was Fannie, the whole McDaniel family with their five children, Ona's father, the Reverend Johnson, even a drifter named Dale Fannin that her father met on the way home. It was such a happy time.

Ona remembered another time when the McDaniels opened up their farm to celebrate the harvest with a community dance. She was small enough to stand on her father's shoes while he whisked her around the McDaniel barn. Her tiny hands fit perfectly in his, and her long dress brushed across the dirt floor in layers of deep green fabric while they twirled to a friendly fiddle song.

The first time Rowland Christie brought Fannie home Ona was very small, barely three years old. Fannie looked at Ona up and down and said in matter of fact voice, "You'll do alright, I suppose."

To which Ona's father, who was sitting with his legs propped by the fire, fell out of his chair from laughter and nearly caught his boots on fire. Ona's father thought Fannie was the funniest creature alive.

The first time Rowland Christie was called away to fight in the battles with the Indians on the Southern border in Tennessee, he was gone an entire year before granted release. He was called to battle again and again, before he was called to suppress Indian resistance of the Federal Road planning.

Rowland Christie was a fighter his whole life. He fought to survive hardship in Ulster. He fought thousands of other people for a spot on a ship to America. He fought to stay in the United States, working as a servant in Virginia for years with Ona's mother before they were free of their debt. He fought for the land he owned in Kentucky. He fought to save the life of Abigail Christie, who died in childbirth having Ona. He fought to win new states for America. Named his only child after the country he loved. He fought for everything he had in life, and what did that get him? It didn't matter how loyal a countryman he was. Rowland Christie was dead.

In the darkness, Ona lay on the soft leaves in silence. She could not bring herself to move. She lay with her eyes closed for a long time, listening to the eerie sound of the barred owl calling out into the night. After some time, Ona began to chill in the nighttime dew and her body shivered with cold. She felt goose bumps rising on her arms and wrapped her mother's shawl tightly around her.

Above her, she felt the first of autumn's leaves settle weightlessly on her back. Ona hoped the leaves would bury her. She imagined her father and his body, resting cold in the ground in a nameless grave. As Ona drifted into a welcome slumber underneath her cover of leaf litter, it occurred to her that in this moment, perhaps they were just alike.

Ona stirred when murmuring voices filled her ears. She pulled her shawl over her head, trying to ignore it. The voices quickened, growing louder, so that she could no longer pretend it wasn't there. Ona peeked out from her shawl and lay very still; listening to conversation fill the space around her and watching many pairs of feet move soundlessly toward her. Perhaps her thoughts were jarred from sleep, but she could not figure out what the voices were saying.

Ona breathed in smoke and suppressed a cough. It smelled like the same tobacco stuff Fannie used in her pipe. Without much say in the matter, she began to relax and her vision became foggy. Four paws stepped lithely through the forest and Ona's eyes narrowed in confusion.

These were not the human feet she had seen a moment ago. These were large, hairy feet attached to rusty colored legs, all lean and muscular. A cold, wet nose loudly investigated the top of Ona's head, and floppy ears brushed across her face. Ona reached out her hand to the big hound dog that gave a friendly lick before uttering an excited bellow into the night.

A violent cry echoed through the trees and two hands collided with hers, ripping her outstretched fingers away from the dog. Ona looked up, terrified, into the steely gaze of a fierce looking man wearing many animal skins. The dog thumped its tail at the man's feet, flopping it enormous tongue out to one side of its mouth, seemingly pleased with itself.

"Sorry," Ona stammered. Her body trembled uncontrollably. Her feet were glued in place. Her mind could not fully comprehend her situation. Part of her mind whispered tales of people captured by tribes and who were never seen again. Or children who disappeared from towns only to stumble out of the forest decades later stark naked, tattooed and speaking not a lick of English. Should she run? Ona had been running all day. She was sick to her stomach with tiredness and her head was pounding. There was no more run left inside her.

"The Gihli for you is not for touching." The man's voice was stern looking down over her. His accent was so thick Ona strained to understand him. He was so large; Ona barely came to his chest. This man was starkly different from the dying man Ona cared for. That man had a fearsome gaze, but simple enough attire and hair. These men wore clothes dyed elaborate colors and layered with animal skins and tails.

The hair of the man who yelled at her was shaved, except for a spiky strip down the middle of his head that shot out in every direction. The others were entirely shaved smooth, except for a small lock of hair on the back of their heads. All of the men were covered in strange geometric tattoos. Ona studied her captor and the four other people that stood near him for a long time. In return, they seemed to be watching her too. She was overcome with convulsions and the last thing she remembered before passing out was falling to her knees and vomiting.

Chapter 4.

Ona stirred at the smell of smoke from a cooking fire. She sat up from a bed in a small cabin and examined the unfamiliar surroundings. She was draped in a combination of deer skins and brightly colored quilts. On the table, there was a pitcher of water and a plate of some funny looking bread, still warm in its pan. It smelled delicious. Ona looked around and saw people outside, and suddenly it occurred to her that she must have been rescued from the Indians. She left the food alone, unsure if she was allowed to eat it, and went to meet her saviors on the front porch.

The same, impossibly large man from the night before nodded his head toward Ona. Her heart stuttered, and she stood very still, so as to not stir the man into action. Her captor was talking quietly with another, but this new face did not have the unusual haircut. His hair was styled similarly to Mr. McDaniel's. It was short and parted to the side. The men were wearing suits, as nice as anyone's, however they were barefoot just like Ona. Ona could see in the distance two young women pulling weeds out of a sizable garden while the men rocked easily in wooden chairs, sharing a small stone pipe.

"Eat some food, then help the girls to earn your lunch," her captor said gruffly.

"Yes, sir." Ona's voice was numb.

The other man seemed to be in a much friendlier mood, and he openly smiled at Ona, waving hello and saying, "Welcome! I'm Rayetayah. Don't mind Kanagagota, he's in bad spirits. His daughter is stealing away my first born tomorrow." Rayetayah winked at Ona. Kanagagota huffed at his companion while Rayetayah continued, but Ona cut him off.

"Did you take me to be a slave?"

Kanagagota did not turn to face her. "We took the sickly woman trespasser from the forest so that tlvdatsi would not draw blood so near my home."

"A what?" Ona was incredulous.

"A panther. I am glad your health is improved from last night. What winds carried your feet to this side of the mountain?" The man Rayetayah was much gentler, and his warmth was genuine. Ona snorted. He spoke English better than most of the people in Calico.

Ona shrugged her shoulders. "I suppose I just like to run."

When Fannie and her husband were free from their indentureship in the Bluegrass, they followed French traders east to God's country in order to scrape a living off the land. They were used to

59

the cities and farms of Lexington and were completely helpless when the French traders dropped them off at a small trading post in southeast Kentucky.

Fannie said they would have starved to death if it hadn't been for the Cherokee who took them in. The Cherokee taught Fannie all the names of the plants and which were used for food and medicine. They also taught her husband how to hunt, and in exchange, Fannie and her husband taught them how to speak English and swapped farming strategies. Fannie remembered those times fondly and often recounted tales of her travels on cold winter nights by the fireplace.

In Fannie's stories, the people lived in round houses made from branches packed with mud. She said they wore clothes made from animal skins and furs and did not speak any English. But this family lived in a cabin, although smaller, otherwise it was very similar to where Ona lived with Fannie. They wore nice clothes like someone who worked in town and spoke English with ease. Why were things so different from how Fannie described?

Ona haltingly made her way to the small table and poured a cup of water. She examined the flat piece of bread, it looked crispy and fried. When she bit into it, it was sweet and soft inside and Ona remembered this wasn't her first time trying this food. Fannie had once made something she called fry bread, a sweet food she loved to eat when she lived with the Cherokee.

Ona sipped the clear drink and spat out what was definitely not water. Corn whiskey scorched down Ona's throat like liquid fire, burning a hole straight to her stomach. Through watery eyes and fits of coughing Ona managed to stuff another piece of fry bread into her mouth to help take away the burn. After composing herself, Ona marched forward to help in the garden, passing Kanagagota and Rayetayah, who were struggling to remained straight faced in their rocking chairs.

The sisters were Kanagagota's daughters and they were not much older than Ona. Ayita was seventeen and Awenasa, fifteen. Ayita was all smiles, just a day before her wedding. Happiness over-flowed in her heart, spilling into the work of her steady, productive hands. The sisters worked well together, but were welcoming of some extra help a day before the celebration.

"Am I to be a slave here?" Ona asked once more.

"I do not know. Our brother took our slaves recently to sell for different ones. Until he returns, we need help in the gardens, and certainly through the joining. We've never had a white woman be-fore, but others have." Awenasa turned her head sideways, taking in Ona's figure with curiosity.

"I don't want to stay." Ona let the ear of corn fall to the ground.

"Cooperation for you is best." Ayita stooped to hand the ear of corn back to Ona. Chills ran down her back, and she spoke no more. They finished harvesting corn and began shucking in the field.

"So, you have never been to a joining celebration? Not even a wedding?" Awenasa couldn't believe Ona was so sheltered. She spoke English more naturally than her sister, with a flat accent like someone from the North had been her teacher.

"No." Ona tried to keep her guard up, but it was hard not to like Awenasa. She seemed honest and pure of heart. Ayita was more serious and reserved, like her father.

"It's a beautiful sight and there is enough food to feed everyone in town. You will attend it with me?"

"If I'm able." A small smile threatened at the corner of Ona's lips. It was impossible to say no to one like Awenasa, her spirit was radiant.

Ona's time with Awenasa's family proved to be a distraction from thinking of her father. No one asked her questions about her family, but they did ask her when she was hungry or thirsty. She helped Ayita and Awenasa through their chores, watching a dozen or more women come and go throughout the day. They brought gifts of jewelry for Ayita to wear at her ceremony and took food to a place called the Meeting House where it would all take place tomorrow at sunset.

Not every woman who visited wore dresses like Ona and Kanagagota's daughters. Some came in traditional clothing wrapped in layers of animal skins and brightly dyed cloths and beads. Tomorrow, Ayita would trade her Western clothes for a special dress that belonged to her mother.

"I'm envious! I don't remember mama at all." Ona worked a thin piece of thread through her needle to mend a pair of blue blankets with Awenasa.

"You call her mama? Strange." Awenasa wrinkled her nose.

"Yes, Mama and Papa. Don't tell me you don't have names for ole Kanagagota up there. That's just plain too long to keep track of."

Awenasa giggled. "It's not hard for people who speak Tsalagi. And I do have a mother. She is not here now; because her daughter is to be wed, she has been praying at the Meeting House to bless the site. She will perform the ceremony tomorrow. We've already delayed waiting for my brother to return, but it has been long enough he will simply miss the celebration."

"What sort of blessing?" Ona folded her blanket up, searching Awenasa's deep brown eyes with interest.

"First Ayita and her promised one, Tewa, will sit on either side of the mothers. Once everyone arrives, we will all go outside and my mother will lead the ceremony. People will bring food and there will be singing and dancing all night long."

Ona was bewildered by the joining ceremony. "I ain't never gone to a wedding, but people in Calico marry with the Bible so Jesus can bless the marriage."

"We took Jesus last year. A man came and said Jesus was like our Unetlanvhi. He built us a church that we visit, even appointed one elder to be the minister and taught him to read the Bible. You perform joinings with that book?" Awenasa's eyes widened in surprise.

"If you can, you go to the church to get hitched. The couple stands at the front of the church alter and the preacher reads you verses from the Bible and he wraps your hands in cloths with knots and ties them together. Then you're hitched." It was all very simple. Ona couldn't believe Awenasa had never heard of it before.

Awenasa crinkled her brow. "But if you're inside the building when you... get hitched...then how will the spirits know you've joined? The joining ceremony has to be done outside under the sky for Unetlanvhi to know it happened."

Ona shrugged her shoulders, laughing. "It seem kind of like a heathen ceremony! Do you even go to church?"

Awenasa spoke gravely. "I do. Every Sunday with my family. If you don't go to church Jesus will let you burn alive for all eternity."

Ona's eyes sparkled with mischief. She knew full well to keep the ten commandments and live according to God if she wanted spend eternity in heaven. On the other hands, heaven also sounded a lot like an eternity of Horace Wexlers.

"Heathen religion do seem a lot more exciting though."

Awenasa revealed a shy smile as she worked her needle, but did not respond.

The day of the joining ceremony was sunny and cool without a cloud in the sky. Ona had a chance to finally see the Meeting House, a large enclosure made of tree limbs and river cane with a thatched birch bark roof. Inside was a spacious room with a stone fire pit in the middle. A dozen cabins like Awenasa's dotted the town and were scattered alongside the steep hillside, each with a lush garden. The Meeting House was the only traditional looking building in sight, positioned in the center of town. The little community was completely isolated on the far side of the mountain, hidden behind densely growing calico bushes.

Awenasa fixed her hair in elaborate braids that ran down her back. She changed into a crimson skirt with a beaded suede top. Awenasa wrapped herself in a multi colored shawl and encouraged Ona to do the same, "It gets colder than you think at night, be sure to bring a shawl. Do you have nothing to cover your feet?" Ona shook her head awkwardly, and Awenasa pursed her lips before leaving the cabin to speak with her father.

Kanagagota entered a few moments later, scrutinizing Ona's filthy, cut and bruised feet. She curled her toes self-consciously before he began rummaging under the quilted bed in the cabin. He pulled out a pair of moccasins, decorated with brightly colored beads, handing them to her. Ona accepted them wide eyed, slipping into the most beautiful things to ever touch her feet.

"Thank you," She stammered.

"Everybody needs something for their feet when it gets to be this time of year," Awenasa giggled. Ona draped herself in her mother's blue green plaid shawl. Awenasa marveled at the deep blue color of Ona's shawl and the complex green stripes and bars in the fabric.

"How did you make this?" She gasped.

"I didn't— Mama done made it a long time ago, before she died."

Ona examined the exotic geometric shapes, with their stars and diamonds that appeared in Awenasa's traditional attire. It seemed just as complicated as a plaid pattern and they discussed different techniques for making Cherokee dyes and patterns until it was time for the ceremony.

Kanagogata shook his head when he saw the girls. "Stay home tonight, Awenasa." Awenasa burst out speaking heatedly in Tsalagi, a string of sounds Ona did not understand that dramatically rose and fell in pitch in a way that was unnatural to the English language.

Kanagogata laughed, "Calm, my child. You look a woman tonight and I am not yet ready to send away my youngest daughter on the night of her sister's joining."

Awenasa smiled kindly at her father, her face resuming placidity. She took his side and walked with her hand in his toward the Meeting House, where Ayita and her mother were already waiting. Ona watched the father and daughter walk hand in hand and felt her heart tighten. A lump appeared in her throat and she refused to think of his face. Ona was not ready to mourn Rowland Christie yet.

At the Meeting House Ona was stopped at the doorway by a stern looking woman who began bickering with Kanagagota. Awenasa whispered in Ona's ear, "She says you are not from the family, and you are not allowed to come inside this sacred space because you are a stranger. My father is saying that you are in his possession and you cannot be left alone." Awenasa cast Ona an apologetic look.

"I'm sorry Ona, but I must go inside for my sister." Ona stood behind Kanagagota, her spirit deflated. Ona imagined Fannie had been told that she took off and was probably scouring the mountains with an axe ready to put Ona out of her misery for running away. She kicked at the ground and sighed.

Possibly the oldest woman Ona had ever seen approached them. She walked with a staff and her voice was raspy, speaking quietly with the upset woman. The woman did not argue with her. She went inside and sat, not looking at Ona. The elderly woman gestured inside the Meeting House saying, "Welcome, friend."

Her accent was thick, but Ona understood her easily and was warmed by her act of kindness. She passed the old woman and wrapped her arms around her frail figure in a hug. All eyes in the Meeting House watched in alarm as Ona broke away from the hug and found a place beside Awenasa. The old woman smiled widely without a tooth in her head and sat placidly beside Awenasa's mother in the large circle. Awenasa couldn't believe what Ona had done. "You just embraced the high elder!" she whispered in disbelief. "I can't believe you did such a thing!"

"Where I'm from that's how you say thank you!" Ona snapped back in a hushed voice. "Why all the fuss?"

"That woman, she can talk to God." It was clear the admiration Awenasa held for the woman. Ona started to feel like she had done something wrong.

"Don't worry," Awenasa continued hurriedly, "I think she appreciates your spirit. I mean, you're still alive, aren't you?"

Ona smiled awkwardly, "Yes, I suppose I am."

The ceremony kicked off with the old woman singing in a rhythmic fashion in the same unfamiliar way that made her voice rise and fall in time. Even though Ona couldn't understand what the woman was saying, her voice was soothing to the effect that Ona found herself lulled into a rhythm that nestled itself into her consciousness so that all she could hear was the crackling of the fire in harmony with the elder's raspy chant. When the room was filled and the old woman's song finished, Ayita's mother raised to address the town.

"Ayita has received the blessing of her family." Awenasa whispered in Ona's ear.

Ayita's mother led the way out of the Meeting House and around a stone fire pit that blazed high against the setting sun. Ayita and Tewa stood before their mothers, each wrapped in a blue blanket that Ona and Awenasa had mended earlier in the day. Ayita's mother spoke to the people, who whooped and cheered back before the blue blankets were stripped from the couple. She then wrapped the couple lovingly in a white cloth and spoke loud enough for all the heavens to hear. She tilted a unique clay pitcher with two mouths so that both Ayita and her husband could drink at the same time. The couple laughed, choking down the harsh drink of corn whiskey in the pitcher. Her husband whooped loudly, thus beginning the celebrations.

The feast was incredible. Ona eyed the food hungrily. She wanted to try everything. There was more fry bread, as well as bean bread and wilted greens with stewed potatoes. There were blackberry cobblers and huge platters of roast duck and smoked deer. Someone had even brought out a basket of pawpaw fruit and Ona smiled to herself as she picked one up and ate, spitting out seeds and chatting amicably with Awenasa.

As with the tradition, Ayita brought a hefty basket of corn that was later cooked over the fire, as part of her promise help support her future family. Her husband killed a deer, keeping his part of the promise to help provide for his loved ones, and people picked at smoked meats all night long.

When the dancing started, Ona could not tear her eyes from the scene. People jumped up and down, shouting and singing. There were elaborate dances that sometimes just the men, or just the women, or sometimes both participated in around the fire.

Several men had buffalo hooves fastened to soft leather that slipped over their legs, turning their steps into music and their leaps into something loud and riotous. The music swelled inside of Ona and she wanted to join in on the fun, but didn't want to intrude on dances she didn't know the steps to. She was happy sitting outside the dance ring, stuffing as much corn bread and smoked venison as she could fit into her mouth.

Hours had passed since sunset and the party was still carrying on. Ona had eaten herself into a stupor and stared up into the stars dreamily. She was beginning to think of the straw pallet bed she shared with Awenasa waiting for her back at the cabin. Tomorrow it would be time to make her way back to Calico Ridge. A man with short cropped hair approached Awenasa and spoke quietly in her ear. She got up to follow him and Ona followed after her friend. Awenasa sighed, giggling to herself.

"This is my uncle, but he does not speak English. The men are out of whiskey, but they are in luck. Word must have gotten out about the celebration tonight because there is a man here with a wagon and two barrels or corn whiskey. This is my job when I am not working in the garden. I speak English very well; I learned it from a Frenchman who lived with us when I was young. *Je parle français, aussie.*" Awenasa winked at Ona, who was amazed at her talents.

Ona and Awenasa followed her uncle behind the cabins to the edge of the village. Ona could see a small lantern ahead of them. As they neared, she saw none other than Jeremiah Sunday holding up the lantern with Enda Cambor at his side, pulling a wagon of whiskey. Ona froze in her tracks.

It was well known that Jeremiah Sunday made all Indians his sworn enemy after his family was murdered by a raiding party. It was possibly more well known that he would never part with a drop of whiskey that he stumbled across, let alone two whole barrels. Something was very wrong here. Ona could not shake the image of the fallen Indian from her mind. Enda Cambor recognized Ona about the same time Ona saw the trap in front of her.

"Be careful!" Ona shouted, "It's a trick!" She grabbed Awenasa, pulling her back and reaching out for Awenasa's uncle. Her warning did not reach him though, for he did not speak English. Jeremiah Sunday shot Awenasa's uncle before her very eyes, and he fell to the ground clutching his stomach. It was only a moment before his body became still. Jeremiah Sunday was crazed. His eyes were wild and he was stuffing more gun powder into his rifle. Enda Cambor dropped the wagon handle, hands shaking.

"What was you thinking? Why'd you do that? Do you want to get us killed, old man?" Enda's voice cracked with shock and rage. He acted as if he did not know the attack was planned. Awenasa fell to her uncle's side, wailing and speaking quickly in her native tongue.

Jeremiah Sunday spat at the feet of Awenasa's uncle. "Good riddance. We best get on, boy. They'll be coming after us soon." He turned around and started back into the forest, already out of sight.

"Enda, Enda, what happened?" Ona began to cry. Awenasa was inconsolable. Ona felt herself being overcome with emotion and she felt the raw weight of her father's own death suddenly hit her. So much life wasted on this earth.

"Ona. I don't know what's going on, but we got to get out of here. They gone find us, and they gone blame us. We ain't them, Ona, they gone say it's our fault." Enda pleaded with Ona.

"But it wasn't us, Enda. We didn't do it!" Ona's voice was straining against Awenasa's wailing. Awenasa stood to her feet. She was trembling all over.

"You know this boy? You brought this boy with that white man here on the day of my sister's joining?" Her fists were balled tightly together.

"Did you plan to be found by my father? So you could continue to murder my people, after years and years. Isn't it enough? Hasn't it happened enough? Walk like you, talk like you, work like you, live like you, go to church like you, get hitched like you! When will it be enough?" Awenasa's pleasant face had crumbled into a visage of pain that ran deeper than her own being.

"You're with this boy? He's not white. He's not Cherokee or even negro. He's not any of us. And you let him and that white man murder my own flesh and blood?"

Awenasa wasn't sobbing anymore. Fury began to mask her anguish. Awenasa's breathing steadied and her eyes were set in a hard gaze. She spat on Ona's moccasins and took off toward the bonfire, which still blazed impressively in the background with music and laughter flooding out all other noises.

Enda Cambor took Ona's hand. His voice was low and steady, "Run."

Ona and Enda tore through the forest, as fast as their feet could carry them. They skidded and tumbled down the mountainside, making their way as far from the Cherokee path they could manage. Ona wasn't sure where they were going, but Enda at least seemed to have an idea. Behind them, Ona heard the sharp sound of cries filling the night. Enda led her to a ravine where they splashed through a shallow stream bed. Ona could hear shots fired nearby in the trees and she forced herself to run faster. Finally, the land flattened and the trickling stream turned into a creek. After a while, Ona had to swim to keep up– Enda was much taller than she was.

"Duck!" Enda shouted. He submersed himself in the creek and Ona mimicked him, feeling something strike the water from above. Caught in the gentle current, she was able to pick up an arrow being carried downstream and her heart nearly pounded out of her breast.

They swam downstream for a long while, only surfacing for air when it was necessary to breathe. Ona choked back a scream when she kicked off from the creek bottom, finding instead of silt and stone, a massive catfish every bit as big as her stirring from its murky bed. At long last did Enda crawl out of the creek on the opposite side they entered, and they scrambled up steep banks and sharp hills, soaking wet. The moon was high in the sky, and they marched on silently into the cool night.

Enda led Ona by the hand silently past an old shack made of tree bark and pieces of salvaged tin in a small clearing. All around the

shack there were animal skulls hanging from the trees like orna-
ments. Through a candlelit window, Ona could see old man Sunday
downing shine from a glass bottle. He threw his emptied bottle
against a wall, laughing gleefully as it shattered. Ona tightened her
grip on Enda's hand and he held his fingers to his lips, motioning
her to stay silent.

They slipped past the old shack and crossed another small
stream before the bramble turned into tracks of mud that smelled
of rotten food and human filth. Ona slowed to a halt when she realized where she was. They had stumbled into the far side of town,
behind the shops. They were also at least still a two hour walk from
the cabin. Walking through town, Ona finally began to feel her heart
regulate. Her side was sore from running, but she eventually caught
her breath. Ona wanted to walk through the brick streets, but Enda
insisted they stay in the muddy alleyways.

It dawned on Ona that Enda may not be a welcome face in town.
After all, Awenasa was right about one thing: Enda wasn't white,
and he wasn't black, and he wasn't Cherokee. In one sense a part of
him belonged to all three peoples. In another sense, he wasn't fully
claimed by any of them. Ona eyed Enda up and down out the corner
of her eye. She thought he seemed harmless enough.

Ona and Enda made their way up the alleys of downtown Calico,
past the brick manors that lined the streets just outside the market
district. Houses were dimly lit with candles in every window, while
perfectly planted roses bloomed in flower beds beside the houses.

Ona paused after hearing music outside of a particularly striking home, made of brick and a balcony supported by tall white pillars. She could see through the window none other than Blanche Beaudin sitting at a piano bench with her father. They were performing a psalm in the form of a duet that her mother and younger brother sang along to.

Ona squished the mud and filth from the alleyways felt it growing warm and sticky inside between her toes. The stench of urine was turning her stomach. She took off her moccasins and raised her arm to chuck one at the Beaudin window, but Enda grabbed it up from her.

"Don't." Enda pleaded. "Don't do that."

"And just why not?" Ona's spirit was beaten.

"Because. They can't appreciate a fine shoe as this." He wordlessly knelt to the ground, gently removing her remaining moccasin and carried them for Ona all the way back to Calico Ridge.

Chapter 5.

Ona slept late the next morning and was slow getting started on her chores. Fannie could be home at any time and the place was, most unfortunately, in the same disarray from the night she learned of her father's death. She swept up the shards of the shattered clay bowl and put away her slate board. The fire had gone out with no one home to tend it and she shivered underneath her shawl, sipping on cold soup for breakfast.

Later in the day, she hauled a basket of clothes over her shoulder, making her way down the rope ladder to the pooling spring over the cliff. Ona scrubbed her clothes with a stiff bristled brush, watching the muck from her clothes and body swirl around her. She was even able to work the filth out of her moccasins.

Scrambling out of the spring carrying a basket laden with dripping wet clothes over her shoulder was more difficult than the climb down, but she managed to make the climb up and hang her belongings out to dry under the sun. Ona changed into a green and white checkered dress that she made with Fannie, and wandered to her favorite tree near the edge of the forest

It was a massive white oak that took five men to wrap their arms around. Ona hiked her dress up to her knees, grabbing knobs and branches until she reached her favorite vantage spot high off the ground. Ona spent the afternoon letting the sun warm her face, watching orioles flit in and out around her. She drew pictures of scarlet tanagers and cerulean warblers darting through the trees and listened to woodpeckers busy themselves deep in the forest. The last of the season's jar flies hummed all around her and after a time, she let her pencil slip her grasp and sketchbook droop into her lap as she drifted into a peaceful slumber.

"She's been missing for how long?" The crackly voice of Fannie, who sounded altogether exhausted, cut through the early evening breeze.

"Two days, now. I done sent my girl up yonder yesterday when we couldn't find her the other night, but there weren't no sign of her. She ain't been to town neither." Mr. McDaniel was deeply worried, walking up the path with Fannie.

Ona stirred awake in the oak tree. She heard Fannie and Mr. McDaniel considering her whereabouts and clumsily began her descent back to earth still half asleep. Groggy, she missed a hold and fell the last 6 feet of her climb, landing in front of Fannie and Mr. McDaniel. Ona rubbed her eyes sleepily.

"Welcome back, Fannie." Ona yawned.

Fannie didn't miss a beat. "Wash here's been telling me you decided to quit civilized living and become remiss. What say you, Cricket?" Ona gave a small laugh. Just like Fannie to lighten the mood.

"Well, I wouldn't expect that to work out so well, Fannie. I couldn't very well make medicine with you if I ain't here to begin with."

Fannie smiled, "That's my girl."

Ona, Fannie and Mr. McDaniel made their way into the cabin which was, to Fannie's delight, in impeccable condition. They finished off the cold soup and Mr. McDaniel bid a reluctant farewell on the promise Ona stop in the general store to say hello every so often.

It was all a little unclear what would happen with Ona. Although it only just occurred to her, Fannie was no longer earning pension from Ona's father. Fannie could leave whenever she wanted.

Fannie strolled with Ona through the yard, plucking mint and sassafras. She mashed the plants together, heated water over the fire and poured them each a cup of tea. Fannie sighed deeply, rubbing her achy knee and lit her long tobacco pipe.

"Your father was a strong man. A warrior, even. I know he loved you with every bit of himself, the best he knew how. It's a hard loss, Cricket. Leaves us left to wander this mean Earth just a-wondering how we hurt so much, and how we're supposed to get on with it like there's not a hole the size of this here home missing in your heart."

Ona stared into the dregs of her tea. She felt the heavy bricks she'd come to associate with her father's death weighing down on her, collapsing her lungs and filling her stomach with mortar. Her breathing increased while her lungs tried to compensate for the crushing effect of conversing about her father, but she could not seem to fill them up with air. She felt herself becoming nauseous. All at once the room seemed to be too close to her, the walls were crushing her, the tea was scalding her; Fannie's very breath encroached on the space of Ona's fragile senses.

Ona's fingers tapped her cup obsessively and she thought about how much faster she could move than Fannie. Leaning forward on her seat, preparing to make a run for it, to get some fresh air and finally breathe, Ona caught Fannie's gaze in the corner of her eye. Fannie held her pipe, puffing silently behind her watery gray eyes. Ona scooted her chair out from the table. "I'm going for a walk."

"Come back tonight, Cricket."

"Yes, ma'am."

"Cricket?"

"Yes?"

"How you holding up, girl?"

Ona recalled the empty gaze of the Indian man tucked under Fannie's covers, looking up at her the morning she found him dead. She replayed the murder of Awenasa's uncle in her mind a dozen times. She imagined her father beginning to rot in his grave, fingers turning gray. Do people mold like spoiled food? She pictured Enda Camber back home in the dilapidated shack with Jeremiah Sunday, who threw glass bottles at walls. She thought for a minute that the Cherokee could still find her and scalp her and Fannie both at any time.

"I'm fine." Ona said simply.

"Ham and greens for supper, Cricket. Don't be late."

Ona spent the next few weeks trudging through school on Monday mornings and learning to set traps with Enda each evening. Enda it turned out, had never been to school a day in his life, so in exchange for teaching Ona how to snare rabbits and other small game, Ona taught Enda how to read and write. Fannie hadn't mentioned leaving at all, so Ona never brought it up.

Although Ona and Fannie suffered great losses during Jeremiah Sunday's escapades nearly a month ago, they were managing just fine. It seemed that Fannie was highly resourceful not just in her knowledge of medicinal herbs, but edible ones as well. It also helped that every time Ona stopped by the McDaniels' shop to say hello, Mr. McDaniel sent her home with bags of flour, beans, thread or as much as Ona could carry on her long walk home.

Their meals were strange, but filling. Enda helped Ona set snares, so they nearly always had meat alongside some assortment of root vegetables, wild greens, onions, and mushrooms. They were able to plant their winter crops: cabbage, turnips, greens, and radishes, which meant they would not starve over winter. Ona finally convinced Enda that Fannie would not put the evil eye on him, and he slowly began to come around for meals.

Fannie made quick work of Enda, employing him to build a root cellar, in exchange for meals and clothes. Enda spent weeks moving debris from deep inside a small knoll not far from the house. He carried flat limestone rocks from the creek bed, stacking them against the exposed earth to create a storage room that kept cool, and unfrozen year-round under the soil's protection. He crushed limestone and broken clay crocks Ona had piled up in the yard into a powder mixed with water to create cement paste that sealed the front facing cellar from water seeping in.

At the Bible School, Zelma stuck to Ona like glue, worrying over her like she could drop dead at any moment. Even though Zelma's family owned the general store downtown, they still lived outside of town a ways. Zelma's father rode a mule in every morning to town and was never home until after dark. Wash McDaniel might have been the only shop keeper to live outside of town. He was also the only shop keeper from Ulster; the other merchants moved in from Virginia and Pennsylvania, already established in their place on this earth.

Ona wore her moccasins to school and church. She wore them partly because she adored their bright colors for she truly owned nothing so beautiful, and partly because she missed Awenasa's company. She wondered what they must think of the girl who ran away like a guilty criminal on the night Awenasa's uncle was murdered. The headmaster Horace Wexler called the shoes sinful for their beaded adornments, taking people's eyes away from God.

After weeks of waking up with tears streaked down her face from garbled nightmares of Rowland Christie sometimes dying in battle, sometimes rotting underground, sometimes buried alive on accident, sometimes being shot in the stomach by Jeremiah Sunday, and nearly always ending with Ona being hunted by an angry Cherokee party, her nightmares began to dissipate. The raw pain of her father's death no longer crushed her lungs so that it was impossible to breathe. In time, Ona's life began to form into her new normal.

At school one brisk September morning, Zelma stood in a simple pink dress hiding a shy smile behind a stack of envelopes. She passed around envelopes to every girl in the school, about thirteen altogether. Ona scrunched up her eyes and tore open the letter:

You are cordially invited to celebrate the twelfth birthday of one Miss Zelma McDaniel on this day of Saturday, October 23rd from noon until three.
Sincerely,
Mr. and Mrs. Wash McDaniel

Ona looked up at Zelma. "A birthday party?"

Zelma smiled widely, nodding her head. Ona had never been to a birthday party before. "That's wonderful!"

On the day of Zelma's party, much to Ona's horror, Fannie had presented her a new white dress with a pale blue ribbon that tied around Ona's waist into a delicate bow behind her back. Ona agreed to wear the waist ribbon but could barely be coaxed into swapping out her moccasins for her old pair of worn leather walking boots to protect her from frost. Fannie sent Ona with a gift for Zelma wrapped in cloth, a pair of deep maroon mittens that she had been working on over the past couple weeks.

Ona escaped out the door before Fannie could do any more damage with ribbon, passing Enda, who was moving potatoes into the newly finished root cellar. He caught sight of Ona and dropped his armload of potatoes before clamoring over himself to pick them back up. Ona giggled, "What's got you all shook up?"

Enda collected himself coolly. "Nothing. Just figured you were someone else with a bath and all. Give me a fright looking like some kind of ghost once you wash the dirt off. Hope you don't expect me to clean up like that for your birthday, Little America!"

Ona rolled her eyes. "And here I was hoping to put you in a dress come January, Enda!" She laughed before pausing to think, "Say Enda, when is your birthday anyhow?"

Enda shrugged, "My father kept track of dates differently. All I know is I'm 15 summers old."

"He never said when?"

Enda just shrugged his shoulders, uncaring.

"Well we better tell Fannie then."

"Why's that?" Enda was confused now.

"So we can have you a bonafide birthday!" Ona exclaimed.

Enda huffed and turned around, carrying his load of potatoes toward the cellar and muttering about work to do.

Ona strolled down the road to the McDaniel farm, careful not to step on her white dress. White was such an impractical color. When she arrived at the McDaniel farm, Ona was greeted by girls of all ages running and screaming through the front field playing tag, hide and seek, shooting marbles, and singing rhyming games. There were even a few older girls Ona's age leaning over balconies to jest with Zelma's older brothers, especially Ezra, who had become very popular since he started working with his father in the general store. Zelma was the youngest of five and the only daughter in her family. Chickens bustled around the home, flustered from all the activity, and a puppy with a large pink ribbon tied to it chased after a ball that Zelma threw gleefully over and over again.

"Ona!" She picked up her wriggly puppy and ran to greet her. "You're here!" Zelma was dressed in a getup more like Blanche than ever, but Ona figured it was alright since she still acted like the same old Zelma.

The afternoon sun had melted away some of the mountain morning chill and everywhere, children were losing shoes to play in the soft grass. Blanche Beaudin sat primly, wearing a pink dress with puffy sleeves and white satin gloves at a small table laden with cookies. She eyed the cookies hungrily but didn't take one. Ona ignored her, grabbing handfuls of cookies to take back to the game of hide and seek.

"Seems like they let just anyone show up today. It figures, since the McDaniels are so poor, they probably can't afford to be picky."

"Don't ruin my appetite, Blanche." Ona tucked a stray coil of hair up into her cap and downed a delicious looking cookie.

"They're barely making it with the store in town, you know. My father had to give them a loan just last week. It's sad really." Blanche sighed daintily.

"Perhaps if they were not involved with so much charity, then they wouldn't be in the spot they are in." Blanche looked up with a small smile on her lips and held Ona's gaze.

Ona drew a long breath and wiped the cookie crumbs from her mouth with the back of her hand. Blanche's eyes bulged in horror, but it was too late. Ona really only got in one good punch before Mr. McDaniel ripped her off of Blanche, who was crying on her back with a black eye and grass stains on her dress.

From a window inside the McDaniel home, Ona watched the other girls awkwardly resume playing in front of the house. It was a nice house. Two stories and made of brick, but it didn't have any pillars or roses; just the same old tiger lilies, now gone for the year, that grew everywhere by Ona's house and that was just as well. She loved the smell of tiger lilies in summer. Ona sat at a long wooden table, polished smooth and made of red cedar. Her fingers traced the pattern of a lace table cloth, watching out the window at the whole group of girls joining in playing ball with the new puppy. Blanche was upstairs resting in Zelma's bedroom.

"Ona, why did you do that?" Mr. McDaniel shook his head, sitting down beside Ona.

"She's meaner than a snake and you can't trust her for nothing. She's lying whatever she say." Ona inspected the ornate pattern of the table cloth closely. It must have taken a lot of time to craft such a beautiful, delicate thing.

"Was it a lie that you attacked her and give her a black eye? We seen it happen, Cricket." Mr. McDaniel's voice wasn't accusing Ona. It was stating the facts.

"She said some awful bad things, sir."

"I don't doubt that Ona, but you can't just haul off and get at someone because they say something upsetting," Mr. McDaniel laughed, stroking his beard.

"You know, before you was born, your father used to be the exact same way. I never saw somebody get so hot and bothered over little things. But you know what, Cricket, when you was born he learned something. He learned that people talk. People do all kinds of terrible things to get you down. We know that better than anyone, coming from where we did, having to do the things we done just to survive. Fannie knows it, too. But you know what?"

Ona would not make eye contact, but she paused from tracing the lace pattern. Mr. McDaniel continued, "Your father decided once you was born he don't care about none the things people say. See, it's easy to fight someone. That's what they expect from you. They don't think you got any self-control. They think you can't succeed in life. They're rooting for you to fail, Cricket, you and Rowland both. They will say things your whole life and it's just a matter of being tough enough to prove them wrong. You beat on that little girl upstairs? Sure, she deserve it. But you do that and you letting them win, sweetheart. That's all they ever think you're good for; but you know what? I know you're so much more than whatever they say, so don't let them win, Ona."

Ona stayed at the McDaniels' long after the party ended. She ate dinner with them and spent time reminiscing over days with her father. Zelma's brothers all found the fight hysterical and one of Zelma's brothers who was Enda's age, Nash, staged the fight with his knife and fork animatedly. Zelma's oldest brother Ezra was laughing so hard he had tears in his eyes. "You should have seen it, Mother. Ona showed that spoiled brat how to two-step!" Ezra choked between mouthfuls of roast duck, brown gravy and potatoes.

"I don't think she's ever touched the ground before!" Zelma giggled.

"Will you kids hush. It's not polite to jest at someone's suffering." Anna McDaniel sounded severe, but the corners of her lips twitched into a small smile. Something told Ona that more than one person was happy to see the judge's daughter eat dirt this afternoon.

The McDaniels were very close with the Christies and it had been a while since Ona visited. Ona began her walk home at twilight. Ezra offered to walk Ona home, to which Ona stared blankly at him.

"Why? I've done it a hundred times before by myself. I'll be fine." Ona stopped, startled at the harshness of her own words. Ezra was just trying to be polite. She chewed her lip, searching for better words. "I only meant—"

Ezra shook his head and smiled in graceful defeat. "Never mind, Ona. I'll see you around, alright?"

Ona hadn't talked with Ezra lately. He'd been apprenticing under his father at the general store in town and she'd seen him busy, learning to do things like accounting and numbers. Ezra was seventeen and had grown tall. He grew his hair just long enough to part on one side, letting the curls only he and Zelma inherited from their mother frame his face like an Englishman.

"Yes." Ona agreed. Ezra started back toward the door when Ona caught him by surprise.

"Ezra?"

"Yes?"

"Next time, alright?" Ona said in a rush.

Ezra laughed kindly. "Alright, Ona. Anything you wish."

The McDaniels and the Halsteads were about as close to neighbors as Ona and Fannie had, and they were still a couple miles away.

Ona's walk was quiet with thoughts of her parents swirling in her head. Dinner with the McDaniels was a lot like the old days when she and her father would go visit them.

Mr. McDaniel and Ona's father would drink sour ales and break out Wash McDaniel's dulcimer and Rowland Christie's fiddle. Anna McDaniel led them all in song around fires, somber ballads and lively jigs, and teaching all the children the different dances she grew up with. Those were beautiful times. Ona absently kicked chestnuts up the hill along the dirt road to her house when a man on horse overtook her.

"Get out of the way, girl! There's been an attack! Go home! Fly home! It's not safe!" The man shouted at her, his hat tilted precariously on the side of his head with coat tails flying out behind him and horse spraying Ona's white dress with mud as it raced past her.

Ona's heart sank into her stomach. She bolted home to Fannie through the steep muddied road up Calico Mountain, ruining the hems of her dress. Enda was gone for the night, back to the shack with Jeremiah Sunday. Fannie was safe at home knitting more winter clothing, completely unaware of any attacks. Relief flooded through Ona. Upon her account of the horse and rider, Fannie decided they should go to church the next morning.

"There's bound to be more news on what's happened from Brother Johnson. We can't be leaving ourselves unprotected. If someone is attacking the homes we best know about it so we can be prepared. You know, we'll be needing bullets for your father's gun. We ought to be ready for it."

The last attack Ona had ever heard of near town was the massacre of Jeremiah Sunday's family before Ona was ever even born. Fannie made sure she lodged the front door tightly shut with a broom. Ona tossed and turned all night in her sleep. Every creak in the floor seemed to be someone sneaking through the house. Every gust of wind was like a person howling outside the window. Ona could see Fannie's lamp light long into the night before finally being snuffed out. Ona wondered if Enda too laid awake in his bed tonight.

A brisk chill clung to Sunday morning, making Ona shiver over her bowl of grits. Ona changed into her deep navy-blue dress for church, pulling up her stockings under her leather walking boots and wrapping herself in her mother's plaid shawl. Fannie donned a simple white blouse with blue checkered skirts and a gray shawl. She hid her wispy white hair under a pale blue scarf that tied under her chin. She stopped Ona before they left the house, "Fix your cap, Cricket."

For the first time she could remember, Ona looked at herself in the small mirror above Fannie's bed. Ona considered her appearance so infrequently that it did not occur to her to request a mirror in the loft. She was not particularly beautiful, and she did not particularly mind. Ona did not dwell on pretty little things, like baubles or mirrors.

Ona toyed with her wild curls, thinking of Mrs. Lafayette's radiant beauty. Ona would never have Mrs. Lafayette's fine bone structure or soft hands or silk muslin evening wear. What was the point? Ona sighed in frustration at the untamed curls spiraling out in every direction. She picked up a lock of hair and began to braid, framing the top of her head in a braid. She stuffed the remainder up underneath her cotton cap, for the sake of time. Ona managed to cover the worst of it, but there wasn't much she could do about the stray locks escaping containment.

They walked the dusty road to town in silence, leaving shortly after sunrise to make it on time. There was the little church that served as Ona's school, the one room Methodist establishment, but that wasn't the church that would draw in the crowds. The Primitive Baptist Church in downtown Calico was an ornate brick building that stood erect two stories with numerous, tall windows. This was the church that would generate conversation about the attacks; and as the church bells sounded, the sanctuary drew in crowds of people squishing into pews as if it were Christmas or Easter. The higher than normal attendance meant people would hear word of the attack before Monday, seeing as the shops were closed on the Sabbath.

The minister was a fearsome man when pressed for a sermon, though was kind enough to speak with and wasn't nearly as cruel as the headmaster Horace Wexler. In fact, the Reverend Johnson occasionally consulted Fannie for water witching work to help new landowners find the best place to dig a well. Even though Fannie kept some old heathen ways, everybody in Calico (except Horace Wexler) understood the importance of water witching to dig wells. The reverend called it a gift from God. Maybe it was because the reverend and Fannie were both old, white haired, and widowed. Maybe it was because they were both blunt and practical to a fault, but Fannie and the minister always got along so long as they didn't talk politics

Ona and Fannie took seats besides the McDaniels. Zelma sat in her yellow, flowery dress bundled in a thick, white shawl with her face hidden by a straw bonnet. She listened in earnest to the minister. Ezra was hunched forward in his seat, glancing back at Ona every so often. Ona waved hello to Ezra, but Ezra simply sat up straighter to listen to the sermon.

The Beaudins sat across the aisle, and Ona noted with smug satisfaction that behind Blanche Beaudin's silk bonnet, a deep purple bruise ringed the bottom of her left eye. Ona let the offertory basket pass her empty-handed, but Fannie reached into her skirts and tossed in two large potatoes. It was not the strangest offering however; the offertory baskets were often filled with not only coins, but smoked meats and bottles of whiskey.

Reverend Johnson made an announcement while the offertory made its round. "The Methodist Bible School will hold class tomorrow and bids caution due to unknown safety of road conditions. Headmaster Horace Wexler encourages youth to walk in groups."

Ona scanned the room, surprised to find her Methodist teacher among the Baptist congregation on a Sunday. He sat stiff and up-right in his pew and did not interact with the people around him.

Ona clicked her shoes against the pew repetitively, forcing her-self not to let her eyelids droop as she slouched in her seat. She was not long slumped in her seat however; Reverend Johnson, led any-thing but dull sermons. The minister started off in a monotone voice reading from the book of Acts; but as he lectured, his voice rose higher and higher, gasping in between phrases. Reverend Johnson's words came with dramatic emphasis before rather abruptly ceasing to speak altogether. His sudden pauses allowed people to ponder the true weight of his words, allowing his message to be absorbed before he jumped to a new point in his sermon.

Reverend Johnson gasped and shouted and flipped furiously be-tween his notes and the Scripture, sometimes slamming his hands on the podium or stomping his feet on the hardwood floor. Ona watched in awe, her attention captivated as he spoke rhythmically, rocking back and forth on his heels to preach the word of God. Ona didn't believe everything that came out of his mouth, but the way he said it made her want to. Periodically the minister was affirmed by the audience with shouts of "Yes, Lord" or "Amen, brother!"

For three hours the reverend shouted in this way. By the time he closed for prayer, sweat drenched his collar and he swayed on his feet from sheer exhaustion. Reverend Johnson concluded his ser-mon by praying over the people of Calico: the children, the women, the families, especially the heathens. He prayed with great conviction and invited sinners up to the front to win Jesus in their hearts.

Ona had never formally been saved before, and today the message was particularly compelling. She considered raising her hand and running to the front, to join the community around her and find out what she and Fannie were missing way up on Calico Ridge. Her heart stirred, and she gripped the smooth wooden pew in front of her. Before she could make a decision, the minister ended his prayer and led the congregation in song.

In comparison to the sermon, the solemn hymns deflated the immediacy of Ona's spiritual yearning. Members of the church sang in every key, a slow and somber tune. As the final verses found their closing notes, Reverend Johnson hovered behind his podium. He looked on into the crowd of people who now sat with bated breath to hear the minister speak.

"It comes with a heavy heart that this news must be delivered. Some of you probably noticed the Halsteads are not present with us this Sunday." The reverend paused and whispers from the congregation threatened to overtake him. He held up his hand to silence the crowd. Ona sat up straight in her seat. Reverend Johnson was talking about Talmadge's family.

"The Halsteads are God-fearing people. Argus ran an honest business in timber. His wife spent good time raising their children to read the Bible. " The murmurs grew louder, but Reverend Johnson spoke louder still.

"Last night, not long after sunset, a band of Indians raided the Halstead house on the far side of Calico Ridge. They slaughtered Argus Halstead and his wife but was driven off by the brave Halstead sons. The youngest born is just barely weaned." His voice broke and the crowd rose to an uproar. Ona's spirit plummeted. She had known Talmadge all her life. What would all those children do without a mother and father?

Cries rang from the crowd. "Bless them, Jesus."

"Save them, Lord."

"What of the children?"

"The Halsteads are a hard loss, but there is more still." Reverend Johnson continued, nearly shouting to be heard.

"The party of hostile Indians also raided the home of Jeremiah Sunday, just outside of downtown Calico." Ona's heart stuttered. The crowd paused in shock. Ona's eyes widened, and she moved to the edge of her seat.

"Where is Enda Cambor?" Ona nudged Fannie in a panicked whisper.

Reverend Johnson continued, "We suspect these attacks were calculated to seek out residents living on the fringes of Calico." A collected gasp resounded through the crowd.

"As for Jeremiah Sunday, it seem to be that haunting the poor man with visions of his murdered family no longer satiated the villains to the East. They shot Jeremiah Sunday in the stomach with his own gun and took his scalp for a prize." The congregation of the church turned riotous.

Reverend Johnson stamped his foot, shouting, "Will the people of Calico stand for such injustice?"

The collective jeering in response organized all willing and able men to launch an attack on the perpetrators. Rumors circulated about a hidden Cherokee town deep within Calico Mountain, where it was suspected the raiding party came from. The women were ushered out of the church and boys fought with their mothers to join the group of men. Ona felt herself tremble and she grabbed Fannie's shawl.

"What of Enda Cambor? They didn't say nothing about him!" Ona didn't know about the Halstead family, but she knew the murder of Jeremiah Sunday was by no means random. Jeremiah Sunday was shot in the same way he murdered Awenasa's uncle only weeks ago.

Fannie turned around in silence, heading back into the church and sticking her foot in the closing doors. She was just in time to interrupt the hall full of men dressed from rags to coat tails dragging out maps of Calico Mountain and marking certain areas with X's. Ona followed Fannie, still clutching the old woman's shawl, listening to Mayor Cambor and Judge Beaudin discuss the murder of Jeremiah Sunday and members of the Halsteads as reason to scour the land in search of the rumored Cherokee town. Such an attack would just so happen to leave the leaders of Calico in control of the extremely valuable and highly profitable salt deposits beneath the Cherokee lands.

The murders seemed like a bad excuse for the rich to get richer by rallying behind brute force of the shaken working-class men of Calico. The men were all too willing to act in the face of the attacks. They would do anything to protect their families and the fragile life they built in the hills. Fannie walked deliberately through the chaos, forcing the men to clear a path for her, refusing to move herself out of the men's way. Ona, who was on the verge of hysteria, followed mutely behind. Fannie finally stopped in front of the podium standing before Reverend Johnson and two surly looking men holding pens and leaves of paper.

"What about the Cambor boy?" Fannie asked above the clamor. Mayor Cambor's icy blue eyes narrowed with disdain. He turned his back on Fannie, continuing his conversation with Judge Beaudin.

"This ain't a place for women, Fannie, you best be on your way now." Reverend Johnson waved his hand dismissively in Fannie's face. Fannie remained planted in her place. She sighed heavily at his rude manners and returned the gesture by loudly hocking chaw tobacco on the sanctuary floor. The men paused to look at her, stunned by such blatant disrespect for the church. Horace Wexler's jaw fell open from shock.

"I said," Fannie spoke louder this time, "what about the boy? Enda Cambor."

"You mean that bastard mulatto old man Sunday tossed his scraps to?" one of the men asked incredulously.

"The half-negro wasn't found at the scene. He's either been captured or run off." Reverend Johnson stroked his beard thoughtfully. "Perhaps he took up with the Cherokee on his own account, in the fashion of his father. If you're done, the men have work to do." Reverend Johnson was clearly irate.

Fannie turned on her heels and strode silently out the church doors, with Ona in tow. Ona's temper boiled over into the sanctuary of Calico's most powerful men. "You don't care who lives or dies! Shame on you! Shame on this house of God! Where is He? I don't see no God living here. Only men worshiping greed and selfish hate!"

"Fannie, control that whelp! I will not tolerate your damning the house of God, young Ona America. Hysterics are for the lunatic asylum!" The Reverend Johnson's face changed shades of purple in his outrage.

The church doors slammed behind Ona and Fannie and the noise picked up once more from inside the building. Fannie started home muttering to herself with Ona dragging behind her, kicking up dirt and contemplating the men from the Baptist church. By early afternoon it was clear that the men of Calico would raid the Cherokee town soon, if they hadn't left already.

Fannie discarded her head scarf, collapsing into the old wooden rocker. Ona paced beside the old woman, wringing the hems of her skirts in hand. She had raised her voice at the Reverend and Fannie had spat chewing tobacco on the sanctuary floor.

"Fannie, what are we supposed to do? He could be anywhere!" Ona was pacing through the cabin back on Calico Ridge, twisting her skirts in her hands and rambling on.

"What if the men actually find the Cherokee?" Jeremiah Sunday appeared to be the only one who knew their whereabouts with certainty, and he was gone now.

"They'll fight them like the others, Cricket. It's the same reasons your father gone off to fight. The Indians come out of secret and killed innocent people. It's a natural consequence." Fannie sat slumped in her rocking chair, puffing on her tobacco pipe.

"Those men ain't concerned about the Halsteads or old man Sunday," Ona spat. Fannie stood up slowly, cracking her knees and hips and back as she righted herself.

"Are we going to look for Enda?" Ona asked hopefully.

"No, I'm a-fixing to make supper." Fannie said dryly. Ona's temper flared one more.

"What if Enda's done been captured by the Cherokee?"

"Innocent people died last night. And no one knows where that boy's loyalties lie." Fannie said simply.

Ona shook her head, "Jeremiah Sunday was not innocent."

Fannie raised her eyebrows, "And what about the Halsteads? People say they was kind people, honest as they come."

Ona had no response to that. "Would you rather simply wait for blood to wash down the creek and never know who it belongs to?" Ona stormed out the front door, letting it slam shut behind her. Fannie did not call after her.

Ona passed Jeremiah Sunday's shack by late afternoon. She hurried past the animal skulls suspended from trees and did not dare to look inside the windows. His property was eerily silent save for the turkey vultures lingering low in the sky. Each time the vultures swooped towards the earth she felt goose bumps rise on her arms.

Ona waded across the stream that Enda and she swam weeks ago and followed it uphill until the sun began to sink in the sky. She climbed the hill with no real certainty she was going the right way, using bulging tree roots and exposed rock outcrops to pull herself up the steep mountainside and through slick leaf litter.

Finally, Ona found the narrow-worn path that she recognized as the one leading into the isolated Cherokee community. Ona walked cautiously into the clearing and was greeted by silence. Not a single man, woman or child appeared to be around. Perhaps the residents got wind of the onslaught and took cover in some nearby caves. She roamed the village until at last she found the Meeting House and beheld the sight around her.

Bodies. Dozens of bodies disfigured and scattered around in front of her. Cherokee that had been shot or cleaved into pieces, scattered amongst the fallen men of Calico, including one of the surly men Ona recalled standing beside Reverend Johnson in the church sanctuary. Her stomach lurched at sight of the frail woman who once spoke out on behalf of Ona. The high elder of the Cherokee now lay with each hand clasped by two women. One of the women was Awenasa's mother. All three were still before her. Warm tears cut through her chilled cheeks. In the growing cold of autumn evening, Ona could not smell the massacre until the breeze shifted. It was then that the sharp winds pressed her into motion, covering her mouth with her shawl.

Ona walked slow through the village; passing the stone fire pit she remembered being the center of life at the joining ceremony. Staring into the empty stone circle, Ona could hear flames cracking in the distance, but they were not coming from the fire pit. She looked around to find the source of the fire, and noticed the church not far from the Meeting House smoldered in ashes under the blood orange evening sun.

Ona started toward the building when she stumbled over something in her path. She looked down, discovering the outstretched fingers of a small toddler girl. She wore a bracelet with elaborate geometric designs etched into its surface. The girl stared past Ona through glassy eyes. Bile rose in the back of Ona's throat. Screams echoed from all around her, and it was several moments before she realized they were her own. Ona wailed, stepping away from the still child.

"Somebody, please help!" Crows returned her cries from high above in the trees. Ona's breaths were shallow, running through the destruction. She passed even more people, but not a single one cried out to her. Veering down the dirt path that led to Kanagagota's cabin, Ona turned her face away as she passed two mutilated men from Calico. One was her classmate, Talmadge's younger brother. He was the same age as Ona.

Ona walked past the fallen body of Kanagagota, and the lump in her throat became unbearable. She neared the cabin where rocking chairs now sat empty, moving just slightly in the breezy autumn sunset. To Ona's torment, the cabin door was already ajar. Keeping her eyes on the ground, Ona pushed the door open just wide enough to poke her head through.

"Hello?" Ona called into the darkening room.

Ona heard a strangled cry in response to her call. She flung the door wide open, squinting into the darkening room.

"Awenasa?" She managed to squeak out.

"Ona?" A sob came from within the cabin and Ona found Awenasa curled up with her arms wrapped around her knees, hiding between the wall and the bed.

"Is it over?" Awenasa's eyes were clamped shut.

"I think so." Ona sank to the floor beside her friend. They sat in silence while the skies faded from orange to pale purple and the cabin became all but dark. Wolves cried out into the hillside, shaking Ona to her senses.

"We can't stay here. It ain't safe. All this blood. It will bring animals." Awenasa nodded her head in agreement. She was able to stand on unsteady legs that could only take small steps at a time.

"I cannot look at what's happened," Awenasa whispered. Ona took her hand, carefully coaxing Awenasa up from the floor. Ona wrapped her shawl around Awenasa's face, making sure she saw none of the devastation during their exit. When they found the trail that crept into the forest, Awenasa gave back the shawl.

"Everyone is gone." Awenasa stumbled through the forest, receding within herself. The girls were not running down the mountainside the way Enda and Ona had done so many nights ago. They took their time through the rugged terrain. This time, nobody was being chased. Not anymore at least.

"There might could be others like you." Ona hoped she sounded convincing. The girls followed alongside the deep ravine for a while, watching it grow from a small trickle of water into the wide stream that ran deeper than Ona's head. Awenasa began to sway precariously with exhaustion before they had even crossed the creek. If they crossed now, the swift moving current would be well above their heads, but Ona was unfamiliar with this stretch of mountain.

"Awenasa, do you know a place where we can make camp tonight?"

Awenasa simply nodded, changing course by moving away from the stream. She struggled wordlessly up a small knoll onto flatter land. Ona followed her some ways away from the stream to a stretch of forest thick with trees much larger than Ona had ever seen before.

"These must be ancient." Ona eyed the massive silhouettes that cropped up from the gentle rolling base of the mountainside. After some time, Awenasa collapsed at the base of the widest tree in the stand. Its massive branches that shed enormous brown leaves in every direction.

"I just need to sit for a moment," Awenasa strained through shallow breaths. She collapsed against a massive bur oak that split open just above their heads, forming an enormous shelter, before meeting back into a single crown that dominated the forest canopy.

"What is this?" Ona ran her fingers up the rough bark, marveling.

Awenasa managed to curl the corner of her lips into a small smile. "This is a safe place for travelers." Awenasa sat up against the tree, shredding a fallen leaf between her shaky fingers. Telling the story seemed to have a calming effect on her, because as she spoke, her breathing returned to normal and her fingers steadied.

"A long time ago, this tree was struck by lightning. Any other tree would have caught fire and died; but this tree was different. Instead of burning up in the flames, it kept its roots planted firmly in the ground and formed a scar inside the hollow where it was wounded. It still grows, even despite its injury. Now the tree offers shelter and protection for hunters in the area."

"It's breathtaking." Ona craned her neck to glimpse the canopy.

"It's truly a remarkable tree."

"But how're we supposed to climb this thing?" Ona felt around for low lying branches without luck. Thick scars along the trunk from where old branches had fallen jutted out like knobs in every direction. The girls clamored up these knobs into the basin of the tree hollow and nestling in for the night. Ona lay awake unable to sleep, toying with her dress. Heaviness crept into heart, and her thoughts drifted towards one person who had not been seen since the attacks in Calico.

"Awenasa, did you hear… if the boy who carried them barrels of whiskey on that night your uncle was murdered…was captured during the raid?"

Awenasa opened her eyes, looking squarely at Ona.

"No, he was not captured. They could not find him the night they came to Calico. They searched all around the hillside with no luck. They searched for you too, but they went to the wrong house." Ona's voice caught in her throat, but after a time she managed to find it.

"He's innocent, you know. He had no idea what would happen that night. Neither of us did." Ona said quietly. Awenasa's deep brown eyes held Ona's gaze a long time before nodding silently.

"I would like to believe you, Ona."

It was a long time before the girls succumbed to restless slumber, shielded under the protection of the massive bur oak tree

Chapter 6.

Songbirds shrieked from every direction piercing Ona's ears and causing her to swear loudly while she stretched, sitting upright. It was still dark outside, but she could see gray skies rising in the distance. Ona wrapped herself tightly in her shawl, straightening her navy-blue dress. She unpinned her hair the rest of the way from church, letting it spring out around her shoulders. Ona groaned, realizing what day it was. It was Monday. School. She crept to the edge of the tree basin peering over the edge, careful not to wake Awenasa.

Ona held onto the lip of the tree basin and stretched out one foot, straining to find a foothold. The tip of her toes found a small knob sticking out of the trunk that she was able to clamor onto. Little by little, Ona managed to scramble out of the ancient oak onto the forest floor. When she finally set foot on the ground, she breathed a sigh of relief.

Awenasa stirred from above, slowly making her way down the tree trunk after Ona. They started for Calico in silence. Ona gave

Awenasa directions to Fannie's house and would meet with her later. Ona had to be at school, and she had a decent chance of being on time seeing how they made it to town just after sunrise.

Awenasa's pace slowed to a crawl as they approached the first houses at the edge of town. She lost her whole community in one night from the people of Calico. They walked in silence down the filthy side alley that wreaked of human waste and spoiled food scraps. Ona periodically ran to the main street to confirm their location. They passed behind a kitchen house hidden behind the biggest mansion in town. They gazed up at the windows, which towered three stories high.

The back door on the kitchen house swung open, and girl with dark skin, sloshed buckets of slop to a dozen or so chickens, and two pigs rushing to clean up. The girl dropped her bucket when she saw Ona and Awenasa. Ona recognized those familiar braided pig tails that curled just under the girl's chin.

"Adelaide?"

Adelaide did not respond but muttered under her breath while hiking up her plain gray skirts to retrieve her buckets. She slammed the kitchen house door shut, watching Ona with knowing eyes all the while.

Ona stole around the side of the property up to the cobbled street. The house had its own brick driveway, latched shut with a wrought iron gate between two brick columns. Each column held a plaque; one read "315 Rue Royale" and the other read "Cambor

Hall, 1789" Adelaide must be the slave of Mayor Cambor. Mayor Cambor was Enda's grandfather. If Adelaide and Enda were cousins, perhaps more of Enda's family was here too. The idea of parts of him being as close to her as the other side of the fence stirred a longing within her that pained her heart. Where was Enda Cambor?

Ona and Awenasa took to the main roads once more when the shops and large houses and brick streets faded into scattered homesteads surrounded by forest, and dusty dirt roads. Ona smiled, waving on Awenasa when they reached the Methodist church yard. Other students played outside the small one room building, gaping open mouthed as Ona approached. She was filthy, no hair covering, and still in her church clothes, waving at a young Cherokee woman, who continued up the road toward Calico Ridge. Several pairs of eyes watched Awenasa walk in silence up the hill. Awenasa did not look back at Ona; in fact, she pretended as if there were nobody else around, taking proud strides up the mountain.

"What are y'all just standing around with your teeth in your mouth?" Ona spat at the other students.

Zelma giggled from under a tree where Ona joined her shortly, waiting to be called in for class. Ona fixed her cap on top of her hair, accepting Zelma's assistance to stuff the majority of it up inside her cap. She scanned the school yard, but couldn't find Talmadge's face among the students. He was always around for school, except during the harvest season.

"Where's Talmadge?" Ona asked blankly. Zelma looked down at her hands and fiddled with a hem on her dress.

"Talmadge can't come to school anymore. He has to stay home and take over his father's timber business. He's the oldest, after all. " Zelma was sad to see Talmadge go. Ona was too; the three of them hung around a lot together during school hours.

"His little brother snuck into the fighting last night. I heard he was killed," Zelma said.

Ona remembered seeing Talmadge's younger brother's body crumpled on the ground back in the Cherokee town.

"Yeah, I know." Ona said darkly. "He had no business being there. Not a one of them did. Jeremiah Sunday had it coming to him and look at all the mess he caused."

"It's not kind to speak ill of the dead." Zelma traced the pattern of her dress without looking up. "His family is having the funeral tonight on their farm. Everyone in Calico is invited. My father's going to bring his dulcimer. You should come. It's a memorial for the whole town after the dead are buried."

It was hard to focus on the lesson at school, and Ona drew even more attention to herself since her desk mate Blanche Beaudin was no longer beside her. Apparently the Beaudins thought it too dangerous to send their daughter so far into the country for a meager education. Blanche had started up with private tutoring once more. Ona was ecstatic, except now there was no teacher's pet to appease

Horace Wexler with a proper answer every time Ona responded in-correctly– which happened more often than not.

"You cannot tell me the meaning of this proverb?" Horace Wexler was sneering over Ona, with his cane touching her nose.

Ona closed her eyes, breathing deeply. "I told you Sir, I don't know. I ain't been here none this last week to learn it."

Students eyed Ona out of the corner of their eyes. She hadn't bothered making an effort to speak the way they were instructed to. She hadn't learned much at all in the way of books lately, though Ona felt she had been learning more than ever here recently. It was a strange situation.

"'You ain't been here to learn it,'" the headmaster repeated slowly, shaking his head up at the ceiling. "The fatal flaw of moun-tain folk is in these slothful ways. Miss Ona America Christie, too lazy to make the effort to communicate usefully and cannot be both-ered to attend to her studies. I'm certain we would find much sin-fulness in her idle hours."

"You never ask me the questions I know!" she spat.

"And what, pray tell, could you possibly know?"

"I know I'll poison your coffee with that pretty snakeroot on your desk!" Ona spat. His eyes flickered to the delicate white flowers pok-ing out of a small glass vase on his desk. He always had a flower of some sort to put in his vase. It took his mind off the depressing state of his classroom. Rarely did the headmaster pause to consider the unnamed flowers he plucked.

Horace Wexler's eyes hardened. He grabbed Ona's loose hair and knotted it around his fist, lifting Ona off the ground until her toes were barely touching. She cried out in pain.

"Please! Stop it, Sir!" Zelma shrieked. The headmaster did not hear Zelma. His eyes glinted with the same rage Ona recognized in Jeremiah Sunday the night he murdered the Cherokee man.

Ona turned her eyes away from the headmaster and looked out the window behind the students' desks. Enda Cambor was approaching the school with a preoccupied look on his face, carrying a small cloth package under his arm. He peered through the windows to the backs of the students and locked eyes with Ona. The vibrancy of his skin faded, and his blue eyes grew wide in shock. Ona was mortified to be caught in such an embarrassing predicament.

"Little girl. Do you threaten me on the morn you arrive with an Indian in your company not less than a day after they murdered one of your classmates?" The headmaster's voice was slow and ragged. Ona felt warm droplets of saliva on her face.

Enda burst through the church door, no longer wearing the kind, mischievous face Ona had grown fond of. His eyes were hardened and his mouth set firm. This face belonged to someone else altogether.

"Pardon interrupting the class. Ona must come with me now. She got called in by Fannie for work needing to be done!" His gaze did not waver from the headmaster. Horace Wexler dropped Ona to the floor and went back to his desk.

"Your place is not in this room, boy." He smoothed his shirt, casting a hard look between Enda and Ona.

"You are behind in your studies, Miss Christie. It is ill advised to miss any more school if you're to become anything more than the low-lying filth with whom you associate," the headmaster shot back. Ona lingered standing beside her desk, feeling uncertain. Her father wanted her to go to school as long as possible.

Ona America Christie deliberated only a moment before her attention was drawn outside the window once more to the loud honking of a flock of geese flying overhead, casting winged silhouettes onto the earth, utterly unconfined. Just the way she wanted to be. She kissed Zelma on the cheek, whispering, "I'll see you tonight!"

Ona exited the doors of the school house with a great weight lifted off her chest. Enda Cambor walked beside her in a daze, surprising himself with his own boldness back in the school house. At last, he broke the silence as they made their way closer to town.

"I don't know if you should go back to that place, Little America. It ain't good for you there," Enda said quietly.

"I know," Ona met his gaze squarely, changing the subject. "Where have you been? You disappeared during the attack and we couldn't find you."

"I never even knew there was an attack. I left for home from the cabin, and by the time I make it home, Sunday was—" His voice dropped off.

"Are you alright?"

"—He was unrecognizable."

"What happened when you found him?"

"I ran to tell the mayor. He's the one who sent out the alarm." Ona pondered his words silently for a while, before noticing their surroundings.

"Wait, this ain't the way to the cabin. You said Fannie had work for me to do."

Enda grinned down at her unexpectedly with a lopsided smile that made Ona's heart stutter. "She do, she's in town, though. She said it was time for you to learn the water witching. She sent me to fetch you, saying you'd either be dead up on Cherokee Hill or in school causing problems. I tried school first."

Ona laughed and Enda shook his head. "Guess she was right. She's a smart ole witch, that Fannie."

"Where we headed to?"

"A property just yonder from town. The landowner is looking to dig a well there. I ain't never heard of him before, I don't know where he's from." He handed the package to Ona who eagerly tore into it.

"This is just my old dress!" Ona was disappointed. She owned exactly three dresses and Fannie had packed Ona her clean, green and white checkered dress along with Ona's leather walking shoes.

"Fannie sent it along with me for you. You're supposed to wear it today."

"Really, Enda. What is all this?" Ona didn't understand what all the fuss could be that she had to wear something nicer than what she had on.

"It's probably someone important." Enda spoke with his back turned toward her while she quickly changed behind a tree.

Enda and Ona made their way down the ridge until he guided her to an uncut plot of woods just outside of town. They wandered the tract until she saw Fannie standing beside a young man wearing black coattails over fine breeches. He completed the outfit with a beaver topper hat and a cane. His hair was perfectly styled. Behind his linen gloves, Ona imagined his hands to be perfectly smooth. Beside the man stood Ezra McDaniel, the accountant at the general store, chatting animatedly with the man.

Ona slowed her pace to examine the peculiar group when she noticed Enda disappeared several paces back, seemingly melting into the forest. Clearly, he had no intention of meeting these people. Ona backtracked to discover Enda leaning comfortably behind a tree.

"Don't be a child. Come with me!" She grabbed his arm.

"Let go! I ain't going nowhere!" Enda shot back in a hushed voice. "Do I look like I'm supposed to be meeting men like that?"

Comprehension dawned across Ona's face, and her hand fell away. She circled him slowly, eyeing him up and down. Enda stood awkwardly, waiting. It was true; the pants Fannie had made him were no longer new and his white shirt was unbuttoned at the collar. She smoothed his hair down and buttoned his collar and straightened his soft leather vest.

"You're perfect." She kissed him lightly on the cheek, surprising herself with her own boldness. Enda stood frozen in silent shock so that Ona had to guide him by the hand, dropping it just before the others could see them through the trees.

"You're late, Cricket." Fannie sounded bored waiting around with the men while they talked business. Ezra's eyes lit up at the sight of Ona, but his expression fell somewhat when he saw Enda beside her.

"Sorry. What are we about to do?" Ona spoke formally in front of the stranger, trying her best to appear like this was not an unusual thing to occur. The young man with Ezra, probably in his mid-twenties, broke into a wide smile that highlighted youthful dimples in his cheeks.

"Mr. John Francis, thank you. It's my honor to finally meet the aspiring witch herself. Ezra here has had nothing but praise for your miraculous talent." The man bowed gallantly.

115

"It's extraordinary really, Miss Christie, the work you and Fannie do. Now, the hills here around Calico are very special. We have located a number of salt caverns in the surrounding mountainside and until very recently, were never able to access."

"Until you slaughtered the people living on top of them." Ona pointed out, arms crossed.

Mr. Francis' winning smile faltered only slightly. "Since we have assumed ownership of the caverns on and around the illegal Indian camp, we have been able to explore our state's riches more deeply than ever before. The situation is much more impressive than we first believed! Do you realize the treasure of wealth that your community rests upon?"

"No."

"These salt mines could change your whole way of life! You could all be rich!"

"It'll be wonderful," Ezra exclaimed. Fannie huffed, unconvinced. Enda eyed the man in the topper hat carefully, like there just might be a snake underneath his hat. Ona seemed to feel exactly the same way about the situation.

"What's that got to do with water witching?" Ona narrowed her eyes.

"Well," Mr. Francis was only mildly disheartened by her poor attitude. "As a serious investor in the town of Calico—"

Ona snorted. "I ain't never seen you around here before."

"Well, the good news is that I will be building my estate right here on this property. It's already been discussed with my good man, Ezra here. He's helped me secure the resources I need to move here, permanently. He even brought me to you!"

"So you need to find water for your new house where you will live because we have minerals to make you rich," Ona surmised.

"Us," Ezra corrected. "It will make us all rich. Everyone in Calico will have more money than they'll know what to do with!" Ezra was hanging off every word that Mr. Francis uttered. He even spoke with a plain accent for the first time in Ona's memory, just like Mr. Francis.

"That is, if you're willing to help me." Mr. Francis removed his hat to look Ona in the eyes.

Ona crossed her arms, looking over to Fannie. Fannie ushered Ona to follow her. "This way, Cricket."

Ona removed her shoes, chucking them back in the direction of the men. Ezra smiled politely, pretending shoes hadn't just whizzed past his face as he entertained Mr. Francis in the grassy clearing. It wasn't for nothing that Ona removed her shoes; she was testing the ground for soft, porous earth and moss. She lowered herself to the ground sitting back on her heels, heedless of her dress, to examine the tiny plants growing up around her feet.

"These are all water loving plants, Fannie. There might could be water here!"

Fannie twirled a small purple flower between her fingers.

"Go and fetch me a willow branch. Be sure you get one with a nice fork and break it off even, you hear?" Fannie instructed.

Ona returned without looking too hard. She managed to collect a black willow branch with two even forks.

"Take one fork in each hand. Face your fingers up. And point your thumbs out. No, like this—"

Fannie stood beside Ona, demonstrating how to place her fingers accordingly. Ona glanced up at Mr. Francis and Ezra McDaniel. They peered through the thinning forest under story, observing Fannie and Ona curiously. Behind them, Enda watched in earnest.

"Never mind them, Cricket. Think on the direction of the water flowing under our feet. You know it's here. Now tell us where." She stretched her finger out across the ground. Ona took small steps forward and Fannie's feet kept in time with hers. With no encouragement of Ona's, the forked willow pulled her toward the left. Ona startled in surprise, letting out an audible gasp. Mr. Francis was standing on his tiptoes, craning to get a better look at them. Ezra and Enda gaped in amazement.

Ona veered left as well, obediently following the direction of the forked willow rod. Ona walked in slow time, deferring to the bend of the willow rod. Nearly an hour passed before the rod began tipping downward. Ona's eyes widened excitedly. The rod turned sharper left and Ona walked in a straight line for several paces, stopping when the rod was completely vertical in her hands. Ona watched the ground to which the willow rod pointed. Fannie spat chaw alongside her, nodding her head in approval.

"Well, Cricket?" The old woman paid no mind to a tiny orange salamander that flamed as brilliantly as Ona's hair as it walked right across Fannie's big toe.

"It's here," Ona mumbled, feeling shy for the first time in living memory. Fannie waved the men over.

"Ezra did not lie when he spoke that you two could perform miracles, Fannie!" Mr. Francis bowed gallantly, scooping up Fannie's hand to kiss it. He removed a heavy purse from his pocket and paid Ona a handsome sum for her work. Ona could not believe her eyes.

"It is a shame that the lovely Fannie did not perform her art today as well."

"I'm old and tired. It's about time the girl started to carry some weight." Fannie spoke dryly. "We wish you luck on them endeavors of yours, but we must go. We have a funeral to prepare for."

Ezra's gaze softened. "Yes, ma'am. I will see you both there tonight." He nodded his goodbye, completely ignoring Enda.

They made their way back to the cabin and Enda bid them a quick farewell before he disappeared in the thick of the trees. Awenasa sat on Ona's pallet while Ona changed clothes for the funeral of the Halstead parents and second oldest son.

"Where do you think he goes when he leaves here?" Ona asked absently, hanging up her green checkered dress in exchange for the simple white dress she wore to Zelma's birthday. It wasn't black, which Ona knew to be funeral colors, but it was the simplest piece of clothing she owned. Ona took a black shawl and wrapped herself in its warmth.

"Wherever he wants, I suppose." Awenasa quietly braided Ona's hair into something modest for mourning. Her hair had a similar braid, and Ona understood it was not in mourning for the Halsteads that she wore it.

"I'm envious. He's really free out there," Ona sighed.

"Mhm. He is. He's also probably lonely too, though. He's all by himself now."

Ona froze, horrified with guilt that played across her face. "He lost someone too. Who helped him bury Jeremiah Sunday?"

"The loss he mourns is not worth memorializing." Awenasa tugged Ona's thick hair mercilessly into plaited obedience.

"He was important to someone," Ona countered.

"How much blood has stained one man's hands? You would honor someone like that?" Awenasa's hands fell away from their task. She turned to face Ona directly.

"I'd stand by someone who was grieving. Their feelings are real, no matter who it is lying cold in the ground." Awenasa did not respond to Ona's remarks, but her hands busied themselves once more. The geometric designs on Awenasa's shawl reminded Ona of the beaded belt. She brought it out to show Awenasa who snatched it up desperately.

"Where did you get this?" She demanded.

"Do you know it?" Ona asked, surprised.

"It belonged to my brother. He disappeared months ago after he left for trading trip. He was supposed to be back in August." Awenasa's face hardened as Ona unfolded the story of Jeremiah Sunday and the Cherokee man.

"Where is he buried?"

"Just outside," Ona led her outside to the little headstones in the yard. Awenasa knelt close to the ground, whispering in Tsalagi for a long while. She gently reached out to touch the rock above her brother's head.

"Oh my brother, you've been here this whole time. With our dog, too." She shook her head, the ghost of a smile touching the corner of her lips.

"You and the witch doctored my brother?" She asked, still kneeling on the ground. She reached her hand out for Ona to join her.

"We tempered the bleeding and got him to keep comfortable." Ona sunk down beside her.

"You buried him, and his dog, all by yourself?"

"Yes, but Enda Cambor placed the stones, and planted the daffodils." Awenasa clasped Ona's hand.

"Thank you." She breathed a sigh of strange release, gently placing the belt back in Ona's hands. Ona stood up, murmuring her thanks. Inside the cabin, she looked down at her ankles sticking out from under the dress. The dress fit better last time Ona wore it, but she must have grown. Ona pulled on her stockings and slipped into her leather shoes.

"Awenasa," Ona began, twisting her handkerchief in her hands before tucking it up her sleeve. "Maybe it'd safest if you wait here tonight." Ona did not have to imagine what would happen if Awenasa appeared at the Halstead place. She would strung up to hang.

"As if I would bow in solidarity to those who died so needlessly in their own blind hatred." She reflected darkly. "You are going to send off your dead. And my people? Who will lay them to rest?" Ona could say nothing to that, so she poured Awenasa a cup of soured cider from off the fire. It simmered piping hot and made the whole cabin smell of cinnamon and cloves.

Fannie had been cooking all afternoon; maybe some days she was a granny witch, but today she was a kitchen witch. They made rabbit and dumplings to take for dinner at the Halsteads and Fannie wrapped an apple stack cake in cloths to take over for the memorial. Awenasa watched Fannie with fascination as she stacked seven thin spice cakes on top of each other with apple butter slathered in between each layer.

Awenasa sat comfortably on the floor near the fire. She was wrapped in a thick blanket with a cup of soured cider and a large helping of dumplings when Fannie and Ona set off for the memorial. Fannie carried the pie expertly and Ona carefully carried the heavy pot of dumplings up the ridge.

The sun was low in the sky for the brief twenty-minute walk to the Halstead place. Ona had never been to the Halstead place, but her father often did business with Argus Halstead before he was called away to fight. Argus harvested timber and Rowland Christie had timber. They always got along well.

Ona was somewhat shocked when she followed Fannie into the Halstead home. It was a small cabin with a loft the same exact size as the cabin Ona lived in, only the Halstead home was furnished with a chimney, which her father was never home long enough to build at the Christie cabin. Ona set the dumplings on a small wooden table, noticing a bed near the fireplace with two large shapes covered with a blanket.

Ona followed Fannie outside and joined all seven of the McDaniels walking toward a recently cleared plot behind Halstead home. Zelma held her brother Nash's hand, looking like a porcelain doll in her black dress. Ona peered over Zelma's shoulder into the three deep holes that had been dug into the clearing. Ona's stomach twisted into knots and she looked away at the grass, sniffling back tears.

Ona could imagine somewhat what Talmadge was feeling. She was still shaken by the sudden loss of her father. She was somewhat envious that Talmadge had the closure of burying his loved ones, but she would not trade for his place being left as the care taker for nine hungry mouths.

It was likely that it would just be the three families for the burial and others would perhaps show up later. After all, many families in town were burying their loved ones tonight after the massacre at the Cherokee town. The McDaniels, along with Ona and Fannie were the Halstead's closest neighbors and, having none participated in the fray, they all came to support the Halstead children. The youngest of the Halstead children drifted toward the McDaniels and the Christies. Twin girls, maybe six, carried a plump baby boy in their arms. Following the two little girls were other children, ranging from eight to Talmadge's age of fifteen.

Talmadge drove his father's two mules up Calico Ridge pulling the flat skid used to haul lumber. Instead of lumber however, a small shape wrapped in blankets was carefully laid in the back, with some of the older Halstead boys walking somberly beside it. The boys must have been able to find their brother in the wreckage by Awenasa's home.

Talmadge helped his brothers carry out his parents from the cabin and lay them on the skid. The McDaniel boys helped the Halstead boys lay to rest their dead. Zelma bounced the little Halstead baby on her hip to coo him and Ona held the hands of the little girls while the older children said goodbye to their parents.

"Talmadge said he's the man of the house now." One of the twins, Mercy, whispered in Ona's ear.

"That's right." Ona spoke softly.

"Talmadge said mama and papa met Jesus." Mercy's eyes were searching Ona's face to see if it was really true.

"That's right." A tear escaped down Ona's cheek.

"Why have y'all been crying?" This time it was Mercy's twin, Sarah Jane who spoke. Instead of responding, Ona turned to observe the funeral closing. Talmadge and the two oldest of his surviving brothers worked to move dirt into the graves. Mr. McDaniel and his sons, Ezra, Jonathon, Dane, and Nash brought shovels enough to help.

After the plots were filled, the families stood around the Halstead graves for a long while. Ona pondered the people before her, squeezing tightly the hands of Mercy and Sarah Jane who were barefoot in the frosty night. These were her people. They were all each other had way out on the ridge, so far from town in such rough country. The people in town with their pink roses and brick homes had no understanding of what life is like when it is carved from nothing.

"Well," Talmadge said after a long while when the oldest Halstead girl Vernie and younger siblings had begun to settle their tears, "let's eat."

The McDaniels had more hands and more money and consequently brought more food. Mrs. McDaniel made a venison stew and walnut pies. The boys had carried a small barrel of sour coriander ale. There were too many people to fit in the cabin which had only two chairs anyway, but people gathered round a fire outside and rolled up logs to sit on, offering up the chairs to Mrs. McDaniel and Fannie. Mr. McDaniel brought out his dulcimer and Ezra tested out a handsome new fiddle. They sat around the fire and played songs, some lighthearted and others somber ballads singing of the unbreakable backs of mountain folk, unyielding to the rigid mountain's sentence.

Vernie brought out the Halstead's family fiddle, playing a lively tune that lifted spirits. The youngest Halstead children were the first ones up and dancing, but Anna and Wash McDaniel were soon to follow. Ezra bowed low before Ona, offering his hand to her. Ona shook her head with a shy smile that played across her face, but Ezra smiled and nodded despite Ona's objection. Their silent conversation took form when he grasped Ona's hand, leading her to dance. Two cups of ale left Ona feeling flush and tingly, and spiraling around to the happy tune helped her forget for a moment the sadness of the past couple days. Too soon the song was over, and Ona was sad to part from the warmth of their closeness.

Through the evening, they danced two more times before Ona joined the younger girls to gorge on a second helping of dumplings and stew. She sat perched between Zelma and the twins when movement in the forest caught her eyes. Ona stood slowly and made for the trees, pretending to relieve herself.

"Who's out there?" Ona hissed. A hand reached out from behind Ona, pulling her behind a large cherry tree. Ona yelped in surprise, only to find her mouth covered by second hand. She was trapped in the grip of someone embracing her from behind, which quickly moved to a hold around her neck. Ona felt the sharp cold of a knife against her throat.

"Shh." A woman's voice hushed close in Ona's ear. "Calm. I am not here to hurt you. Yet. Where is my sister?" Ayita's spoke with an altogether different voice than the laughter and stories shared leading up to her joining.

"Your boy Enda told me you're keeping her."

Ona nodded, her mouth still covered. She winced as the blade turned closer to her skin.

"You will take her to Ice Cave and leave her there. Do you understand? You have until the moon is peaked, or your boy will know what it feels like for the crows and worms to whittle his flesh into nothing."

Ayita shoved Ona to the ground, disappearing into the thick of the forest. Ona's heart hammered, and she stumbled to her feet, desperately seeking out the moon. She had a few hours to meet Ayita, but she had no idea where Ice Cave could be.

"Ona?" Ezra called into the trees, concerned. "Are you alright?"

"No," Ona stammered, making her way back to the others. "I'm so sorry," She spoke to Talmadge and his siblings sitting around the fire. "I'm just not feeling well. I need to go lie down. Now." She shot a look at Fannie.

"Sure thing!" Talmadge hurried to his feet. "We got plenty beds up at the house."

"Thank you, but I think it'd be best if I just go home and sleep it off." Ona smiled weakly. Fannie's knees cracked and popped like the blazing fire before them, but she made it to her feet, rubbing her wrists.

"Alright, Cricket. Cold is getting to my bones anyhow. We'll be back soon for the kettle. Just enjoy the food, Halsteads." She bent down and whispered to Mercy, sitting nearest to Fannie, "We'll make sure you keep fed this winter." She winked, poking Mercy's belly. Mercy smiled warmly up at Fannie, waving them off.

When Ona explained what had happened in the forest, Fannie was only mad she was too old and slow to go with Ona and Awenasa. Luckily enough, Fannie had in fact been to a place called Ice Cave. Awenasa also knew of it and although she had never been, she had a general idea of its location which confirmed Fannie's recollection. Awenasa slipped into the moccasins once lent to Ona, just as Ona changed hurriedly into her more practical green checkered dress.

"I can't believe my sister is alive!" Awenasa said breathlessly on their way out the door. They walked by moonlight; Fannie and Awenasa both believed a lantern would be a bad idea.

"I can't believe they kidnapped Enda," Ona said dryly. Awenasa ignored her.

"I wonder how many of my people are alive?"

"I wonder if they will actually let me and Enda out in one piece?"

Awenasa stopped to face Ona, placing her hands on Ona's shoulders to look at her squarely. "They will. You took me to shelter from the massacre. You cared for and buried my brother. They owe you safe passage home."

"Then why didn't they just ask me? Why'd they kidnap Enda?" Ona argued.

Awenasa shook her head, exasperated. "Because, Ona, you are not a clear ally! You knew where we lived. You ran away from us after my uncle was murdered. For all they know, you helped organize the attack."

"It wasn't me, though! Me and Enda had nothing to do with it!" Ona shouted defensively.

"Well I know that, but the thing is Ona, they don't."

Ona hoped Awenasa was right about her and Enda getting safe passage home after delivering Awenasa to her sister. They made quick work getting to town keeping warm from their pace despite the frosty air. They crossed the creek behind the house where Jeremiah Sunday once lived and they did not slow to fuss over the freezing water. Where was Jeremiah Sunday buried?

Ona's balled her fists, frustrated that her legs were not working fast enough. She began to run up the ridge to Cherokee lands and followed Awenasa's lead under the rising moon once they reached the Cherokee trail. They marched away from the path, downward through steep terrain until they were scrambling over boulders down a cliff face. Ona watched a lazy river erupt from the mountain, meandering through a valley she had never laid eyes on.

Awenasa pointed to the mouth of the river. "Ice Cave is through there."

They made their way carefully along the steep cliff face toward the mouth of the river, struggling through ancient hemlock stands and dense thickets of calico bush. Ona saw a dark opening through the still green rhododendrons at the source of the water. Awenasa picked up her pace, just as Ona slowed in contemplation.

"How will we see in there?" Ona wondered aloud.

"We will not get lost. They are expecting us, after all." Awenasa seemed non-pulsed.

Ona tried to be as trusting as Awenasa but was coming up short. They approached the river's head and discovered a rock shelter around the opening of Ice Cave with a recently put out fire that still smelled of smoke.

"They're here!" Awenasa squealed.

"It sure looks like it." Ona couldn't muster near the enthusiasm.

They squatted against the back of the rock house, watching the water flow through an opening wide enough for several people to fit through. Lucky for them, it had not rained recently, and the water was maybe only waist deep. The thought of crossing the water in the late autumn chill was miserable. A breeze picked up in the hollow of the rock shelter and Ona shivered, clutching her shawl close to her.

"Don't worry," Awenasa smiled. "It'll be warm in there. It's warm all the time in a cave."

"Then how will there be ice?"

An orange light flickered from behind the water, inside the cavern. Awenasa squeezed Ona's hand, plunging into the waist deep water. Awenasa was right. The water was warm.

"Shall we?" Awenasa let go of Ona's hand, ducking her head to make it through the cavern entrance. Ona exhaled slowly, following after her.

The first thing Ona noticed were the brilliant white crystals, coating the walls and ceiling of the cavern. Some hung elaborately from the ceiling, exactly like an icicle hanging from a roof. It was like stepping into a snowy winter day.

Awenasa's piercing scream bounced painfully around the crystal gallery, tearing Ona's eyes to the chaos within the cavern. Two men who were not Cherokee, held lanterns and cussed as they dragged Awenasa out of the water, kicking and flailing to wriggle out of their grasp. The larger man knocked her unconscious with a single fist.

Ona audibly gasped, her sharp intake of breath magnified tenfold in the cavern drawing the oppressors nearer to her. She submerged back into the water, retreating from the cave. The same large man caught the hem of her dress near the mouth of the cavern, reaching for Ona's hair and pulling her out by the elbow. Ona did not see the second man behind her who knocked her out with a hunk of glittering rock.

Chapter 7.

Ona stirred, groggy and unsure why she couldn't move her arms. Beside her, Awenasa was already awake. Her arms were tied behind her back and her ankles were tied together. Ona looked down at her feet. She was tied up the same way. The men stood not far away, arguing with each other. Across the gallery of gleaming white crystals, glowing beautifully against the lamplight, the two men argued. A small man with shifty eyes and sort of a rat nose, and a tall man who looked like he could do some serious damage if he wanted to.

"We'd do best to kill them now and toss them to the river." The larger man suggested, picking under his fingernails with a large hand blade while the smaller rat-faced man filled potato sacks with some kind of root plant.

"We can't kill them, Saul," the small man hissed. "The Indians would go looking for their girl. Then we'd be the ones to die."

"No one would go looking for the Irish whelp." Saul argued. "They'd think she left to be a whore. We could take her with us if we don't kill her."

"That Indian girl will haunt us from the grave for all eternity if we kill her."

"Thomas, you superstitious idiot. That Indian girl won't do nothing but rot once we kill her."

They bickered back and forth for a while and Ona learned the men had used this cave as a hideout all summer while they harvested ginseng root. Now there had been other white men poking their noses around the area the past few days. They also heard about the raid at the Cherokee town. The two men were moving the root to the coast of Virginia a little at a time where it was sold all over Asia. Mounds of ginseng root lined the walls of the cavern. Fannie used ginseng in some of her remedies to help sick people. Ona had no idea it was such a valuable plant outside of Calico.

Subtle movement beside her drew Ona's attention to the corner of her eye. Awenasa had shifted to a sharp crystal formation jutting out of the cavern wall and was quickly wearing down her ropes on the crystal's pointy end. Ona shifted her eyes on the men once more. They were now thinking of leaving Ona and Awenasa tied up for the next few weeks until they could finish moving the last of the ginseng. Ona turned only slightly toward Awenasa and followed her idea.

Lucky for them, the ropes seemed to be mostly dry rotted. Awenasa cut through her wrist ties first and immediately bent to untie her feet, and Ona mimicked her. She brushed the sweat from her face, puckering immediately when some of the white crystals hit her lips. Salt. Ice Cave was a salt deposit. It was one of Calico's coveted prizes that came with the victory of the Cherokee massacre. Ona felt acid building up in her stomach and she spat out the salty taste in her mouth.

The men dropped their debate on whether or not Awenasa and Ona could be sold down south when Ayita's melodic voice pierced the cavern, echoing loudly through the chambers. Male voices rang out beside hers, speaking jovially in what Ona recognized as the Cherokee native tongue, Tsalagi. Many pairs of feet clamored against the chambers' quiet halls. Awenasa bolted toward the sound of her sister's voice, shouting in words Ona did not understand. The voices fell, the even paced steps turned into chaotic scuffling that amplified in the cave, grating against Ona's ears.

The men tore after Awenasa. The tall man Saul dragged her to the ground by her hair. Ona didn't stop to think. Her feet moved faster than her mind. Ona launched herself at Awenasa's captor, wrapping her legs around his waist and jamming her fingers into his eyes from behind. Awenasa managed to crawl out from under the man Saul, but when she tried to stand up, but her ankle gave way and she collapsed to the ground. She continued to speak in her native tongue, making her voice low and deep so that it carried through the chambers.

Ona held onto the sides of Saul' face so hard she saw trickles of blood sliding from underneath her nails and down his face into his shirt collar. The man's screams filled the enormous chamber, drowning out the cries of Awenasa's friends as they approached. Awenasa threw chunks of crystal rock at the men that she gathered from the ground around her, aiming for their knees and heads and making her mark more often than not. Ona felt a thick pair of hands ripping her away from the man Saul. The small, round man Thomas had a hold of Ona's arms, but Ona kept her legs wrapped around Saul's waist in a firm grip. Her target was blinded from where her fingers stabbed. The holes in his face overflowed with scarlet and suddenly that strangely captivating crimson color was the only thing in the world Ona could focus on.

Ona screamed, writhing out of Thomas' grasp and jamming her thumbs back into Saul's eye sockets while finding her feet on the ground. Saul's hands found Ona's hair and pulled with all of his might. Ona cried out but managed to keep control over the large man by shoving him with her fingers still lodged in his face. She drove him all the way to the cavern opening, smashing his head against a large boulder that lined the mouth of the river. He rolled into the water face down, caught between stones in the current at the mouth of the cave. He did not get up.

Thomas' arms were around Ona before she had time to turn around. She struggled against him and managed to fall on top of him, but he was much stronger than Ona. His thick fingers had an iron grip, flipping her underneath him. Ona struggled under his weight, but he sat on top of her and she could not move her arms. His fingers wrapped around Ona's throat and she felt her air supply being cut off. She gasped, but no sound came out of her mouth. Tighter and tighter the man squeezed until Ona's eyes hurt and her head throbbed. He averted his gaze, and would look at her, but remained flush with determination. Sweat beaded on his nose, dripping onto Ona's face. She felt his fingers pressing deeper into her throat and the pain shot through her veins, erupting across her eyes as spots colored with that familiar shade of red Ona saw so much of tonight.

A whizzing sound flew above Ona, and Thomas' grip went limp. He slumped off of Ona and fell sideways into the cavern floor. Ona blinked, and it was several moments before the ringing in her ears quieted somewhat and she was able to turn her eyes to see the dead man facing her. There was an arrow sticking out of his forehead. Once again, his eyes seemed to stare right past her, this time in a vacant sort of way.

"Ona!" Enda's screams were agonizing.

"Ona!" He shouted again. Ona tried to swallow, to respond, but she could not muster a sound. It was like she swallowed a jagged piece of stone that caught in her throat. The ache shot up through her jaws and down into the hollow of her neck. She could move her lips, but not open her mouth. Ona felt warm tears sliding off her cheeks onto the cavern floor. She stared at the dead man and wondered why she was crying. After all, she wasn't the one who died.

Enda rushed toward Ona, leaning anxiously over top of her. His face was contorted into an expression Ona had never seen on him before. Ona realized this must be the face one makes when they think their friend is dead. She reached out to Enda's hand squeeze Enda's hand. Immediate relief flooded his face. His clear blue eyes did not stare past Ona. They pierced right through her. His dark fingers gently brushed strands of Ona's fiery red hair out of her face. He bent slowly, pressing his lips to her forehead.

"Can I help you sit up?" He whispered close to her so that only she could hear. Ona nodded slightly, the effort doubling the pain from moving her head.

Enda carefully helped her into a seated position against the wall. Ona's ears pounded from deep inside her head. The ache in her throat seemed to at least have piqued into a steady throbbing and she was seeing spots again. This time, the spots were black.

Awenasa limped along upright, supported between her sister and her sister's husband, Tewa. They made their way slowly to Enda and Ona. The cavern seemed to spin around them.

"My sister told me how you secreted her after the massacre," Ayita spoke formally. Her western style blue cotton dress was damp and dirty around the fringes, but her Cherokee winter style boots, layered with thick animal furs seemed to remain dry.

"She told me how you went to look for her after the massacre. How you and a witch hid her from your community. How you worked together tonight." Ayita's body was stiff. She still did not trust Ona or Enda, but she did not deny Ona's acts of friendship, either. Ayita's husband Tewa took up where Ayita left off.

"I will return to help you back to your home in Calico after my family is safe on the other side of the mountain. Wait for me. I will not abandon an ally of Awenasa."

"We'll wait for you." It was completely different from Enda's usual jovial banter. Ona wondered how much time he spent with his Cherokee father before he was murdered by Enda's grandfather, Mayor Cambor.

Ona and Enda watched six pairs of feet disappear through a corridor, taking one of the lamp lights with them. Enda stood up, taking the second lantern with him and set it in the middle of the gallery. The fire burned low and dimly lit the cavern in its glow.

The softly lit room made minimal sounds aside from the shuffling of Enda's feet and bubbling of the river through the cavern's mouth. It was a wonderful respite from the earlier chaos echoing in her ears. Enda did not disturb Ona. He did not bother her with questions and he did not ask her to move. He worked quickly enough without her help. Enda dragged the bodies out of sight into a yet unexplored corridor that followed the course of the underground river. It was a different direction from the path Awenasa and her family left in. He did not go far into the corridor, just enough so that they did not have to spend the night in the presence of corpses.

Had Enda seen? Did he know that Ona killed a man tonight? The man called Saul bobbed lifelessly in the current. Her hands were stained dark with his blood. It coated her fingers, drying in drips down her hands. The sight of it made bile rise in the back of Ona's throat. She clawed at her fingers, trying desperately to scrape away the blood from her hands, only stopping for fear of retching. Enda sat down beside Ona, easing a quiver of arrows off his back. She noticed for the first time a modest wooden bow rest on the ground beside him. Ona shot him a knowing look, for a moment forgetting her hands.

"What? You didn't know I could shoot?" He teased, pulling her into his arms. Ona was still soaked to the bone from wading into the cavern and didn't protest his warmth. He sat against the cavern wall and she used his legs as a pillow, stretching out on the cavern floor.

Ona reached up, tracing the outline of his jaw with her sullied fingertips, pulling a strand of his dark brown curly hair to watch it bounce back into place. Her whisper was hoarse, like an old woman's, and caught painfully in her throat.

"We are abominable," And she was not one bit sorry for it.

"If that's what it takes, Little America." He delicately traced bruises on Ona's neck with his dark fingertips. Ona fell asleep not long after, waiting for Ayita's husband to return.

The moon was still out when Ona was woken. It was time to head back to Calico with Tewa. Enda helped Ona to her feet, and she took small steps to test her balance. A couple hours of sleep seemed to cure the spots in her vision.

The walk home was slow. They relied on Tewa's guidance to get back to the familiar Cherokee path. When Ona recognized the trail, her eyes followed the path leading towards town. Tewa followed her gaze.

"We will not see you again, Ona America and Enda Cambor. Ayita, Awenasa, and I will go south. It's safe for us down there. In the southern mountains we can live peacefully. The white people will not acknowledge you, Enda; but you were not born a slave, either. There will be a place for you if you decide to come with us." Ona turned to face Tewa, wide eyed. She had not considered the possibility of Enda ever leaving Calico. Enda exhaled slowly.

"That's generous, Tewa. I'm grateful for the offer, honest." He looked around wistfully at the thinning forest canopy and the mild frost settling over fallen leaves that once concealed the Cherokee town.

"It seem like I've given my whole heart to these hills and all the life that manages to survive in them."

Tewa smiled kindly at Enda's words, "Good luck to you then."

"You the same."

Tewa turned back towards the caves and Ona's heart swelled with a gladness she did not anticipate. She watched Enda shyly out of the corner of her eye for a time before linking her red stained fingers through his brown ones. A small smile twitched at Enda's lips, though he said no more during the journey home. They neared the familiar sights and smells of downtown Calico, still sleeping quietly in the dull gray morning light, when Ona felt her knees buckle underneath her.

Ona coughed, and the force pained her greatly, raking against her tender throat. She was so tired. When Ona could go no further Enda scooped her up, carrying Ona through the back alleys of downtown. Ona did not know what Enda was meaning to do, but she knew there was no way he could keep that up all the way to the Christie cabin on Calico Ridge. The bounce in Enda's steps brought back her dizziness.

Ona vaguely registered Enda turning down the lane of beautiful brick homes on Rue Royale, making his way past a wrought iron gate, toward a few scattered one room cabins behind the mayor's mansion. He pushed open a door to one of the cabins, and Ona saw Adelaide's eyebrows nearly hit the ceiling with shock. Enda walked past Adelaide to face an impossibly old woman, with nearly twice the wrinkles as Fannie and maybe half as tall.

"Please," He pleaded. "Help her."

Chapter 8.

Ona remembered only flashes of arriving at Granny Trinity's cabin. Unlike Fannie, Granny Trinity was Enda's actual granny, and she was a slave at the Mayor Cambor's mansion. Ona drifted in and out of consciousness, after being laid out on a straw pallet on the floor of the cabin. The elderly woman spoke decisively, delivering orders to Adelaide that Ona couldn't hear from the floor.

"Yes, ma'am." Adelaide cast Ona one more puzzled glance before hurrying out the door to fetch whatever Granny Trinity had asked for.

"Good girl," Granny Trinity's voice was raspy, but cleared somewhat after lighting a pipe.

"You got to set her on the table, son. These old bones don't bend so good."

Enda obediently bent over Ona, but she was determined not to be fussed over. She sprang up wildly, briefly standing on her own before being swallowed by the tide of the dirt floor. Enda was quick to move however and managed to catch her as she collapsed. Granny Trinity studied them in silence. Enda sat Ona upright on the rough wooden table in the cabin. She was grateful for the stability of the table surface and tried to slow the spinning room by staring pointedly at her toes. When she began to teeter sideways Granny Trinity instructed Ona to lie down on her back.

Granny Trinity examined Ona with dainty, cracked finger tips. She touched Ona's temples and adjusted her arms. She barely glanced over the bruises on her throat. She complained that Ona's clothes were wet, and she would get sick. By this time, Adelaide returned with a handful of herbs that Ona recognized to be dried sumac and something else that she didn't recognize.

There was already hot water over the fire and Granny Trinity poured Ona a cup of tea, withholding it until it had cooled, and the herbs had steeped to her satisfaction. Ona took a small sip of the liquid which provided instant relief to the throbbing as it trickled down her throat. She examined the unfamiliar bitter tasting plant in her cup that swirled around the sumac leaves.

"It coltsfoot," the old woman explained. Comprehension dawned on Ona's face. She and Fannie used coltsfoot alright. It was one of the earliest spring flowers to bloom and they were in the completely wrong season for it. Ona never know the plant was useful when dried. She met Granny Trinity's eyes with new interest. Fannie was not often matched in her own trade.

"Sleep," The old woman instructed, once Ona had drained her cup.

Ona felt more stable and managed to climb in the straw pallet just as the sunlight broke through from under the cabin door. Adelaide had come and gone, bringing Granny Trinity a bundle of linens to mend at the table. Enda left out back behind the cabin to chop wood for his grandmother's fire.

Ona woke to the sound of the front door scraping against the dirt floor. A booming voice filled the room. She squinted into the sun, realizing it was past noon. Ona moved to sit up, finding that her limbs sore but sturdy. She was glad the room had stopped spinning.

"That boy been by here today, Trinity?" The Mayor Cambor held a split log in his hand that he waved accusingly. His white hair glistened in the sunlight shining behind his head and his maroon suit appeared freshly washed. His icy blue eyes scanned the room and fell on Ona's face. Ona knew those eyes. She'd know them anywhere. She looked the mayor up and down and wondered how the man who murdered his own daughter could share the same eyes as a boy like Enda Cambor.

"He come and chop wood for his granny. Then he go. I ain't feed him."

"Boy needs a job. He's nearing a man." He took a seat beside Granny Trinity, lighting his cigar. Trinity kept her eyes on her work, saying nothing. Ona thought it the oddest pair in the world discussing their grandchild like this. His gaze drifted back to Ona, who was sitting silently on the pallet.

"Where'd you come from, sugar?" He stood helping Ona to her feet. Ona realized she had been changed into a cotton night gown. Her green plaid dress was drying by the fire. She stood up to meet Enda's grandfather. When Ona did not immediately speak, the mayor continued with questions.

"You in school, sweetie?" He tucked a lock of Ona's hair behind her ear. Ona stiffened up, feeling her skin crawl with revulsion.

"No, sir." This was the first time she tested her voice since the night before. The tea had helped with the pain, though her voice still sounded hoarse and groggy. Mayor Cambor's fingers, clean and kept, traced the bruises on Ona's throat.

"You got a man treating you bad?" The mayor's fingers lingered over Ona's collar bone, sticking out through her gown.

"No, sir," Ona said firmly. She took a step back, glaring up at the mayor.

The mayor chuckled through his thick mustache. "Listen here, girl. That's my gown you're wearing. That's my bed you're using. That's my water you drink from." The mayor gestured toward Ona's empty cup. "And that's my Trinity you'd be bothering. Let me guess— you little Irish whelp ain't got no money to pay for my trouble. You best help old Trinity here before I find you a job myself. Everybody needs to work. All this," he gestured out the open door to his mansion, "is not built on idle hands and charity." He strode out the door, leaving it wide open for the leaves to blow in.

Granny Trinity waited for the mayor to disappear before she closed the door. Ona sat down beside Granny Trinity and began threading a needle from the thread basket. She helped Trinity mend the linens for most of the afternoon and changed back into her checkered dress. Then it was time to help Granny Trinity and Adelaide's mother Iris serve up the food. Ona did not know how to serve food the way the Cambors liked it, so she stayed in the back with Adelaide, washing dishes until dusk.

Ona overheard Iris given strict instruction by the mayor's wife for the Irish girl not to be left alone with anything valuable and not to let her leave spots on the silverware. Adelaide had spent the day feeding the dogs and the pigs, and waiting on the mayor's wife. Ona spent most of the day in silence, listening to the daily conversations of Enda's family.

Adelaide's mother Iris was Enda's aunt. Since Adelaide was younger and smaller than Ona, it was Iris' gown that was lent to Ona. Iris was twin sisters with Enda's mother, and she shared the same icy blue eyes as Enda and the mayor. Adelaide looked a lot like her father Elijah; a tall, thin man with an easy smile and kind eyes.

Ona wondered aloud where Enda stayed before his parents were killed. Neither Adelaide, nor Granny Trinity spoke a word, however Adelaide's mother Iris put down her dish cloth.

146

"Enda live with his daddy and his mama before they been killed. Axe come into town one day for trading, and he took sight of my sister. After that, he been coming for months sneaking behind the mayor just to visit Emmaline. He bring us meat, even herbs for Mama. Then one day, she done run off with him without even saying goodbye. She caught child after that, and they be living with them Indians for a long time."

"Why don't Enda stay with the Cherokee now?"

"All his kin be gone. Probably for the best. Emmaline hated living with them Indians. They treat her about like Mr. Cambor do her here. Those Indians don't speak no English; they ain't even believe in God. It weren't no time before that whole village got burnt up, and then there was Axe and Emmaline and Enda just a child, living in a cave all by themselves. Emmaline was better off to have just stayed put and raise her baby here." Iris put the dishes up after Adelaide and Ona washed them.

"That town got wiped out too?" Ona couldn't believe it.

"Emmaline better off to stay, but the best thing she ever did for that baby was leave. Look at him now, he a free man." Trinity countered. "You know, it ain't always been like this." Trinity wrapped loaves of bread up for the next morning. "My father live a free man, even with his skin as dark as his journey in chains across the ocean. Him and my mother, a white woman from England, both servants at the same house where they work over in Virginia. Us kids even learn to write some. We lived at a city built up in the low land marsh,

147

where us kids and my father, and my mother all got to working in the community."

"Your Papa was a free negro."

"Yes, ma'am. We lived in a special kind of town, called Maroon town, and gone to work for an honest living."

"How did you end up a slave?"

"Does it matter? I am who I am now. The past don't mean nothing."

"That's not true, Mama. Your story in our blood. It matters." Iris put her dishcloth down.

"I be taken. Me and my sister been walking home from taking care of house for an old woman in the village. My father's brother ask us to follow him and help him carry some goods back to his house, only he ain't take us home. He take us and sell us to a white man hiding with horses in the woods, and we never seen our family again. I ain't seen my sister since we was sold apart back when we wasn't knee high to a grasshopper."

"Is that when you first was a slave to the mayor?"

"Lord no, I got some years on that man," Trinity laughed.

"He the reason I'd rather see my Emmaline dead than here right now. She free today in heaven, and Enda better off an orphan than to grown up here with his cousin Adelaide."

"Where did Enda go when his parents died?"

Emmaline wiped the kitchen counters down with a rag, directing Ona to do the same. Adelaide mopped up the floors around them.

Emmaline continued, "After Axe's people all died, they stayed in the woods and the caves with that baby boy, blue eyed Enda, raising him up that way for years. They come see his Granny Trinity one Sunday, but the mayor already decided to stay home from church."

"That's when Enda got discovered by the mayor?" Ona scrubbed with harsh smelling lye soap.

"Enda about ten years old with his mama and his papa when the mayor came to call on my mama Trinity the way he do. He found his runaway slave with the Indian Axe and he shot them both for their sins. He threw Enda out, told him not to come around, but Enda still comes around to help his Granny. She been good to him and he knows that. I don't know exactly what he did when his parents died, but he made it this far."

Ona sat back, aghast. "How much blood will run off this mountain? The river can't possibly carry away the whole of Calico's sins."

Iris snorted. "It can carry away an awful lot of them."

"Jeremiah Sunday." Ona said quietly, looking up from her dirty dish rag.

"Jeremiah Sunday took him in and kept him fed."

"That ole drunken fool? Help him, Lord." Granny Trinity cast her eyes to the heavens, exasperated.

"What he fixing to do now that old man Sunday's been killed?" Adelaide asked

"He ain't come round here no more than usual," Iris noted.

"He's been working for Fannie, the midwife up on Calico Ridge." Ona interjected.

"She a tough old granny witch." Granny Trinity nodded her head in approval. "I met her twice when the mayor's wife took sick. She ain't let me work on her none, so he called in a witch named Fannie. If Enda works for her, she keep him fed I bet. How do you know this, girl?"

"I'm the granny witch apprentice. Fannie raised me."

The women finished cleaning the kitchen and made their way back to their cabins. Ona looked around Trinity's quarters and thanked her for her hospitality. Granny Trinity gave Ona more of the herbs for tea. Thanks to a day of relative silence, her throat was feeling less tender. Although by the looks Adelaide had given her earlier, Ona guessed her bruises were turning colors.

"Most nights we have a fire tonight and listen to the Scripture. You want to stay before you go back?" Granny Trinity asked. "We feed you."

Ona sat between Adelaide and Granny Trinity on large, flat rocks arranged around a fire. Adelaide's father told stories and pulled out a funny instrument Ona had never seen before. It was a hollowed-out gourd with a long wooden neck and strung tight like a fiddle. It made wild, uplifting music to sing and dance to, but unlike a fiddle, it was played with only your fingers.

"Call it a banjo." Adelaide's father, Elijah said fondly. His voice was low and smooth, like a slow-moving creek in the hot summer.

He plucked a tune, singing a song Ona had never heard before. The whole family joined in the song, Adelaide clapped alongside her father, keeping time while Iris sung beside her husband.

Ona was moved by Elijah's telling of the story of God. It was easy to see where people would follow a God who knew what it was like to be poor and human and ridiculed. She was especially glad when it was time to eat; filling her belly with hot corn mash drizzled in molasses.

She was feeling warm and sleepy around the fire when she heard a rustling coming down the road toward them. In the dim firelight, Ona could just make out the hunched over shape of an old stubborn woman making her way to the fire. Fannie did not speed up or slow down when she made eye contact with Ona. She spat out her chaw tobacco before reaching the group.

"Heard you wasn't fit to walk home this morning, Cricket." Fannie said nonchalantly, nodding to the Cambor slave family.

"Is that true?" Fannie asked Granny Trinity.

"She about knocked clean off her feet." Granny Trinity laughed.

"She feeling better?"

"Seem so."

"Good, then. Come along, Cricket. The Lafayettes will be needing us in the morning." Fannie turned back up the way she came. Ona stood up to follow Fannie, waving goodbye to the family.

"Thank you." Ona smiled.

"Get on now, girl." Granny Trinity waved her on, with half a smile on her lips.

Ona and Fannie stood at the door of the Lafayette's two story French colonial around noon the next day. Ona admired all the empty planter pots on the second story wraparound porch, imagining how beautiful the home must be in the warmer months. Fannie made sure Ona was clean and prim in her white dress with blue ribbon. Her leather shoes were looking haggard and ugly, so Ona did her best to minimize the attention on herself. It proved nearly impossible, since the bruising on her neck had ripened to a horrible shade of yellow and black.

The doorman eyed Ona's bruising curiously but said nothing. Ona could hear a baby crying relentlessly somewhere in the house. The doorman led them to Marie Lafayette, who was lounging in a chaise sofa sewing cross stitch patterns while Mr. Lafayette hovered over paperwork with John Francis, the mineral investor who requested the water witching. All three turned to face the new company, the men bowing politely.

"Good afternoon, Fannie, Miss Christie. Thank you so much for coming today. The health of our son is quite distressing recently." Despite Mr. Lafayette's concerns, the baby remained screaming upstairs, seemingly unattended.

"Miss Christie!" Mr. Francis was in shock.

"My God, are you alright?" Mr. Lafayette was stunned, only just noticing Ona's bruising.

"Oh! Those are some rather hideous markings indeed," Mrs. Lafayette chimed in.

"Perhaps it's not best to be up and walking with such injury! Tell us, what has happened?" Mr. Francis crossed the large room in a few long strides, to examine Ona's injuries more closely.

"Surely the girl is feeling well, else she would not be up and working." Mrs. Lafayette concluded soundly on Ona's behalf. "Honestly, I'm glad you came. The little monster hasn't given us a moment's rest in weeks."

Mrs. Lafayette led Fannie and Ona upstairs, trailing her fingers along the wooden banister in a slow, deliberate way. The new Lafayette baby, Charles Clovis, was suffering from colic. Fannie cooed the baby from his crib while Mrs. Lafayette sat in the far corner of the nursery, as if afraid to touch the child. Ona stood awkwardly beside Fannie watching her play with the boy's fingers and toes and he settled somewhat. When her cold fingers brushed his belly to feel his stomach, the boy began to wail.

Ona could not listen to the crying any longer; it was maddening. She picked the child up in her arms, holding him close. Immediately, the boy ceased fussing. Marie Lafayette sat hunched over in her chair, hands covering her eyes. She peaked through her fingers when silence replaced the child's cries.

"You ladies are angels! He has been crying incessantly for weeks! What in creation did you do?" Marie Lafayette exclaimed. Her porcelain complexion really was something unusual. Her pale blue veins ran underneath her translucent skin. Some of the veins even appeared to be painted on. If Ona concentrated long enough she could separate the actual veins from the painted ones.

"Mrs. Lafayette, do you remember the last time you held your baby?" Fannie did not let any sign of judgment penetrate her voice.

"I... well..." Marie Lafayette flushed the palest tinge of pink. "I have a wet nurse from the Beaudin household who comes in the day. It's been hard on us both... adjusting to the little thing." She said. "I believe the wet nurse picks him up when it's time to feed him. She changes him and turns him in his crib." Mrs. Lafayette seemed uncertain. Fannie watched Ona soothe the baby, sighing.

"Massage his stomach twice a day to help with the colic. It has to be you; it won't work if anyone else does it. Change him often or he will take sick." Fannie instructed.

"If he cries, pick him up and sing him a lullaby. Tinctures won't fix what's wrong because the only thing this child needs is to be loved. Can you do that? Will you love him fiercely?" Ona turned with the child in her arms to look at Mrs. Lafayette. Marie Lafayette nodded, her eyes wide. She took the baby in her arms and a new softness fell over her. Her voice was strained when she spoke and she had to clear her throat.

"Ona, come with me. I can hide your bruising with powder. It will last you at least the rest of the day." Mrs. Lafayette offered. Ona glanced at Fannie, unsure what to say.

"Go on, Cricket. I need to collect payment from Mr. Lafayette anyhow. Meet me in the foyer when you're finished."

Ona followed Mrs. Lafayette to a room with an enormous bed and ornate furniture. The wood was all beautiful dark cherry and the chairs and benches matched, their cushions all made of pink velvet with golden leaflets embellished on the fabric. Mrs. Lafayette gestured Ona to sit on the bench in front of the bed. Ona obeyed and Mrs. Lafayette tinkered over the table, looking at jars and containers of innumerable paints, fragrances and powders before selecting one and joining Ona. She dabbed at Ona's throat tenderly while Ona held the baby.

"You are young yet Ona, but you are nearly a woman." Mrs. Lafayette said kindly. "You are passably attractive." She tugged one of Ona's fiery locks hanging loose from her cotton cap. Mrs. Lafayette kept her dark curls hidden behind a beaded silk cap that glittered with sapphires.

"In life, a woman can only do so many things. You can marry for love, or you can marry rich. Being where you come from, you might not get a chance to choose either." Mrs. Lafayette said softly. "Mr. Francis is intrigued by you, Ona. Some say he's not quite right. That he takes men for lovers, though my husband doesn't believe so. But even still, he must marry. You are young yet, but in time you may

155

grow close. Mr. Francis suspects the oldest McDaniel boy may already have a claim on your heart, but I tell you this, Ona." Mrs. Lafayette stopped powdering Ona's neck and slowly put the lid back on her container.

"Love will not fill your belly. Marry rich while you are still young and attractive and if he's good to you, you've done even better than you could have hoped for." Mrs. Lafayette rose, and Ona hesitated. So many things Ona had never considered before. Marie Lafayette put the baby back in his crib.

"I ain't in love with Ezra McDaniel," Ona said haltingly.

"It makes no difference to me, darling."

In the foyer of the house, the doorman waited silently beside Fannie, while Mr. Lafayette and Mr. Francis discussed investments. The men were headed to the tippling house. Mr. Francis was interested in becoming an investor of the place, to help build an Inn above the bar. He was convinced the natural resources would draw prominent businessmen from all over the country.

"Investing is the most important thing you could do with your money! If you play your cards right, you can start with peanuts and end with caviar. That's the beauty of America!" Mr. Francis winked at Ona, thinking he had offered her a rare, profound tidbit.

"He's right, Miss Christie." Mr. Lafayette agreed. "Say, you've been given a chance opportunity not too long ago, yes? Didn't your father pass away in the militia?"

"That's correct, Mr. Lafayette." Ona said evenly. For some reason, Ona sounded different when she was interacting with the Lafayettes. It was like at school, when she worked to switch off her accent. No one told her to speak more slowly and enunciate her words a certain way around them, she just did.

"Surely the military has compensated you for your loss?" Mr. Lafayette inquired.

"Dear, that's not polite conversation." Mrs. Lafayette chastised. Mr. Lafayette waved her off.

"That's right." Ona said cautiously. "I was given his salary for the year, plus compensation for the loss of a Lieutenant. And his gun and sword." Ona had not revisited her father's possessions since the night she received them. She was vaguely aware that Fannie had put them under Ona's pallet bed for safe keeping until Ona was ready to take them out.

"Marvelous. A true war hero, he must have been." Mr. Francis bobbed his head in admiration.

"Ona, have you ever considered investing your father's pension? What he left behind would set you up for maybe a little while, but you could earn so much more." Mr. Lafayette's suggestion was earnest.

"Thanks for an honest interest in Ona's welfare," Fannie interrupted the men. "We got more stops to make before we leave town, so we can't stay today." Her voice was firm. Mr. Lafayette ignored her.

"At least consider putting his pension in a bank, Ona. You're not earning any interest if it's sitting around hidden away!"

"Thank you for all the ideas, Mr. Lafayette, Mr. Francis. Fannie's right. We best be leaving." Ona had no idea if they had other stops to make or not, but she wanted to get out of the Lafayette home.

Fannie was telling the truth, they really did have more stops to make. They delivered a tiny vial of red liquid to Mayor Cambor's wife, Virginia. Mrs. Cambor's hands were growing unsteady in her years, so she reached out to Fannie's medicine for help. She was aging and in poor health, despite being at least two decades younger than Fannie. Virginia Cambor stood cloaked in a golden gown, hair hidden in a matching silk turban. Standing in the entrance of the large home on Rue Royale, Mrs. Cambor's nostrils flared when she laid eyes on Fannie's apprentice. She ushered Fannie into the house, but instructed Ona to stand in the foyer and wait. Virginia Cambor insisted on privacy. She reminded Ona several times not to touch anything, even leaving Adelaide behind to keep eyes on Ona.

Ona wandered into the next room, examining the severe paintings of the Cambors that decorated floral papered walls. She had never seen wallpaper before. Ona started to sit on a soft velvet sofa in a large room lined with bookshelves and a fireplace, but Adelaide clicked her tongue.

"She gone throw you out and not pay your witch if you do that."

Ona immediately rose, standing straight and still with her hands clasped in front of her.

"What's the matter with her?" Ona asked, crinkling her nose. Adelaide shook her head.

"She don't trust ones that used to be indentured. Thinks y'all thieves."

"My parents was indentured. Fannie was too. I never was, I was born right here on Calico Ridge. But Mrs. Cambor will take help from Fannie and not me?"

Adelaide took a rag out of her skirts and began wiping down the surfaces of the room. "Fannie ain't running round with the mayor's bastard grandchild. In her book, you tainted. Untouchable." Adelaide said simply.

"Bet she still manages to touch her husband." Ona spat sardonically.

Adelaide's head whipped around to face Ona, a smug grin tugging at her lips. She did not respond to the comment, but quietly resumed dusting the mantle until Fannie returned with the old hag Virginia Cambor. The mayor's wife seemed pleased with her remedy and Fannie seemed equally happy with a change purse growing rapidly heavier as the day progressed, clinking merrily around in her skirts. Fannie gave Ona money to pay off their tab at the general store and headed back to the house for a nap.

Ona barely heard the bell above the door chime over the chatter of customers as she entered the busiest shop in town. The general store was always buzzing with people sending mail, purchasing dry goods and household wares and catching up on gossip while waiting in the never-ending line from sun up to sundown. After the general store closed, the tippling house across the street became the most popular place in Calico. Ona made her way to the back of the line, watching Ezra balance sales in a large accounting book while his brothers Jonathon, Dane, and Nash darted in and out of customers finding goods and fetching mail.

Ezra's eyes scanned above the frenzy before finding a clock in the back of the store and sighing. Ona's found the source of his displeasure: Still three hours before closing. His gaze found Ona's face and Ona dropped her eyes to the floor. When Ona finally had her turn at the counter, Ezra could not see the bruises concealed on her neck.

"Come to pay my tab," Ona slid the coins across the counter toward Ezra. The place was quite noisy with all the shoppers, but Ezra did not seem to notice it.

"Right, thanks." He flipped through his book of accounts, adding the figures to Fannie's tab. He crossed her name through with a pen. They were all paid up.

"Come to dinner with my family tonight," Ezra said suddenly, looking up at Ona.

"I'm sorry, I can't." Ona's face turned bright red.

"Having dinner with Mr. Francis?"

"Hardly!"

"Who then? Who dines with Ona Christie to keep her company at night?"

"Fannie. I dine with Fannie." It was no business of his how often Enda came around to work for Fannie, or guests like Awenasa who seemed to turn up periodically.

"Fannie was alone last night. I came to check on you since you were feeling ill. You weren't even there. You don't come to parties or dance. You rarely go to church. You lose your things and let your hair fall loose from covering— the disregard for propriety drives away any honest man, Ona. Just you and Fannie alone on the ridge? What are you doing up there? Two hours I waited for you." Ezra's words stung Ona, but she masked her hurt.

"I went for a walk and lost track of time."

"Lie! Fannie told me you were too sick to see me. What are you hiding?" Ezra's eyes narrowed.

Ona was contemplating a rude comment for Ezra McDaniel but was interrupted mid thought by a knocking at the window beside Ona and Ezra's hushed argument.

Enda Cambor waved at Ona from outside the window. Ona's eyes drank in Enda's messy mop of curly brown hair that framed his face, matching his warm brown skin in complete contrast to his icy blue eyes. His energy radiated with enthusiasm for life. Ezra, mirror opposite of Enda save for the curly brown hair, lost all coloring. His face went pale, comprehension dawning on his face.

"You... Surely not... *him*." Ezra stammered. "That is absolutely vile, Ona. A downright sin against God himself. Not to mention illegal!"

"There ain't nothing between me and that boy, don't you dare even suggest!" Ona hissed low over the counter.

"He ought to be hung; he will be if word gets around." Ezra spoke low under his breath.

"That would be a downright waste of human life considering no law has been broken. Thank you for handling the account. Please let us know if any problems turn up with it." Her formal tenor left a frigid air between the two of them. She gathered up her empty purse, taking proud strides out the door without another word.

Enda was ecstatic about something but wouldn't say what. Ona watched his distracted thoughts, following his eyes to the winter cardinals and chickadees that flitted through the trees.

Once the last patch of town had vanished, Enda took Ona by the hand, leading her underneath a magnificent chestnut that stretched high into the canopy. He gathered her other free hand in his and they stood across from each other, linked.

"I'm getting an apprenticeship." Despite his nonchalant tone, Enda's body was tightly coiled, and Ona could see him fighting a small smile coming to his lips.

"What? Where? That's wonderful!"

"With the blacksmith. He says I can be his farrier assistant and work my way into the rest."

162

"With Talton Messer?" Ona asked. She knew the town black-smith. He was gruff and surly as his job required, but nice enough with fair prices and good work. Fannie had treated a few of his particularly nasty burns in the past, an occupational hazard it seemed.

"Not with him. With Billy Titus." Enda corrected. Ona searched her memories, trying to place the name. Calico was a small town; everybody knew everybody, and she'd never heard of Billy Titus.

"He's not from around here. He's new to the area. He ain't even moved here completely yet. He said he'll be ready for me by Spring." Ona chewed on this news silently.

"Do you know what this means?" Enda continued.

"What?"

"We are both apprenticed now. We will have both have a trade, Ona. We might could really..." He didn't finish his sentence, but his words lurched a kind of pang in Ona's stomach. She looked up into Enda's eyes, the small thought of possibility reeling through her mind transformed a flickering feeling into a blazing realization. For a moment, she leaned closer against him. Adelaide's words and Ezra's horror flashed through her mind like an ice bath.

"We are abominable." Ona repeated the words from inside Ice Cave, pulling away from him to straighten her dress. She clasped her hands together, holding them at her waist.

"Maybe," Enda didn't deny it, grabbing her hand and pulling her back close.

"What if they find out?"

"What if they never know?"

Chapter 9.

Ona woke up shivering one November morning and stirred from underneath her blankets to find snow falling off her bed. She peaked through the cracked chinking of the cabin, where slight gaps between the logs had allowed snow to drift inside. Ona slipped into her leather walking shoes, aware that the thin soles offered little protection from the elements. She stoked the fire's embers from last night's supper: turnip and onion soup and took to the forest, searching for pine needles. She wrapped herself in a thick shawl but did not bother to change out of her night dress.

Melting snow leached through Ona's boots and she crunched through the trees, seeking out the long, soft needles of white pine. Ona hiked up her dress, lithely scaling the tree's dead and broken limbs to the upper, living branches. She broke off as many bundles of needles she could stuff in her shoes and dress, slowly making her way back to the cabin. She lined the soles of her shoes with the soft needles, hoping to add more protection from the cold. Ona considered Talmadge, who had no shoes at all and worked outside all winter.

Ona spent most of the morning outside and returned to the cabin with a surprise waiting for her and a note written in Enda's uncoordinated scrawl, "For Little America." Ona bent to examine delicate ice clusters laid out in front of the door. Fannie poked her head outside, admiring the surprise. She stooped down beside Ona, a small smile turning the corners of her lips. Ona gingerly picked up one of the fragile formations, marveling at the streaks of ice, glittering like gems, folding in thin ribbons around itself. As quickly as it was in her hand, it collapsed and melted into droplets on her palm.

"Frost Flowers. They bust from plants during the first of the winter freezes," Fannie explained.

Enda fared better than Ona lately, with thick animal skins wrapped with leather strings around his feet that rose to his knees. He was spending lots of time at the mayor's house, helping his Granny Trinity. The mayor himself was kind enough to set Enda up with the blacksmith. If you asked Enda, Billy Titus was arriving by the first day of spring. If you asked anyone else, Enda was absolutely mad. No one else had ever heard of a Billy Titus, either. Enda insisted he signed a contract and would be collected first snow melt of spring to begin his apprenticeship.

As the weeks passed, winter crept into Calico like the thick morning fog that fills the valleys. As the snow piled, the shelves of the general store became barren until finally Wash McDaniel closed shop for the season. None of the traders could make it into town to keep the shelves full. The whole day was spent outside trying to keep warm, busy with chores to keep warm inside at night. Enda spent nearly all of his time chopping wood for his home at Jeremiah Sunday's little shack, or for his Granny Trinity, or trapping meat for the both of them.

Ona chopped wood from seasoned downed trees, using large sacks to carry back firewood from the forest one load at a time. Since their properties touched, sometimes she spotted Talmadge out working in the woods with his brothers and was able to catch a ride with them on their sled pulled by two sturdy mules, Whiskey and Old Boy. She would pile on as much firewood she could stack on top of their massive cherry, oak and pine timber and ride on top of the felled trees back to Fannie's.

"Thank God for whiskey and fire. Without them, I think we'd all be dead." Talmadge passed Ona a bottle of horrible turnip mash liquor and she choked it down in little sips, relishing the burning warmth that came with it. Ona and all ten of the Halstead children were sitting around the stone fire place in the Halstead home huddling with blankets on the floors, on the pallets, anywhere they could find warmth. Little Mercy sat curled up in Ona's lap, sharing Ona's shawl. The Halsteads were now skinny children. You could see hollow cheeks on the same plump baby boy from fall. Mercy felt like a feather resting on Ona. There was nothing to her.

"How's your daddy's business doing for you?" Ona asked.

Talmadge spat on the floor. "Can't make a sale even to give it away."

"Don't you meet those traders from the city?"

"Traders holed up for the season. I bet they ain't left their homes since November."

"Really," Ona was shocked.

"Lexington people is fragile." The oldest Halstead girl, thirteen-year-old Vernie, giggled. Ona rolled her eyes, placing a sympathetic hand over her heart.

"Well God bless," Ona pleaded with mock sincerity.

Mercy could not control her laughter after that. Her full-hearted laughs seemed to make the whole room radiate with warmth. It was not long however, before coughing overtook her laughter and Vernie sent her to lie down. The Halsteads offered to feed Ona dinner—they were having boiled water and pine needles, but she politely declined and managed to trudge the grueling mile through knee deep snow back home before dark.

Ona examined her grits with butter somewhat guiltily during supper.

"What's the matter, Cricket. Why won't you eat?"

"It's the Halsteads, Fannie. They ain't got nothing to eat!" Ona was ashamed of herself for ever thinking a winter without canned beans or apple butter would be too difficult.

"Well, don't them boys feed the little ones?" Fannie's brow furrowed.

"It's just, they work all the time and all, but I don't think they know *how* to feed them. Seem like they was mostly able to always trade for meats when their father was around."

"Well that boy Talmadge is sure big enough to kill a deer, Ona. Is he not taking care of his brothers and sisters?" Fannie was upset now.

"He ain't got a gun."

Fannie clicked her tongue. "Tomorrow you find that Enda Cambor and take him on up there to those kids and teach them Halstead boys how to snare a rabbit! Nobody's allowed to starve on this hill, Cricket. We take care of our own. And you better eat girl; there ain't one good reason for you to go to bed with an empty belly when there's food sitting right here waiting to be eat."

The following morning, Ona crunched her way through the back alleys of downtown Calico. Although nightmarish to march through in the warmer, smellier months, they were peaceful enough on a slumbering winter morning. The sun was just peeking over the morning sky and Ona knew she had a good chance of catching Enda still at home.

Veering away from town and into the bramble, Ona examined the creek trickling underneath a thin layer of ice. She had to cross it to get to Jeremiah Sunday's shack, now Enda's shack, really. It was too wide to make in one jump, but small enough she might only have to get one foot wet. Ona quickly undid one shoe and sock, dashing across the icy creek. She ignored the throbbing cold on her foot. It was only a moment before she stopped feeling anything on that foot anyway. Ona hopped as fast as she could through the snow to Enda's shack where she defrosted her icy toes by a small fire.

Enda had dried meats strung up throughout the shack and was busy patching some warped siding that had allowed several inches of snow to pile up in one corner overnight. He was bundled in thick animal skins that seemed to block out the cold entirely. Enda reluctantly agreed to spend the day at the Halstead house, weary of most Calico people, even the ones outside of town.

Enda slipped Ona's shoe back on her foot, using a thin twine to tie around her foot and hold her shoe on. Ona examined the twine carefully. It wasn't rope, exactly.

"What is it?"

"Cord. Made from cat gut." He tightened the knot around her ankle, holding the shoe snugly in place.

"What?" Ona squeaked. Enda shrugged his shoulders.

"I make it to string my bow. You're welcome." He winked, helping Ona to her feet.

"Is it really made from a cat?" Ona dared to ask. Enda burst out laughing.

"No! They just call it that. You can use any sort of gut. This one's made from deer."

"Who taught you how to do something like that?"

"My dad. The Axe." Enda passed Ona a cup of whiskey that she sipped on.

"Did he teach you a lot?"

"Well, it was just me and him and mama for a long time. Axe's home was neighbors with Awenasa. Friends, cousins maybe. They got killed out when I was little and my dad, he just sort took us and kept on living out there."

"How'd he meet your mama?" Ona heard this tale from Enda's Aunt Iris, but she wanted to hear his version of it.

"She was a slave at the Cambor house, and fetched water from the creek every day. The Axe came to town for trading every little while and watched her for a few days at the creek. Thought my mama was sweet." Enda closed his eyes, remembering the story from heart.

"Axe finally gave it the gumption to say hello and it was history from there. Mama would sneak into the Cambor cabins from time to time to visit Granny, but I didn't meet her until the day my parents died. Mama said I had to keep hid and that's just what they did."

"They must of loved each other a lot," Ona smiled. She passed Enda the cup and he took a long drink before standing up.

"They wasn't never married, not really anyway." Enda

"What's a wedding, but a promise to the God who already cursed us at birth?" Ona wondered aloud.

"God didn't curse us, he gave people choices. When people choose to commit evil on their own accord that's part of free will. People like the mayor will get what's theirs in hell."

Goosebumps raised the hairs on Ona's arm. She accepted Enda's hand and he led her toward the door of the little shack. Enda wore a crooked grin on his face and held the door open for Ona, ushering her back out into the cold for the trek up to the Halstead place.

Outside, Ona tripped on one of Jeremiah Sunday's old glass bottles. She stumbled, knocking into one of the skulls strung up and suspended from the trees. This one looked like some kind of dog. Ona stood up, brushing the snow off herself and Enda shook his head, looking around at the shack Jeremiah Sunday had built.

"Ole Sunday sure was a different kind of folk." Enda sighed, scratching his head.

They crossed the creek back into Calico, only this time Enda showed Ona a fallen log just a little upstream that they could walk across.

"How in Sam Hill did you even meet up with a man like Sunday?"

"He could be plenty awful, sure," Enda reflected. "But he wasn't so bad all the time. I was still little when the mayor threw me out after he did what he did to my folks. Granny Trinity and Uncle Elijah help me bury them at the negro cemetery outside of town."

"I ain't never been there," Ona mused.

"It ain't easy to find. It's cut right out of the woods with no signs to speak of. I spent a lot of time there in them first few months.

That's how I met Sunday. He seen me walking around the hills more than anybody else and finally offered me some old corn bread one day." Enda's voice wavered. "He must of seen that I was hungry. He told me about his own kids once. He kept me fed for a long time. He never knew who Axe was though, or he would shoot me dead right where I stand."

When Ona knocked on the Halstead door, they were greeted with mixed response. Talmadge did not invite them inside, despite the long trip that took all morning and early afternoon to get up to the Halstead place. Mercy's twin Sarah Jane hid shyly behind her older brothers. Mercy wasn't shy however; she wriggled her way out the front door and stood tall, looking up into Enda's endless blue eyes.

"You're fixing to get us get some food?" She asked sweetly.

"Truly hoping so," Enda smiled down at her. Mercy took his hand. Vernie gasped, pulling Mercy back to her side.

"You don't touch negroes," Vernie scolded, straightening Mercy's dress. Enda's face became unreadable.

Mercy and Sarah Jane stayed home with their baby brother, but all seven of the older Halsteads followed Enda and Ona into the woods. Enda showed them how to set trap lines in the snow and what kinds of bait to use for different sorts of animals. After a few hours, Enda's snare had caught a rabbit. Enda stood very still behind the rabbit, slowly moving one hand in front of the struggling animal.

"The trick is to just," Enda grunted, scooping the animal up by the neck and twisting its head off in a quick jerking motion. "make it fast and painless." It was all very clean. There wasn't even blood. The rabbit's legs were still twitching which caused one of the younger Halstead boys to turn a concerning shade of green. Vernie watched in rapt attention.

"All this work for just one rabbit? That'll barely be enough for the little ones." Talmage was disheartened.

"You'll get good at it with time and practice." Ona offered.

"I don't have time for practice. Kids is hungry now." Talmadge shook his head.

"Then don't be good, be great. You can kill enough to keep the edge off at first. Next year you won't be hungry again. And don't forget to save every bit."

"What do you mean?" one of the little boys asked.

Enda withdrew a large hand blade from his pants and began peeling skin carefully off the rabbit. Once it was started, the whole pelt slipped right off like butter. He pointed at his feet wrapped in handsome fur boots.

"This is useful." Enda gestured with the pelt. Enda maneuvered his knife around the body cavity of the rabbit, pulling out organs without damaging any of them. He separated the stringy intestines and pointed at the cords that kept Ona's shoes tied. "This is also useful. It can all be used for something." Enda explained.

"Watch your knife. Don't poke the gut. You'll ruin it."

"I ain't an idiot." Talmadge spat.

Vernie picked up the rabbit carcass, eyes glittering.

"Soup tonight, boys!" Her voice rang clear.

On their walk back to the Halstead place, Enda kept offering tips that finally won over Talmadge's dislike for Enda.

"Listen, traps will hold you over with small game, but if y'all don't want to be hungry you got to get something you can shoot. You got a gun or bow?" Enda pressed.

Talmadge shook his head disparagingly. "My father traded timber with the butcher. Now they're both gone and dead after the massacre and lost the gun with it."

"I got a gun," Ona looked up suddenly.

"Really?" Vernie and Enda asked at the same time. Vernie looked impressed; Enda was shocked he hadn't heard about it before.

"My Papa's." Ona said softly. "The McDaniels... they brought it to me after..." Her voice dropped off.

"And you never even used it? That was months ago!" Talmadge exclaimed. Ona flinched at his words, but he was right.

"I should get it out," Ona contemplated.

"Damn straight! Or give it to people who will put it to real use!" Talmage carried on brandishing a stick he found on the ground. Talmadge paused by a large burrow near the edge of the forest.

"What do you think is in there, Cambor?" He whispered.

"Something that'll be awful angry if you wake him up." Enda laughed. Talmage, feeling brave, knelt in the snow to poke his head inside the den.

"Might be a groundhog," He said hopefully, thinking of more food to bring home.

"Might be a bob cat," Ona rolled her eyes.

Talmadge jammed his walking stick inside the den, hoping to spook out the hibernating creature. A strangled squeak preceded angry growling and the most offensive musk Ona had ever been around.

"Skunk!" Vernie cried. They raced home in futile attempt to escape the retched smell lingering on every inch of Talmadge. Vernie held the prized rabbit meat high above her head and took it directly to roast over the fire. It was not difficult for Ona and Enda to take their leave after that. Fannie spent the rest of the evening burning hickory just to overpower the residual skunk odor clinging to Ona and Enda.

Christmas was not an eventful time, although Enda was in high spirits and spent the night with his Granny. On Christmas night, Fannie prepared roasted venison with turnips and onions. It was delicious. They sat beside the crackling fire, gorging themselves on fried apples. Ona's eyes were drawn to the corner by the fire, where her father's gun and sword had been moved to after the hunting lesson with the Halsteads, still partially wrapped in the cloths Mr. McDaniel brought it in months ago.

Ona, suddenly emboldened with the help of spiced Christmas rum, took out her father's belongings and lay them on the floor. There was the letter from President Jefferson. The fat change purse, her father's pension, remained untouched. The flint lock rifle Rowland Christie took to battle. And his military issued sword. Ona again studied the red stained flecks on the golden hilt eagle feathers before unsheathing the blade. She practiced swinging it slowly around the room.

"Watch it, girl, you're about to take my eye out." Fannie waved her hand in front of her, like she was swatting at a fly.

"I could really use this." Ona breathed.

"For what? Fannie exclaimed. "Use it more than the gun? How?"

"I don't know for certain. It's got a weight to it though."

Ona sheathed the sword, scurrying up the ladder to the loft and slung the beaded belt over her shoulder before making her way back down to the fire. She laced the belt through ringlets on the sheath and tied it around her waist. Ona sat comfortably on the dirt floor, spreading her dress out before her. She took the long rifle in hand, staring past the small silver eye sight.

"How do you load this thing?" Ona asked eagerly. Fannie threw her arms up in the air.

"I'm a-going to bed, girl. Girls and weapons. Huh." Fannie mumbled to herself, crawling into bed and turning under her quilts.

Chapter 10.

Ona and Talmage spent the week after Christmas with Enda learning the parts of the gun, how to take it apart and clean it. Jeremiah Sunday died with his gun still in the house. Enda wouldn't touch it for the lives it had taken, but he left out those details and gifted it to the Halstead children.

Ona's rifle was more modern, but they were both Kentucky rifles that operated with the same muzzle loading technique. Talmadge had a few dozen small lead rounds but did not offer to share his spoils. Talmadge was hanging around less and less; now that he was bringing in big game like deer, he was spending nearly all of the short days outside. Ona still needed bullets for her father's rifle.

"You might have to put that gun down long enough to celebrate your birthday tomorrow," Enda laughed.

"I'll celebrate with my gun in hand if I want to." Ona did not look up from cleaning the long barrel with a rag.

"What would you do with that anyway?" Enda asked.

"All kinds of things. I can hunt now. I can keep wolves and mountain cats off."

"Fair enough. You want bullets? You'll have to trade for them."

Ona shook her head, confused. "Ezra said the traders won't come this way since the snow. He said we're stuck until spring."

Enda smiled mischievously, offering an exaggerated bow. "Pardon from your friend the gentleman, but he ain't selling the kind of goods that are worth trading for year-round. Where do you think Sunday got all his liquor? You want lead? I'll take you to get some for your birthday." He winked.

They departed in shin deep snow the following day. Enda surprised Ona with a birthday present that morning: knee high deer skin leather boots. Ona squealed in delight, admiring their warmth and water proofing. Ona bundled up in shawls, sporting her new boots and displaying her father's newly cleaned sword off her hip. Enda carried the gun and a flask of whiskey to keep them warm. He was bundled up in a buffalo skin coat and looked perfectly comfortable in the January snow. It was a beautiful morning, with clear skies and sunshine to warm their backs. Light glistened off snow like brilliant crystals making the earth positively shine in such pleasant weather.

They stopped off at the Halstead home and were able to borrow a mule. With so much success with the gun, Talmadge wasn't worried about slow business for the season any longer now that he could feed his family. He was happy to lend Old Boy to them for the day. Ona eagerly climbed on the mule first, excited to steer.

"Can I just put the blanket on first?" Talmadge shook his head.

Ona slid off Old Boy and allowed Talmadge to toss a small, thick blanket over the mule's back before scrambling back up.

"He don't normally get rode too much, he's really only used to pull skids; but, I think he'll be alright. He's strong and likes to work."

Old Boy was large draft mule. He was tall and muscular with a rust colored coat that was soft and thick for the winter. His massive legs powered through the snow with great force and his movements were surefooted. He had no difficulties carrying two people on his broad back and seemed to enjoy getting out for some exercise.

"Enda... I thought the trading post was West, towards Lexington..." Ona started.

"Sure. There's one that way, halfway between Calico and the next town. We're going south a ways to another one."

"What if no one's there?"

"Look around, it's a beautiful day. There's a good chance for people to be selling today."

"What if they don't have lead?"

"There's lead seams everywhere around here. That's one thing we are practically guaranteed to find most anywhere." His matter of fact attitude laid Ona's worries to rest. For a moment.

"What are we gone to trade with them?" She cried. "How could I not even think about that before now?"

"Don't worry, Ona. It's all taken care of." Enda assured.

They rode south into wilderness until they were practically on the Tennessee border, weaving up endlessly steep terrain dotted with pine and maneuvering around sharp cliff faces hidden by jagged pines and barren forest. By afternoon they joined a well-traveled road that, after another hour or so of riding, passed by a two-story cabin with a chimney.

"Mondry Trade Post," Ona read the sign outside the cabin aloud.

"That's the man who owns it."

Enda slid off Old Boy, hitching the old mule up by the store. He eyed a group of men smoking pipes on the front porch and decided to take the riding blanket with them, keeping it tucked under his arm. Ona appeared quite impressive with her sword and managed to gracefully maneuver off the horse without any assistance. Enda looked downright formidable with Rowland Christie's gun slung over his shoulder and massive buffalo hair cloak nearly tripling his size. His hair grew longer than usual for the winter, brown curls framing his face in the style of Ezra and Mr. Francis. His blue eyes cut across their surroundings and Ona followed his gaze.

Enda was right, there were quite a lot of people milling around despite the cold. Most of the men were more similar to Jeremiah Sunday in appearance, but there were others. Two Indian men standing almost out of sight around the back of the house. A black man packing up his horse to leave. Women could be seen from inside the windows, with loose hair and colorful, if not immodest, garments.

"Enda, look at all these people," Ona whispered in awe.

"Mondry will sell anything people want to sell to anyone looking to buy. He don't care what color so long as you got money."

"Is it like the general store? Do we just go and ask the shop man for what we need?" Ona asked.

"Just let me talk. Don't say nothing. Please."

Ona rolled her eyes. "It's just a trade store, Enda."

"This kind is different." Enda shook his head. "But it's the only place open this time of year, and if you want bullets before spring, we can probably only get them here."

Ona said nothing but followed Enda inside. Warmth flooded Ona, melting her tingling fingers and thawing her face. She gravitated toward the fire place to admire the lovely stone laid into the wall. Looking around, the cabin had a few common travel items behind a bar and several tables set up with a few men drinking at some of them.

Ona turned to find a woman with dark skin wearing a vibrant blue dress with a slinky arm draped around Enda's neck, whispering softly in his ear. Enda stood stiffly, looking uncomfortable and trapped. Ona simply stared in blatant disbelief at the audacity of such public indecency. Perhaps, secretly, she was bit jealous that she was not so simpering and woman-like with perfectly curled locks piled on top of her head and ruby lips so easy to kiss.

"That's your lover, little dove?" A velvet voice purred behind Ona. Ona whipped around to face a porcelain doll of a woman, draped in delicate white fabrics that ruffled around her breasts, to tease the world. She spoke with a thick New York accent.

"What is this, a bawdy house?" Ona hissed, pointedly not staring at the woman's chest.

The little woman cocked her head, frowning; a tragic imperfection for someone otherwise seemingly perfect. Her deep chestnut hair fell in waves down her side.

"Little dove, it is not kind to say such things. Uncle Mondry allows the people to sell anything that people want to buy. I make good money. More than you, likely." The doll's voice chimed like bells.

Ona narrowed her eyes, watching the woman in blue leave Enda to greet a new customer who walked in the door. He seemed to swat her away too, like a fly.

"Go away, whore." He shooed. "I am here for bread and beer only."

The doll shrugged her shoulders. "It's a living. Say little dove, you have a strong body. Nice curls. Do you need a job? The men won't care about your freckles. It's all in the way you speak." A low, sultry laugh escaped her lips.

The woman in blue passed Ona and The Doll, finally with a taker, leading him up the stairs of the cabin. Ona felt like she was going to be sick. Enda grabbed Ona by the hand, squeezing it tightly and completely ignoring The Doll.

"Come on Ona, we can pick up the lead out back."

"It is not nice to ignore people." The Doll chided, drifting toward the crowd of men who were on the front porch and now shuffling inside the room.

"Hello, my loves!" The Doll greeted the men, chatting amiably with them.

"Isabelle!" One of them called. "I have missed you!"

Enda slammed the door behind them, shaking his head.

"Who is this Mondry man anyhow?" Ona asked.

They veered around the back of the cabin and Enda pointed out a large man with an enormous belly roasting a whole deer over an open fire while arguing with one of the Indian men. The antlered buck head sat severed on the frozen ground, blood soaking into the snow. Enda approached quietly, waiting patiently for a turn to speak.

"You can't keep bringing them here!" Mondry exclaimed, waiving a knife in the air.

"They ain't selling. They're flat out depressing to stare at. Who would buy a damn slave in the goddamn winter time? Nobody needs extra work done right now!"

Ona automatically glanced over to the other Indian man who was holding the end of a thick rope. Tied to the other end of the rope were two negro males, slaves, standing barefoot in the snow. Enda's eyes did not wander but remained determinedly rooted to speak with the man Mondry.

"I hear you, Mondry, but I cannot afford to keep feeding them. Surely someone is needing a house built. I know there are plans to build a general store in spring." The man argued.

"Yeah, Ace, Spring! You are taking up space in my shop as of two months ago!" Mondry carved a bit of meat off the smoking animal and threw it in a wooden bowl beside him.

"Space! What space? Outside in the freezing snow all day?" Ace countered.

"They can't come inside. They stink like piss, Ace. I don't know what to tell you. You don't have to take them home, but they can't stay here!" Mondry laughed. Ace scoffed, turning away from Mondry. He threw his hand up in farewell as he walked away, conceding.

"See you in Spring, Mondry."

Ona watched the men as they gathered their horses to leave, leading the slaves by foot back to the frozen road outside the shop. She wondered how far the group traveled only to be turned away upon arrival.

"Crazy Ace," Mondry shook his head, laughing to himself while he cut more meat off the smoking deer.

"Come to get some lead, Mondry." Enda spoke in a voice that was deeper than usual.

"Eh? Oh yeah? What would you give for it?" Mondry watched Enda from the side of his eye, not turning away from the meat.

Enda slipped out of the buffalo skin cloak he wore, presenting it to Mondry. Mondry turned to face the cloak, feeling over the fur in his hands.

"Say, boy, run behind the bar and get me a piece of that plug." Mondry did not look up from the craftsmanship.

"Yes, sir."

"That boy make this?" Mondry sounded impressed.

"That's right," Ona said.

"Here I thought he was only good for sitting on the mash while she cooks down. It takes time to make it just right," He winked down at Ona as Enda delivered the chaw into Mondry's large hands.

"Hey boy! Where's that ole Sunday been at?" Mondry inquired.

"Crawled off and got himself killed." Enda rolled his eyes.

"I'll be. What'd that son of a bitch do? Drown in a whiskey barrel?" Mondry laughed, spitting a large brown wad of chaw by Ona's feet.

Enda shook his head sighing, "Something like that."

Ona and Enda followed him to a stone cellar that was dug into the ground attached to the cabin where they saw a number of supplies like dried meats, cloth, long rifles, and powder. Mondry measured powder in a cloth sack that Enda could hang from his belt. He counted three heavy lead bars and handed them to Enda.

"We also need a cast," Enda added.

Mondry took one of the bars back, replacing it with a small cast that made one bullet at a time. Mondry paused with the cast in hand, hovering above Enda's laden arms.

"You ain't shot any bullets in that rifle?" Mondry raised his eyebrows.

"No, sir."

"What did you kill the bloody buffalo with?"

"My bow," Enda shrugged. Mondry whistled low and impressed. Ona peered inside barrels of dark liquid dripping from copper pipes that went up the walls to the main floor.

"Mondry?" Ona ventured. Enda turned around, surprised.

"What's that, darlin'?"

"What is this liquor? It's got foam. I ain't never seen it like this before."

Mondry slapped his knee laughing. "Sugar, that's no whiskey. That's beer. Isabelle brews the best in house."

"Beer?"

"You drink it instead of water." Mondry explained. "It's her old recipe— they ain't got any good water in the cities. It's about like the ales you got back home."

"I've seen it, I just never drank it." Ona explained, eyeing the barrels curiously.

Mondry sent them on their way with flasks full of Isabelle's beer. The weather turned nasty by late afternoon and they brushed snow off Old Boy before redoing his blanket and heading back north to Calico Ridge.

They arrived at the Halstead place well past dark to deliver the exhausted mule, but they did not stay. The march back to Fanny felt like the longest mile, hiking through knee deep, sideways blowing snow. Enda looked frozen to the bone without his cloak, but just kept increasing their pace to try and stay warm. They pushed open the cabin door and collapsed by the fire.

"Well, y'all look like the snow done nipped your toes off!" Fannie cried.

"Happy Birthday, Cricket." Fannie smiled. She brought them bowls of stewed rabbit pie and cups of hot spiced cider.

"Thanks, Fannie." Ona smiled weakly, staring longingly up at her pallet.

Afterwards, Fannie fed them sugared apples and marched Ona up to bed. Fanny would not allow Enda to go out in such miserable weather after the exhausting trip. Instead, she put him to rest by the fire with a spare quilt and he fell asleep with his head on the dirt floor as if it were a bed of feathered pillows.

Chapter 11.

Blustery February winds carried in with it a terrible influenza that seemed to infect nearly every child in town. Ona, Fannie, and the Reverend Johnson spent nearly every waking moment together working with the families of Calico. Most days Fannie was sending Ona to fetch supplies for this and that, and when their stock of herbs ran low she argued bitterly with Wash McDaniel to re-open the general store. He would not until the trading posts opened up back in spring; there was simply nothing to sell.

Ona cooked up vials of medicines and bone broth while Fannie worked to keep the children of Calico sometimes warm, sometimes cooled, and always to settle the tremors. It seemed lately no matter which family they visited it was always the same: the child felt ill, burning hot then freezing cold, vomiting and then after some time turned incoherent. They convulsed and drooled but would not wake. Once they had the symptoms, they never lasted more than a day or two.

Reverend Johnson prayed fiercely over these children. He would hold his Bible over the babes, shouting verses. Fannie mostly ignored him but sometimes mumbled he was disturbing the children. When the children died, the reverend consoled the parents. He helped them arrange funerals. The past three weeks they had buried fifteen children from town and the reverend had begun performing combined funeral ceremonies. The influenza was not aware of color or wealth. It took without mercy whomever it felt, sliding into homes undetected and robbing families of their light and life. It was said that on the day Mrs. Lafayette woke to her motionless son, her wailing could be heard over even the church bells sounding.

All of this death proved profitable for Enda Cambor. For the first time in his life, he was offered a job. Mayor Cambor knocked on the Christie door late one night shortly after the death toll began rising daily. Enda stood stunned behind Fannie, and Ona openly stared in shock. Fannie was the first to speak.

"Mayor Cambor, come on inside."

The mayor removed his hat, stepping inside the Christie cabin. Enda still could not find his words. The mayor's pale blue eyes scanned the room, hovering over the sizable pile of fur pelts carpeting the space in front of the fire.

"Whiskey?" Fannie asked.

"Please. You been busy this winter, boy." The mayor commented on the furs.

Enda shook his head. "Those are Ona's."

191

The mayor's eyes widened, and he whistled lowly. "Your papa teach you to shoot, girl?"

"No, sir— I mean mayor; Enda did."

"Now that's a bit troublesome. Mind your time with the negro folk, lass. It reflects poorly on your character. Call me Mr. Cambor." He turned from the piles of soft rabbit, stout deer, mink, fox, raccoon, and bobcat to face Enda.

"Listen boy, I know you are apprenticed in the spring to go with the, uh, black smith... Oh hell, what's his name... Billy Titus. But I've been asking around town and it seems to me that you don't have any employment up until the date of your departure. Is that right? You ain't working right now?" Mr. Cambor asked.

Enda spoke cautiously. "I suppose that's right. I ain't got a job proper, but I ain't just laying idle either."

"Glad to hear it. The good Lord hates men who loaf. Listen boy, I've been talking with the reverend in town and— the Reverend Johnson that is, not that Methodist bastard. Anyway, he and I were working the figures and this sickness just ain't showing sign of slowing down. With all these young people taking ill with the influenza, it's just not safe to keep the bodies nearby. They're contaminated."

"Mr. Cambor, won't parents want to bury the dead at their own properties? Community graveyards are just not the way round here," Fannie interrupted.

"Exactly my point, Fannie. Now, the reverend agrees, we've got to get this sickness out of here! We can't be contaminating the rest of town because of a few grieving mothers."

Fannie clicked her tongue but said nothing.

"Surely once they're dead all the disease is gone out?" Ona inquired.

"We can't know that," Fannie said slowly.

"It's best if we remove the bodies from town. Take them out into the woods and bury them somewhere. We'd pay you, boy. They bring their dead to the church. All you have to do is stop by the church, collect the bodies and bury them outside of town." Mr. Cambor continued.

"What if Enda catches the disease?"

"Sweetheart, if he were going to catch any sickness, he would have no doubt been sick by now, same as you or Fannie would have if you were vulnerable. You two are in the thick of it. He's already been exposed. He'll be fine."

"So he's just going to parade around town with the children's bodies? People will despise him for it." Ona was not satisfied.

"No, sugar. He'll do it at night."

It was decided then, that Enda should be employed by the city of Calico to remove bodies lost to influenza to the outskirts of town.

Enda asked only one question. "Where are they to be buried?"

"As far away as you can manage, boy."

It was two days before Ona noticed that Enda was affected by the influenza. It was not the symptoms others were displaying, however. He was not bed ridden, nor feverish, nor anything otherwise typical of influenza. He was quiet. His hands and feet were fidgeting. He slept late. When he declined Fannie's offer for supper, Ona was downright concerned.

Near dusk, Ona decided to follow Enda to the church and check on him. She was sitting on the floor of the cabin slipping into her soft deer leather boots when an urgent knock sounded at the door. Fannie's furrowed brow deepened, expanding the web of wrinkles adorning her face as she approached the door. They had a lot of knocks on the door lately, and she wore that distracted frown all the time now.

"Ezra! What a surprise." Fannie and Ona had not seen much of Ezra since Enda began hanging around.

"Fannie. Ona." Ezra nodded, not stepping inside. His face was sweaty, like he ran the whole way from the McDaniel place. His toes tapped nervously and he fiddled with his hat, taking it on and off, wringing it between his hands. Behind him stood an unfamiliar black horse covered in thick winter fur that stuck hot and sweaty to its coat.

"I-i-it's late. I-I'm sorry." Ezra stammered.

"What's the matter, boy?" Fannie cried.

"It's Zelma!" His voice broke. He bit his sleeve to get a grip on himself, finding his unsteady voice.

"She's sick," he croaked.

"No!" Ona exclaimed. "That's not possible!" Her voice was small.

"She's bad, Fannie." Ezra pleaded.

Fannie's hard eyes hardened. "Lend us your horse, boy. We'll leave now. Ona, get the bag."

Ezra flung his arms around them, desperately hugging them. "Thank you both." His voice was muffled by Ona's thick hair.

"Meet us at the house!" Fannie shouted back at Ezra.

Ona helped Fannie mount the horse. She climbed up in front of Fannie, who was seated behind the saddle. Ona gripped the reins in her hand. Fannie wrapped her thick arms around Ona's waist.

"Hang on tight, Fannie!"

Upstairs in the brick McDaniel home, Anna and Wash McDaniel stood hand in hand with their other three sons, praying without interruption over the seemingly lifeless body of little Zelma. Her face was dotted in sweat and her breathing was labored. Zelma's little yellow puppy, now half grown, paced nervously around the room whining. Ona felt her stomach do little flip flops in the doorway of Zelma's bedroom and she froze behind Fannie. Fannie paused too. Her shrunken shoulders slumped only a little before she took a deep breath and plunged forward. Fannie weaved under the linked arms of the McDaniels, meeting Ona's eyes as she crossed to the opposite side of the bed. Ona lingered only a moment longer before mimicking Fannie by taking a deep breath and joining her side.

Fannie had Ona fetch a bowl of snow and a rag. They spent most of the evening keeping snow on Zelma's forehead, until her small body was overcome with tremors.

"It's the devil himself! He won't release my baby girl from his hold!" Anna McDaniel wailed. Anna leaned over her daughter's body, shaking Zelma by the shoulders.

"I command this devil to leave my daughter! God will strike you down!" Anna McDaniel was hysterical, causing the dog to bark excitedly. Fannie ignored Anna.

"Nash, get her out of here!" Ona instructed. The second oldest McDaniel son obeyed without a word, eager to help in any way possible. He and the youngest boy, Dane, escorted their mother down the stairs where her sobbing reached every room in the house. Jonathon watched silently from the back of the room.

"Is she dying? Is my little girl truly leaving us?" Wash was incredulous.

"She is fighting hard. She ain't possessed either." Ona explained. "She's want to break her fever." Fannie pulled a jar of green paste from her bag and proceeded to dip her finger in the paste and coat the inside of Zelma's cheeks.

"What is that?" Ezra entered the room, breathless.

"Black willow, mostly. To help the fever." Ona explained while Fannie worked in silence. They waited. The family prayed. Ona sat with the dog beside her. At last Zelma's breathing regulated and Fannie announced that there was nothing to do but wait.

Ona and Fannie stayed overnight, dosing Zelma with drops of aconite every hour until dusky dawn. Fannie slept on the floor in Zelma's room and Ona crawled into bed with Zelma, allowing the dog to sleep faithfully at the foot of the bed. Ona spent most of the night pushing strands of hair out of Zelma's face, tucking them safely behind her ears. She smoothed Zelma's blankets and whispered soft words of encouragement to her friend.

"You can make it." Ona allowed quiet tears to escape her eyes. "I know you can."

The McDaniel men took turns sitting up over Zelma, but after a time all was quiet in the house and sleep overtook Ona.

Sunlight filtered past the curtains in the McDaniel home.

"Ona." A whisper woke Ona. Ona's eyes fluttered opened and she turned in bed to face the voice. She realized she had slept with Zelma's hand in hers all night long. The dog was sprawled out comfortably on top of the girls, still fast asleep.

"Can I have my hand back?" Zelma whispered, smiling weakly.

Ona's heart leapt through her chest, releasing Zelma's hand to wrap her arms around her in a tight hug.

"How do you feel?" Ona asked.

"Awful." Zelma half giggled, half coughed.

It was not long before the whole house surrounded Zelma, who managed to sit propped in bed. Fannie gave the McDaniels strict instructions to feed Zelma only water, bone broth soup and wood sorrel tea for three days. After three days, Zelma should try and walk downstairs for simple meals. The family fixed a breakfast feast to celebrate Zelma's health. They gorged on soured ale, sausages, warm bread, seasoned potatoes with onion and candied apples.

Fannie pulled a small herb cake out of her bag. It was wrapped in a cloth from one of Ona's old dresses. "Tie a string for the girl to wear this around her neck. It will keep diseases out from her."

"No amount of money could thank you for the miracle you performed," Wash marveled while Anna cleared the breakfast plates.

"Wash, Anna, you're family. And this? This is our work." Fannie waved her hand dismissively.

"Is there anything we can do to repay you? If not as payment, then as thanks?" Anna asked.

Fannie tapped her fingers on the table, contemplating.

"With me and Cricket back and forth to town so much these days... It would be nice to have a quicker way into town in this snow... At least until things is settled down a bit."

"Of course!" Anna clapped her hands together happily.

"I have a horse." Ezra volunteered. "I am traveling to Lexington in spring and so I bought a horse. He is great to ride, really. Please, use him to get to town and back." Ezra's offer was clear and sincere.

Ona chewed a piece of hay, helping Ezra saddle up his new horse inside the McDaniels' barn. He really was a beautiful horse. His inky black coat was textured for the winter, but Ona imagined it to be sleek and clean in the warmer months.

"This is Jack." Ezra spoke softly, smoothing his hands down the horse's neck. Ona rubbed her hands down his soft nose, before offering him a mouthful of hay.

"He's incredible," Ona admired. She, like most of Calico, was used to seeing only mules be worked in the area. In general, they were sturdier for the mountainous terrain.

"No, he's not. He's attractive, yes; but you and Fannie. What you two did in there last night? That was incredible." Ezra stopped to face Ona.

"That ain't... I mean... We just..." Ona stammered, embarrassed. Ezra interrupted her.

"Don't be so modest." Ezra shook his head. "What you do? That medicine of yours? It's a gift from God. In the book of First Kings, God sent the witch from Endor to aid King Saul. That granny witching of yours is made to help people, given from God himself." He said quietly.

"I'm still an apprentice," Ona smiled.

"I want to be with you, Ona."

Ona choked on her piece of hay, lapsing into a terrible coughing fit.

"Are you alright?" Ezra looked concerned.

"I think so." Ona rasped through watery eyes.

"Ona?"

"Yes?"

"Did you hear what I said?" Ezra's deep brown eyes peaked out from behind curled locks framing his face. His shirt collar was perfectly white, his coat cuffs perfectly measured. How did he get them to be stiff like that?

"I think Fannie and I been needing to get to town. We really must check in with the Reverend and pay our visits. There might be even more people sick, now. It's hard to say, really." Ona felt like she was babbling.

"Of course, of course." Ezra blurted, flushed with embarrassment.

Jack carried Ona and Fannie faithfully through town. Ona was relieved to learn that, while three children had died in the night, four including Zelma had pulled through and were all up and talking. Everyone in town was talking about Fannie and Ona's miraculous gifts from God: The granny witch and her apprentice, whose medicines were healing the sick children of Calico. Late in the day, Fannie turned the horse, heading back to Calico Ridge but Ona stayed behind.

"You need to sleep if you want to keep your strength for treating these folks." Fannie argued.

"I just need a little time, Fannie." Ona persisted. Fannie didn't push and while she began the trek home on Jack, Ona tiptoed into hiding behind the Baptist church. Enda arrived around the back of the church not long into the night. He carried a cart behind him that should have been hitched to a pair of mules, dragging it through the snow toward the church cellar. Reverend Johnson crept out from the church and unlocked the cellar door before scurrying back inside the warmly lit church building.

Enda carried the bodies of the three children who did not survive the night. He moved them individually to the cart, with great tenderness. Ona did not consider how the winter season would impact the bodies. They were not just stiff, they were frozen in the cellar. Enda took care to wrap a large cloth over the children, as if tucking them in to bed for the night. He picked up the posts of the cart, sniffing loudly before beginning a slow pace toward the back alleys of Calico, pulling the cart behind him.

Ona followed some distance behind Enda, so as to go undetected. She planned on following him all the way to the forest, to study him for signs of illness. Ona did not expect the cart to stop behind the little cabin of Granny Trinity on the alley side of Rue Royale.

Adelaide's father Elijah met Enda in the frozen alley. Elijah gripped Enda behind the neck before pulling him into a tight hug, wrapping his large arms wholly around Enda. Iris, Adelaide's mother and Enda's aunt, also left the cabin to meet Enda. Iris walked on unsteady feet, with the help of Granny Trinity, who kept patting Iris' hands and stopping to kiss her cheeks.

Elijah disappeared back into the cabin, returning with a child sized bundle, wrapped in a thick blanket. Ona's breath caught in her chest. Elijah tucked the covered bundle carefully beside the other bodies before concealing them all once more with the cloth. Enda threw his arms around his aunt Iris, who collapsed in his grip. He brought Granny Trinity into his arms, kissing her on the head. By now, Enda had grown so much his Granny Trinity was only as high as his chest. He was a man like Elijah or Wash.

When Enda took leave from his family, Ona followed him all the way into the forest. He stopped at the small slave cemetery outside of town. Past the snow-covered graves marked only by large rocks, a deep pit was carved into the frozen ground. Fifteen small bodies lined the bottom of the pit. They were not covered but lay frozen underneath a thin layer of freshly fallen snow. Enda laid each of the three bodies on top of the others in the pit. He moved with deliberate carefulness. At last, he clutched the fourth and final body closely to him. From behind a large poplar tree, Ona saw a small dark hand, motionless, peep out from underneath the covering. Enda gingerly laid Adelaide to rest among the others in the pit. His demeanor broke into tremors and tears melted the snow beneath his feet.

Ona rushed out of her hiding space, running up behind Enda and flinging her arms around his middle. His surprise curbed his tears, his hand reaching out for hers, seeming to know who it belonged to. Ona turned to face Enda, not letting go of his hand. She took his other hand in hers and held him close for a long time. Gentle snow fall began to cover the tops of their heads.

"I'm so sorry." Ona said at last. "I never knew she even took sick."

"How could you? I went to your house last night, but no one was home." Enda sniffed loudly. "I didn't know what to do. I had to go back there and tell them there was no one to come help her."

"I can't believe she's gone." Ona sniffled.

"Where was you last night, Ona?"

"Taking care of Zelma McDaniel... She took sick. We went to help her. It was late, I'm so sorry." Ona explained. Enda slumped to the ground on his knees and Ona sat silently beside him, not letting go of his hand.

"The church record says, only three children died today." Enda began. "But that's not true. There were four. Four children died today." He spoke softly, but underneath his quiet demeanor something inside his voice hardened.

"This is God's choice for Adelaide?" he asked bitterly.

"Enda, I never heard she was sick or I'd go to her, you must know that," Ona pleaded.

"You ain't telling the truth. That girl and Adelaide was sick at the same time. If you had to choose, you would have gone to the white girl."

Ona did not respond to that; he was right. All of the sudden, the barrier between them seemed impossibly large. Ona had no business dealing with this boy the way she had been over the past several months. It wasn't natural. Her lips were set in a hard line as she rose to her feet preparing to leave, when Enda spoke once more.

"Why are you here anyhow? You shouldn't be seeing this. It ain't good... for the soul to witness to this. I wonder if God ain't mad with Calico."

"I followed you because you're not right lately, Enda. I'm worried about you catching the influenza, being surrounded by all these sick people." She turned to face him.

"I won't catch the influenza or I'd done be sick already; but I ain't right these past few days neither. It's more than sickness of the body, Ona. It's a sickness of the spirit."

Ona's stomach lurched, and she fell to her knees. She surrendered herself to snow covered ground, imagining that at this moment, perhaps the enormous barrier between them was made of cut ice, like that taken from the ponds to store in the ice houses. It was strong and would keep frozen all year long if it was protected from the sun. But Enda Cambor was to Ona, the sun itself.

"If you are sick, then I will wait beside you until you are well again."

"Why?"

Ona kissed him ever so gently on his lips, causing Enda to startle.

"Because Enda Cambor, I think I might love you madly."

In all, fifty-five children were affected by the Influenza and officially, twenty-one of them were taken from the illness. Unofficially, twenty-two of them were. Ona recovered from the shock of such sudden death in such high volume by keeping her fingers busy. She visited Zelma and the McDaniels as often as the snow would allow.

Zelma once told Ona that if they burned a twig to ash it would make the first letter of their future husbands' names. They burned twig after twig until they could pick out a letter, but Ona was not comforted when she plainly saw the letter E before her.

"E for Ezra!" Zelma squealed. Ona brushed away the ashes, refusing to play the game again. Instead, Ona spent time working on the pelts she had killed, tanning them with salt and working the leather into soft, wearable material.

Under Enda's guidance in the solitude of his little shack, Ona pieced together fox pelts into a thick, warm cloak. Ona had never owned a coat before and she was elated to wear something so beautiful as the fiery red of fox fur. The coat covered her shoulders and tied in the front with strong cord and a bear tooth Enda gave her to use as a clasp. She finished the piece by sewing two fox tails on the front bottom of the coat that hovered just above the ground. She even stitched two fox ears into the cloak's hood. Ona did not stop there, however. She also made Fannie an identical covering from black weasel, and Zelma a pair of rabbit fur house slippers. She saved the rest of the furs for soft blankets to last the rest of winter.

Chapter 12.

March snow melt met heavy rains, swelling the ravines of Calico. Springs trickling out of mountains rushed forth into waterfalls, filling little pools within hillside depressions and raising babbling creeks into streams with swift currents. Each day Enda waited at the end of the street on Rue Royale for the blacksmith Billy Titus to arrive. And one day in late March, he did.

Ona loitered around the pillars of Rue Royal keeping Enda company while they waited for the–by now–almost mythic Billy Titus. A gruffly dressed man with faded shirts and rough hands pulled back the reins of two large bay mules pulling a cart laden with metal tools. He hitched his cart to the gate in front of the Mayor Cambor's house, hopping down and collecting a small, dark skinned girl from the back of the cart. He walked her by the cuff of her dress toward the house and she followed behind him barefoot and staring at her toes. Her hair had been cropped short to her head and her small frame was dwarfed by the man walking beside her.

"Mr. Titus!" Enda greeted.

Billy Titus turned to face Enda. His beard nearly covered his mouth, save for the pipe hanging out of it. It was difficult to see where his thick beard and tangle of black curly hair began. His pants were worn, his shirt patched. He did have nice shoes, however; and both he and his horses seemed well fed.

"That'd be me." Billy Titus responded reluctantly.

"It's me... Enda Cambor! You apprenticed me last year for the blacksmith shop you want to build in town?" Enda reminded him. Recognition flickered in Billy Titus' eyes.

"We sign the papers?" Billy Titus asked cautiously.

"Yes, sir."

"I'll be back for you on April 21st. I got business to attend beforehand." He confirmed.

Enda smiled broadly. "Thank you, sir."

"Meet me at the trading post west a here a ways. I'll be training you at the shop in Lexington." Billy Titus stroked his beard.

"Yes, sir!"

"Alright, boy."

"April twenty-first." Enda repeated.

"April twenty-first." Billy Titus confirmed, trailing up the entrance to the Cambor home.

Ona followed behind Enda, badgering him with questions as they made their way out of downtown Calico.

"How do you know this Billy Titus man anyhow?"

"Well, the mayor introduced us. Said I should be trained for a job proper if I'm to make something of myself." Enda explained.

"Why didn't he just ask the blacksmith in town?"

"I signed papers, I saw them myself. What are you even getting' at?" Enda sounded irritated.

"I only wonder... who was that girl?"

"Probably a new house slave for the mayor's wife."

"So, why was she arriving with Billy Titus?" Ona persisted.

Enda shook his head. "Ona, nobody keeps slaves in Calico but the mayor, the Beaudins and the Lafayettes."

"I don't understand."

"I'm saying that the mayor probably had to arrange for his wife to get a new house slave from someplace else. Billy Titus maybe delivered her, but they likely bought her in the city and he carried her on out this way."

"Something's off about it," Ona spoke flatly.

"He's my future, Ona. Every dream that I keep boldly and close to my heart will become reality after training with that man."

"How long are you to be in Lexington anyway?" She stopped at the swift moving creek behind Enda's shack and sat down in the leaf litter, watching the water foam and swirl at the lips of the creek bank.

"Until he sets up shop here, I imagine."

"You're leaving in a just a few weeks and you don't know when you'll be back?" Ona cried.

"This will be good. It's good to travel. See places." Enda nodded to himself.

"You won't find places more beautiful than Calico mountain." Ona frowned.

"Certainly not if you stay here," Enda chuckled. He brushed a strand of Ona's hair out of her eyes, causing Ona's heart to stutter in her chest. She splashed muddy creek water up at him and led the way back to Calico Ridge.

Over the following weeks Ona's stomach was as unsettled and every day she changed her mind between wanting to spend every waking moment with Enda to not wanting to see him at all. Fannie was so fed up with Ona's antics she stopped asking her for help making house calls for the entire week leading up to April twenty-first.

The day before Enda was to depart, Ona spent the evening with Enda's family. Granny Trinity beamed with pride that her grandson would leave to study a trade in the city. Elijah filled the evening by telling stories around the fire.

"What's your name?" Ona smiled sweetly at the little girl brought to the Cambor mansion a little over a week ago. The girl lowered her head and stared at her toes which she wiggled in the dirt.

"She don't talk. Poor thing ain't spoke a word all week. She wouldn't even eat for the first three days." Iris sat next to the small girl and ran her fingers over her short-cropped hair possessively.

"Iris call her Mary. Do you like to be called Mary?" Elijah asked the girl gently. The girl shrugged her shoulders.

"How old are you, Mary?" Ona tried again with her most innocent voice. Mary climbed into Iris's lap and buried her face in the woman's shoulder.

"We think she about seven or eight," Granny Trinity speculated.

"Why so young?" Enda's eyes widened.

"Honey, how in all this world should I know? Look at that baby missing her mama. It about break your heart for watching the poor thing." Granny Trinity shook her head.

Elijah clicked his tongue. "The people in that house," Elijah pointed to the massive brick manner they served, "ain't got a soul to part with for separating that little girl from her family."

"All to keep her in the house with that old woman all day having her get this and that and hitting on the poor thing if she spill or knock anything over."

"I suppose then, that it is a truly an unfortunate thing to be born a slave." Ona stared into the fire. Iris sighed, a dry smile tugging at her lips.

"Is that all it is?" Iris wondered aloud. Ona met her gaze, but did not respond. Mary finally managed to peek her face out from Iris's dress and look sideways at Ona.

It was late into the night when Ona and Enda waved their goodbyes and made their way back to the alleys of Calico. Ona looked out past town, toward Calico Ridge and Fannie. She felt the crooks of her bones stiffen and she could not bring herself to take one step forward. It wouldn't make sense for Enda to walk her home. He was much closer to stay in his shack and make the short trek to the northern trading post in the morning.

Ona thought she saw his warm, brown fingertips move from his side and wrap around her own, pale fingers, but loose strands of hair poking out from under her cap blocked her full vision and she could not manage to turn and face him. Ona took small breaths to fight the nauseating feeling of her heart spiraling anxiously out of control while Enda just stood there kicking at the dirt.

"It's just, I..." She tried to say something, just to fill the void; but for the first time in living memory Ona's words failed her, dropping off in a small whisper. The dark and lonesome walk home to Calico Ridge seemed an impossible distance to manage when it felt like the weight of the whole mountain was crushing her.

Enda slowly moved closer to her, wrapping his arms around Ona to kiss her gently. Ona was certain the only thing supporting her upright was Enda himself and the only thing holding her together was the warmth from his lips. If he left she would fall apart into a million pieces.

"Will you go with me tomorrow?" Enda whispered.

"To say goodbye?" Ona's asked in a croaky voice, fighting the strain in her throat.

"Yes." He spoke into Ona's hair.

"It's bad luck to say goodbye."

"Then don't say it."

"Alright." Ona took a deep breath and stepped back, squeezing Enda's hand one last time before she was to see him in the morning.

Enda did not release her hand. He turned around and started walking. Ona felt her stomach tighten as she followed after him. He led her across the creek, over the moist fallen log so that their clothes would not get wet. He opened the door to his shack, and Ona stumbled inside after him, allowing him to close the door behind her.

As Enda's lips found hers, a tingling sensation stirred within her. Enda's jaw twitched with a small smile when Ona tugged his linen shirt loose. Some small thought registered vaguely that what she was about to do would seal her fate as an unforgivable sinner in God's eyes; though Ona's heart was beating loud enough that it was difficult to hear her own mind. Ona became lost to time with Enda, falling softly onto his meager pallet of furs and hides as if they were covers of down and fleece on the finest of silk sheets. Ona melted into Enda, deciding she did not mind the idea of being damned so long as she remained in the heart of the one she loved most.

Ona stirred the next morning, turning to face Enda. He was already awake and watching her through his pale blue eyes. She brushed his mess of curly brown hair behind his ear and kissed him fiercely, her mind and body succumbing into his for several moments before standing up and offering him a hand up.

"Are you ready?" Ona asked.

"I think so, yes." Enda stammered, flushed and fumbling for his shirt.

They made their way out of the cabin, fingers linked. The first house they passed once on the opposite side of the creek stood a middle-aged woman in the alley behind the shops, emptying her chamber pot. She dropped it on the ground, mouth open in shock, ignoring the acrid scent of urine quickly filling the alleys. The woman dashed inside her house, hiking her skirts up so as not to muck them up with her own spilled mess.

"That's no good," Ona said, half smiling to hide the worry shivering through her.

"It's probably for the best I'm headed out of town right about now," Enda frowned, looking up at the sky.

"They could hang you."

"No, they would have to catch me first. You're about to have a go of it, though."

It was a two hour walk north to the trading post. They crossed a clear, shallow stream that Ona stopped at to splash water in her face before they continued on. It was not long before the narrow dirt path became wider with hoof prints marking up the frequently traveled road. They walked behind mules pulling logs, and arrived mid-morning to the wooden sign engraved with the words "North Hill Trade".

Like Mondry's trading post, there was an inn where travelers were welcomed. Unlike Mondry's trading post, Enda was the only negro walking around and his presence was noted by the suspicious glances cast by the throngs of wandering people. The other traders either wore working clothes or fine-spun threads akin to Wash McDaniel or Mr. Lafayette. There were no bawdy house women around, only respectably dressed wives of merchants who were traveling with their husbands. Ona, with her messy hair and muddy, bare feet attracted the kind of looks Virginia Cambor or Blanche Beaudin might cast her way.

Ona milled around the vendors who set up temporary stalls to sell their wares. She was thinking she should have brought some of her furs to sell when Enda spoke.

"Look, he's over there." He pointed just past a round woman selling clay bowls. Billy Titus drove the same cart from last week.

"I suppose this is it?" Ona asked in an unnaturally high pitched voice. The memory of Enda keeping warm beside her left a remarkable imprint on her heart. It was hard to imagine being away from him for an undetermined amount of time.

Enda grabbed Ona's hand and pulled her away from the vendors. He steered her to a large tree behind the inn and clasped her hands tightly. Ona could see Billy Titus scanning the crowds looking for something, probably Enda, with a scowl on his face.

"This ain't forever. I'll be back sooner or later, and with a trade." He kissed Ona's hands.

"It's not too late to say no."

"This is for us. To earn an honest living."

"You're the most honest person I know," Ona spoke truthfully. She covered her free arm over her eyes. She did not want to cry; she had been so good up until now.

"You can write." Ona spoke in barely a whisper.

"I can barely read." Enda laughed, pulling her arm away from her face. He kissed her softly on the lips.

"It will not be long." His voice was low.

"I love you." She said, finding her voice and staving off her threatening tears.

"I love you." Enda said. He plucked a yellow coltsfoot flower and tucked it behind Ona's ear. He kissed her on the forehead one last time before turning towards the bustling people in front of the inn. Ona watched him flag down Billy Titus. Enda jumped in the back of the cart and it jolted forward, heading back toward the road that led west out of the mountains.

Ona sat against a large tree trunk behind the inn for several minutes before she dragged herself to her feet. Poor Fannie; Ona was out all night and had been no help all week. And by the look of the merchant woman's manic frenzy this morning over the pissing pot, Ona imagined it to be no secret the Irish orphan up on the hill was seen at daybreak with the negro boy, leaving his shack. Suddenly, a spark of cleverness wrapped around Ona's worries and she began gathering as many coltsfoot plants she could find. She plucked daffodils and little blue irises as well. Ona managed to find a large patch of bloodroot in full bloom with enchanting white flowers. She carefully dug with her hands through the mud to collect the whole plant, leaving a few behind to re-flower next spring.

She stood at the corner of the vendors, smiling and offering flowers to every couple she saw. They tossed her coins at her feet in exchange for flowers. For a special price, Ona showed people the magic of bloodroot.

"May I borrow your knife, sir?" Ona smiled sweetly, tucking away her thick accent as best she could.

"Well, I suppose." In a group of four couples, one man in a topper hat offered Ona a fine hand blade.

"It truly is a living plant with soul like you or I. Just watch!" Ona spoke with enchantment. She sliced open the orange root and showed the couples who began cheering excitedly.

"Truly, it bleeds like a human being!" One man exclaimed.

"How much? I must have them in my garden! I want them all!" a woman said excitedly.

"No, I would like that plant. How much? We are willing to pay!" another woman spoke over the first. Of course, bloodroot was neither rare nor novel, however Ona gladly haggled for the steepest price, managing to sell all of her plants between the two women for what Fannie would have earned in a month mixing medicines. Ona picked up all of the coins and stuffed them in the shirt of her dress.

Ona was so busy entertaining travelers she did not notice the large brown skinned man watching her work over the visiting women of Northern Licks Trade. As the last couple departed with the last of her flowers, Ona startled at the sound of a deep chuckle.

"You got a tongue for talking and eyes for charming, darlin'." The man was perhaps in his in his thirties. He was enormous and muscular. He wasn't dressed like the other merchants but wore a simple white linen shirt rolled up at the sleeves. His pants were clean, and his black boots were in good condition, but looked well used. His square, brown face was attractive, and his black hair curled a lot like Enda's. Ona pursed her lips, turning away and ignoring him.

"Hah! I like your spirit! And barefoot too. Tell me young lady, what holler did you crawl up out of?" The man asked, amused.

"I come up from Calico." Ona answered shortly.

"Ah. Pretty country. Right up on the hem of Indian territory, though." The man shook his head. "Dangerous place, I've heard. What brings a wild mountain girl like you to the edge of the hills?"

"To sell flowers, obviously."

"Keep going West toward the cities and they just get stupider," the man laughed.

"What's your name?" Ona ventured, deciding she liked this merchant.

"Marcus Morgan."

"Well, Mr. Morgan, it was a pleasure meeting you." Ona smiled and dipped into a small curtsy meaning to leave; only coins fell out of her dress and she had to stop and pick them up. Mr. Morgan bent to help her.

"I'm here every day— hell darlin', I own the place, and I've never seen you around here before. You sure you didn't come up for a reason?" Mr. Morgan asked curiously.

"Tell you the truth, I came here with my friend. He left with a blacksmith called Billy Titus to Lexington. He's to apprentice under him and come back home to Calico. Honestly, I'm not sure why he wanted to leave, but maybe he'll learn something once he's there," Ona rambled.

Mr. Morgan looked up. "Billy Titus? You sure?"

"Yes." Ona spoke cautiously.

"Billy Titus. He drives a wooden cart for hauling logs?" Mr. Morgan inquired.

"Yes, that's right." Ona's eyes narrowed.

"Darlin', Billy Titus is no blacksmith." Mr. Morgan scratched his beard.

"Excuse me?"

"I said he's no blacksmith. Billy Titus is a hired man. A bounty hunter. Catches runaway slaves from all over the state and brings them back to they keepers. Sells them too."

"He's a blacksmith. Enda signed the papers to apprentice himself." Ona said, confused.

"Has Enda ever committed a crime?" Mr. Morgan asked.

"Of course not! He ain't no slave neither!" Ona exclaimed.

"But he's negro?"

"Well," Ona stumbled over answering that question.

Mr. Morgan looked skeptical. "Does he have manumission papers saying he's a freedman?"

"Papers? What do you mean, 'freedman'?"

"Freedman. You know, like a 'free' 'man'," Mr. Morgan emphasized the words. "Oh, honey. If your boy ain't got papers he ain't free. Billy Titus, that's why he's for hire. Finds lost slaves, gets rid of unwanted ones. What's your negro's story, some kind of bastard?"

Mayor Cambor's icy blue eyes flashed through Ona's mind. Mayor Cambor set up the job for Enda. Enda signed the blacksmith papers. But what did those papers actually say? Enda said it himself, he could barely read.

Ona walked away from Mr. Morgan. She was vaguely aware of him calling back after her, but she couldn't hear exactly what he was saying. She bumped into several disgruntled travelers, including a pair of men who seemed shocked by the sight of her.

"Miss Christie! Are you alright?" Ona looked up at the sound of her name. Mr. Francis and Ezra McDaniel carried armfuls of rolled paper under their arms.

"I think she ought to sit down, speaking honestly." Mr. Morgan spoke. Ona hadn't realized the man Marcus Morgan had been walking beside her holding her elbow the whole time.

"No," Ona finally blurted.

"Ona, be reasonable. You look ill!" Ezra looked concerned.

"No. I need to get to Lexington! He's been taken away!"

"Who? Who's been taken?" Mr. Francis seemed genuinely concerned, however Ona wasn't paying attention to his words.

"Mr. Francis, please. I'm begging you. You are from Lexington. Won't you take me? Please?" Ona's voice was weak.

"Of course, Miss Christie. That is what friends do for each other! We can leave right away!" Mr. Francis spoke, emboldened.

"John," Ezra began in a hushed voice. "The girl needs rest. She's hysterical."

"I will not rest until he is back. Not until he is safe." Ona argued.

"Who?"

"Enda Cambor!" Ona shouted.

"The mayor's bastard grandson? I thought you said that you weren't running around with the negro boy." Ezra's voice stiffened.

"Ah see, I told you there was a reason for Billy Titus to get involved!" Mr. Morgan added.

"Oh, that man," Mr. Francis deflated. "He chills me to the bone."

"I'm not scared of him," Ona said fiercely.

"You know him?" Ezra asked, ignoring Ona.

"Of course! He's famous!" Mr. Francis was shocked there were people who didn't know of him.

"Alright, alright. So a bounty hunter bought your lover? How are you going pay to get him back? You'll need to sell a lot more of them flowers, darlin'," Mr. Morgan reasoned.

"A mulatto boy is your lover?" Mr. Francis gasped. He clearly enjoyed the scandal.

"You've disgraced yourself publicly. Be glad you are rid of him." Ezra said pointedly.

Ona stamped her feet like a child. She was fed up with all of these men wasting her time. She didn't have time for them or their gossip. Ona's hard gaze locked with John Francis. This man was her only chance at finding Enda.

"I have a sum of money." Ona spoke with deliberate annunciation, so as to not lash out at any of the three men who stood before her. "From when my father died. Mr. Francis. John, with your blessing, I would return to Calico in your carriage. I would fetch my belongings and the money and ride with you to Lexington. If you do this for me, you are saving a life. Would you do this, John? Do you want to save a life?"

Mr. Francis blossomed under Ona's flattery.

"Miss Christie— Ona, I would be honored to accompany you." Mr. Francis said earnestly.

"Wait a moment," Mr. Francis added excitedly. "Ezra, why not you come, too? I know you've been so curious about Transylvania.

I'll admit I am biased toward my Alma mater, but listen to me Ezra: you were born for college! This is a perfect opportunity for you both!"

Ezra flushed the faintest shade of pink, straightening his long coat before nodding his head in agreement. "Well, I suppose Ona will be needing looked after, seeing how she's trying to get herself killed over a slave. I've been meaning to inquire with the university anyhow."

Mr. Morgan chuckled at the scene. "I need to visit Calico again sometime. Seems like a pretty exciting place! Darlin', you got yourself some stand up friends to haul you cross country like that. Be grateful for them." He winked at her, smiling.

"Y'all are welcome back any day. And darlin', don't come back without more flowers. Shoot, this lass could sell the very sun if she felt like it."

Ona placed her hand on Mr. Morgan's muscular arm, warm and weathered from the sun. "Thank you for your honesty, Mr. Morgan. Without it, he would be lost to us forever," Ona said graciously. She gave Mr. Morgan a tight hug. He froze, momentarily caught off guard, before returning with bear hug and sending them on their way.

Ona relaxed only a little and clapped her hands together. "Well gentlemen, we best be off!"

Chapter 13.

It was early afternoon by the time Mr. Francis' carriage bounced up the hills of Calico Ridge and parked in front of the cabin. The stage coach tended to the pair of fully papered bay Percheron geldings. Mr. Francis' gaze rested softly on the cabin, as if he had never seen such a humble structure. Ezra followed after Ona inside, livid.

"You are absolutely mad, Ona!"

"Mr. Francis volunteered to help, I accepted his offer." She found the heavy coin purse with her father's pension and letter from President Jefferson. She emptied her own coins from the day into the purse with her father's pension.

"Don't do this to yourself, I'm begging you. Save your reputation." Ona pretended not to hear Ezra. She already wore her green checkered dress, and gathered up her deep blue dress, and fox fur coat. She looped the strap of her father's long rifle over her shoulder, which had tied to it the powder bag, and a small drawstring pouch that held about fifty shots. Ona put her beaded belt and sword around her waist. After she piled the materials up in the carriage and Mr. Francis balked at her.

"That's it?" he asked.

"That's it." Ona lurched forward when the horses started.

Ona was so fidgety by the time they arrived at the McDaniel home she had managed to fold her clothes and pick all the burs out of her coat.

"I'll just be a minute getting a few things." Ezra promised. He closed the carriage door behind him.

"Do you need to stop by where you're staying Mr. Francis, and gather your things?" Ona asked. Picking up on Ezra's cues, she was careful to mind her words and speak more slowly, annunciating each word to help minimize her accent.

"Oh, no. I should be fine. I'm renting a place above the tavern, but the majority of my belongings are still back home in Lexing—" Mr. Francis was cut off by Wash McDaniel flinging the carriage door open.

Ezra was right behind him, looking flustered and embarrassed with two large cloth bags. One was full of things and slung over his shoulder. The other he tossed over his father's head to Ona, only Mr. McDaniel intercepted it.

"Girl, what are you thinking?" Mr. McDaniel cried.

"Dragging Mr. Francis and my boy cross the country to look for some black bastard."

"Mr. McDaniel," Ona began.

"I know he's your friend, Ona, I do. But you're going to spend your father's pension, what he earned on account of dying on something like that. I cannot fathom it. People know you've been running with that mulatto bastard. Have you heard what the people in town seen this morning? You're a loose cannon. If that boy shows his face here, he'll be hung. He's dead either way, lass. Save your reputation and stay home."

"Mr. McDaniel, I ain't got no clue what people are saying, but you're the one who told me people talk. My reputation is reliable medicine, any other stories simply ain't nobody's business."

"No one will take your business if you're breaking the law living like an abomination of the Lord," Mr. McDaniel spat.

"Thank you for your concern, but we must go." Ona stopped arguing with the man she respected as much as her father, realizing it was moot. Mr. McDaniel scanned Ona's face, his bright red beard twitching in silent fury. He shook his head, handing Ona the bag.

"I'm half a mind to drag you out of that carriage." Mr. McDaniel said finally. "You need a good whipping to knock some sense into you. You've got no discipline whatsoever. Your father would not want this."

"My father is dead."

Ezra climbed into the carriage, not meeting his father's eyes as they drove off. With a chill, Ona realized she finally acknowledged her father's death aloud for the first time.

She packed her folded clothes into the bag as slowly as she could manage. The rough terrain and constant jerking and rocking made her nauseous. It was a long ride ahead of them; a four day journey if Ona understood correctly. Mr. Francis was quite excited for their adventure. He could not wait for Ona and Enda to meet his friends in Lexington.

"Ezra you're such a charming young man, you will be quite popular. I have a good feeling about you two coming. Ona, they will adore you! Who can resist a bold girl like you who knows water dowsing?" Mr. Francis chatted animatedly the whole day about the sights they must see in Lexington.

They traveled late into the night before stopping to sleep by small fire in the wilderness.

"I do love camping under the stars like this," Mr. Francis happily admired the stars. "But I will be glad to see an inn tomorrow night!"

Ona remained quiet most of the night. She glanced back at the horses, munching around on fresh spring grass. The carriage driver rested against a tree away from the group. He did not seem interested in conversation.

"How do you know he was even really taken to Lexington?" Ezra asked.

"I guess I don't. Not really, anyway."

"It's possible he was taken somewhere else, but there are plenty of people needing the help this time of year and Lexington is right in the thick of it," Mr. Francis chimed.

"Always a silver lining, Mr. Francis." Ona smiled sardonically. She curled her knees close to her face, soaking in the warmth and light from the fire. Her eyes followed Mr. Francis' to the stars. Was Enda watching the same ones?

Ona and Ezra did not speak much directly to each other. Ona's last conversation with Ezra did not end on an easy note. Mr. Francis filled the void with small conversation, which he maintained for the most part by himself. Ona forced herself to take deep, slow breaths. In a way, she was grateful for Mr. Francis' chatter. It filled a space otherwise heavy and somber with mild conversation that distracted the intensity of Ona's emotions.

Mr. Francis' stagecoach must have wondered at such a different crew. Mr. Francis was a polite, reformed gentleman. Ezra could have been his younger brother, except for the ease which Mr. Francis navigated conversation, Ezra matched with awkwardness and over gesturing. Ona was filthy. Her flaming red hair was ratted and poked out in every direction from under her cap. Her feet were muddy. Her dress was stained with dirt. She wore the beaded Cherokee belt and her father's sword and gun with the fox fur coat she skinned and sewed herself.

Two days they traveled in the manner, breaking to camp at night. On the third night, they stopped at an inn in a small town not unlike Calico, except in exchange for steep mountains there were stout hills.

"Where are we?" Ona wondered aloud.

"Estill County," Mr. Francis replied. "Knobs country." He pointed at the hills surrounding the town. Mr. Francis left his stagecoach with the horse and led the way inside. The two story inn was a brick building with candles lit in every window and a loud raucous echoed from inside its halls with the cheerful banter of bar patrons.

The innkeeper's wife was visibly taken aback by the sight of Ona's fearsome appearance. She spoke nervously, showing Ona to her room. The room contained two proper beds, not just a pallet stuffed with moss and straw. The beds sat up on bed posters and were decorated with lovely patchwork quilts. Her bag had been brought to her room and sat in the corner by a tray of cheeses and boiled eggs.

Five other women occupied the room, some already tucked into bed, and others slipping out of their day clothes. The innkeeper bade her goodnight, leaving Ona to crowd into a bed with two other women. Ona tossed and turned, itching and scratching from bug bites all night long.

She was awake and dressed before daylight, knocking on Ezra's door to wake the others. Ezra shared the same red welts up and down his limbs from the pests inside the hotel. Mr. Francis was slow to stir, but once he was up he proved efficient enough at gathering his belongings in order to make it into Lexington by nightfall.

Mr. Francis was as cheerful as ever, eager for Ona and Ezra to sample some of the finer perks city life had to offer: coffee, chocolate, bourbon and roast beef.

"How big is Lexington?" Ona asked nervously. She wondered how difficult it would be to find Enda in a city.

"It's not a city like Boston or New York," Mr. Francis eased some of Ona's fears. "But it's still the largest city in the state, for now at least. Some people think Louisville will surpass Lexington, it has access to the Ohio River, you see; but how could anything become more spectacular than the Athens of the West?"

They left the knobs region and entered a land entirely foreign to Ona: one devoid of forest and mountain. As they neared the city, the muddied roads transformed into deep trenches hollowed out from wagon travel. Massive farms cropped around them, each one bordered with miles of stone wall fencing around properties and dividing livestock pasture.

"Who made all that fencing?" Ona asked, amazed.

"Mostly the Irish, but slaves will help fetch up the stones for building, and here lately slaves are beginning to take it up being trained under some of the Irish." Mr. Francis said off hand.

"Forgive me; both of your families are Irish, yes?"

"Scots-Irish, more like," Ezra corrected.

"The Francis family takes a historically pro-immigrant stance. We always employ indentured servants. It's only the right thing to do, to help them leave such poverty." He added quickly.

229

"How generous." Ona gazed out the carriage window, only half listening. Fannie and Rowland Christie each worked as indentured servants and held darker views on the politics of such houses. They drove past a pair of white men working beside a black man to reconstruct a collapsed portion of the fence. Were they indentured? Slave? Or freedmen?

The muddy wagon road into the city turned to crushed limestone and the sounds of Lexington captured Ona's attention. There were horses clopping along the streets and people shouting, men hammering, and women tossing rotten food and waste into the alleys. Perhaps not every part of the city was different from Calico. The carriage pulled off the road and a man wearing a fine black suit opened an iron gate for the carriage to drive through.

Ona peered underneath the thick, low hanging clusters of black locust blossoms and gasped at the sight before her. The entire three story Cambor House would have made up only one wing of the Francis Estate. Ona, sitting nearest the carriage door, attempted to open it; however, someone on the other side beat her to it. A middle aged woman wearing a simple blue dress with a plain white smock over it opened the door before Ona was ready and she tumbled out of the carriage to the ground. The woman looked horrified, both by the fall and by the looks of the person who fell.

"M-m-miss? Are you all right?" The woman spoke with a thick Irish accent while helping Ona to her feet. Ona straightened her sword on the side of her hip and slung her father's rifle back over her shoulder. After falling on the ground, Ona seemed somehow even filthier than the past two days.

"I'm fine, thanks." Ona brushed herself off. Ezra and Mr. Francis piled out of the carriage behind Ona.

"Poor Miss Christie," Mr. Francis sighed. "Such a head for herbs and lore. Fewer thoughts saved for sense." He winked.

"Or bathing," Ezra crabbed.

"Complaints are unbecoming, Ezra." Ona snapped. She continued more softly toward her host.

"Mr. Francis, your home is lovely." Ona inhaled the thick fragrance of the black locust blossoms. They drooped down from the leaves, hanging not much higher than a man. Ona felt nearly drunk on their scent.

"Mr. Francis! So marvelous you've come home," The woman smiled. "This way." She gestured toward the house for Ezra and Ona to follow.

"Thank you, Catherine."

"Oh, that's alright, Miss uhm..." Catherine fussed over Ona, who had picked up her bag and slung it over her heavy fox fur coat.

"Christie," Ona spoke dryly.

"Miss Christie, there's no need to carry your bags. We will take care of you, Miss." She smiled at Ona. They continued up the steps into a large foyer with warm, oak flooring, covered by ornately decorated carpets.

"Mr. Francis, shall I call Mr. and Mrs. Francis immediately or would you and your– guests," She cast Ona a sidelong glance. "Prefer to bathe first?"

"Oh I'm sure if we wait to meet them until dinner that will give Grace in the kitchen more time to find wine for all these guests!" Mr. Francis suggested thoughtfully.

"I suppose. Mr. Francis, are you able to show Mr..."

"McDaniel," Ezra chimed in politely.

"To his room? Or shall I fetch James?" Catherine inquired.

"Oh that's not necessary, Catherine, thank you! If you would just show our dear Miss Christie to her room that will be all."

Ona followed Catherine up the stairs, careful not to touch the smooth honey-colored banister after noticing her toes leaving dirty marks on the steps. Catherine's pointed shoes made sharp clicks with every step she took, contrasting Ona's utterly silent bare feet. Catherine opened an upstairs room in the left wing that had windows facing outward to best view the not so distant streets of downtown Lexington. Ona watched Ezra appear from a twin stair staircase outside the bedroom. Mr. Francis opened the door and showed Ezra inside, right beside the room Catherine led Ona to. Catherine closed the door before shutting the curtains tight.

A gentle knock at the door made them turn briefly.

"Come in, Grace," Catherine instructed.

A girl around the same age as Ona managed to open the door while carrying a large pail of steaming water. She poured it in a metal contraption Ona had not seen before. It was like a metal basin to hold water, only it had a metal seat built inside the basin. A small, round water trough with a seat in it, was the only way Ona could describe it.

"What's she waiting for?" Grace whispered in the same accent as Catherine.

"Dear, shall we help you undress?" Catherine inquired soothingly.

"Why am I undressing?" Ona asked in a small voice. She didn't know what she was looking at. Grace's eyes widened. She was completely taken aback by Ona's ignorance.

"To wash? Would you like to wash, Miss Christie?" Catherine asked kindly.

"I suppose I should wash. In that?" She pointed at the trough.

"It's a called a 'bath tub', dear. And yes, if you'd like." Catherine did not push.

"Do you need anything? Help bathing?" Grace asked.

"Why would a person need help with something like that?" Ona blurted nervously.

"Some people just do, dear. You seem like a strong girl, though. I'll be back to check in on you shortly." Catherine smiled with reassurance.

"Wait," Ona stopped Catherine before she exited the door. She picked up a bottle Grace had set down by the tub.

"What's this?" Ona asked.

"Oil. Fragrance to help you smell nice. Some ladies like to use it. Some men, too." Catherine explained.

Ona nodded her head and the women left her. She gently laid aside her father's weapons on the large bed before her. She peeled off her filthy green checkered dress, climbing into the hot water. It burned her skin bright pink. Ona had never bathed in hot water before and she found the experience entirely more desirable than spring water, especially in the colder months.

Ona had no idea what to do with the dirty water when she finished, so she left the tub alone. One benefit of bathing in springs included the dirty water getting washed downstream. Where did this water go? Ona changed into her deep navy dress, which had been brought in by Grace during the bath and suited her sword and gun up. Ona answered a knock at her door.

"Still wearing your weapons?" Catherine asked, eyebrows raised.

"I'm going out." Ona replied. Catherine shook her head.

"I'm sorry Miss Christie, but I don't believe any of the gentlemen you arrived with had planned on leaving again this evening." Her voice was friendly, but firm.

"I'm not taking those two with me," Ona laughed.

"You want to leave all by yourself?"

"Of course."

234

"You cannot leave without a guide, Miss Christie. You'd get lost," Catherine said bluntly.

"I'll find my way."

"I don' think you understand, young lady. It would be improper for a lady to wander the streets alone. It would embarrass the Francis family." Catherine became stern. "There will be plenty of time for tours tomorrow. Now, I've already escorted Mr. McDaniel to the parlor where young Mr. Francis and he are waiting for you. Why not set those weapons down and follow me?"

Ona paused only for a moment. "Sorry, I just need a little more time to finish getting ready. I'll be down shortly." She raised her hands helplessly.

Catherine pursed her lips before exiting the room but said no more. Ona dropped to her knees, looking underneath the door for Catherine's feet to make their way down the stairs. When she was safely out of Catherine's hawk eyes, Ona tiptoed out of her room, opening her door as little as possible. Intuition flickered, telling Ona not to take the same set of stairs she entered with. Ona also bypassed the twin banister upon discovering a narrow set of stairs built into a wall behind what appeared to be a closet door.

Ona made her way down the rickety stairs as quietly as she could manage in the dark space, feeling around for railings. There were none. The stairs took a sharp turn, wrapping around the corner of a wall and Ona stumbled but managed to catch herself. Light appeared from the bottom of the steps once she had turned the corner. Ona paused, hearing voices.

"The brisket is going to be tough if ye over broil it, James." Ona heard Catherine chastise.

"Just pull it out from the fire and leave the kettle to cool on the hearthstone 'til supper."

"Sure thing, love." Ona heard a male voice with a thick accent like Catherine's.

"Grace, would you be a dear and help me with these bourbons to the men?" Catherine ran a tight ship, it seemed.

Ona waited until she heard both Catherine and Grace leave the room, silently counting her blessings no one needed to use the stairs. She dared to place a single toe on the wood flooring of the kitchen room before allowing herself to glimpse the room.

It was a large space with two iron door ovens built inside a brick wall that contained the cooking fire. There was an open window allowing cool spring air to filter inside the hot kitchen on the wall opposite of Ona. She could just make out the front gate through the rows of trees lining the estate entrance way.

"Who the devil are you?" The surly voiced James asked.

Ona startled at the man's discovery and bumped her head on the stair case's low hanging ceiling.

"Hello," Ona rubbed the spot on her head. She did her best to hide her accent and sound important. "I am the guest of Mr. Francis."

The man called James looked incredulous. He wiped his floured hands on a dirty smock and narrowed his eyes. "William?" He asked.

"John."

"Oh, I see." The cook's eyes flickered with interest. "Are you lost, miss?"

"I'm supposed to meet John outside? Is this the door? I'm afraid I'll be late if I go the long way." Ona smiled warmly. "I've simply had too much fun exploring the estate. It's enormous!" She wasn't entirely lying; the house was incredible.

"Oh sure, miss. Back door's just to your left." James smiled, returning to his work.

"Thank you, cook!" she exclaimed.

"Oh, I'm not the cook!" The man chuckled. "I'm the stableman, James Donnelly. Heard we got some important visitors in today and the ole lady gave me a job to watch over the meat!" He uttered a hearty laugh. "Men that cook! Thank you, lass, I needed to smile, what with the wife all wound tight over the young Francis' return."

Ona waved goodbye, letting herself out the back door quite impressed with her own artifice. The kitchen room led out to the side of the Francis estate. Ona followed the curving path that wrapped around the home until she could easily see the front gate.

Climbing the high gate posed obvious complication, so she began searching the perimeter of the property. Ona discovered an unmanned back gate, much smaller and less austere than the front entrance. The gate was easy to cross over and led into a dense line of thick magnolias. Ona struggled through the trees and found a row of the same slanted top stone wall scattered around the outskirts of the city. Beyond the stone fence, was a Lexington back alley that stunk of rotten food and waste.

Ona curled her bare toes at the sight of the alley and decided to walk on top of the stone wall until she made it to the main road. The slanted limestone was harsh on Ona's feet, as were the crushed gravel streets. The dirt roads of Calico were much better for barefoot walking. Ona veered the opposite direction from which their carriage arrived, already knowing what that side of town would bring: several smaller brick and wooden houses before turning into miles of stone fence lined hemp and tobacco farms.

Ona passed many more brick buildings and log structures filled with law offices, newspaper press, coffee houses, taverns, churches and house upon house. Polite women eyed her suspiciously and reformed men eyed her curiously: after all, it was a strange sight indeed to see a young woman walking barefoot down the street wearing an Indian belt with a military issued sword on her side and a long rifle strapped to her back.

As afternoon faded into evening, Ona entered a district comprised entirely of log shops and homes. She heard the clopping of fast approaching horses echoing through the street and flattened herself against a closed hat shop to avoid being trampled in the narrow road. Two boys Ona's age or younger ran after the horse. The rider, a lanky teenager, slid off the sweating animal and patted its flank. The dapple-gray mare looked nothing like the common drafts, or more often, draft mules, that worked in Calico. She carried a lithe frame, and she was faster than anything Ona had ever seen.

"Well? What was the time?" the rider asked eagerly.

"A minute ten!" the smaller boy shouted excitedly.

"Alright! Did you hear that, Sooty? We beat our record! Shall we go again?" He smoothed out frothy sweat from Sooty's body, slinging it to the street.

"Excuse me," Ona interrupted, shyly. "I'm looking for someone, maybe y'all seen him around?"

"What did you say?" The rider asked.

"My friend? Have you seen him? He's lost. Mulatto type. About your age. Curly brown hair." Ona tried again.

"I'm sorry, what?" The rider asked again, half laughing. He brushed blonde hair out of his eyes and walked nearer to Ona, standing with a hand on his hip.

"Where are you from? Your accent is so thick!" the smaller boy giggled.

Ona blushed, embarrassed. She tried to tuck her accent away, but when she got all flustered it was hard. "My friend, he..."

"Wow! Where did you get that sword?" The youngest boy asked excitedly.

"Is that an Indian belt?" The rider tugged the fringes of Ona's beaded belt, and she backed up defensively.

"Did you say you're friends with a mulatto?" The rider asked, suddenly curious.

"Um, yes to the belt, and yes." Ona stammered. "He's about sixteen year old. He's tall, like you, only—"

"Why do you have a gun?" The second oldest boy asked. He was perhaps Zelma's age.

"What, are you looking for your runaway negro or something? Did you lose track of your precious slave?" The rider scoffed.

"No!" Ona spat. She was getting angry now.

"He's a freedman. But—"

"Oh! Well, that's easy; he's probably in the Freedman District!" The smallest boy chimed, desperate to be helpful.

"Well, he's a freedman, but he was taken... Do you know a man named Billy Titus?" Ona asked.

"Sure!" The second oldest boy said boldly. The rider raised his eye brow at the boy, doubtful.

"Well, I mean I know who he is. His advertisements are everywhere. He's a legendary bounty hunter!" The boy carried on enthusiastically.

"He's a kidnapper," Ona countered.

"A public defender, you mean." The oldest boy, around Ona's age, shrugged his shoulders.

"Where can I find the business of this 'public defender'?" Ona asked.

The oldest boy smiled smugly, "It's not like he has an office."

"He's a bounty hunter!" the second boy exclaimed.

"Well, where does he take these people?" Ona cried.

None of the boys could give her a straight answer.

"Y'all don't know!" Ona accused. "Are you even telling the truth?"

"Billy Titus really is a legend!" The middle boy shot back. "It's just..."

"It's not exactly the kind of place you want to tour." The oldest boy finished the middle boy's sentence. "I wouldn't suggest going there alone."

"What's 'y'all'?" The youngest boy asked, confused.

"If you want to find out what happens to the slaves, why don't you ask around the Freedman District? Someone over there might know," the rider suggested. "It'd be better than... the alternative."

"If you're brave enough to risk it," the second boy taunted.

"It's getting dark." The youngest boy squeaked, afraid.

Ona rolled her eyes at the boys. While somewhere in the pit of her stomach she knew it was unwise to wander around a strange place at night, she wanted to show up these street kids.

"Point me in the direction." Ona called their bluff.

Ona made her way to the Freedman District as just as the sun began to dip under the horizon. She had followed the boys' directions, turning down two different streets before stumbling upon a series of small, one room log cabins that seemed to all be built on top of each other. There was virtually no space between each house, save for the narrow alleys that were barely a shoulder's width apart.

When Ona heard music, she carefully approached the lively song and stopped short in front of the two dark skinned players. They were both seated on a front porch and looked up in surprise as Ona approached. A woman picked at strings on an unfamiliar instrument, while a man tapped his shoes playing an instrument that flickered in Ona's memory.

"Banjo?" Ona asked shyly of the man playing the hollowed-out gourd instrument with a long neck and tight strings.

"Yep, that's right. Honey, are you lost or something?" The man asked. The man wore a gray beard not unlike the Reverend Johnson with nice pants and a coat over his shirt.

"I don't think so. Is this the Freedman District?"

"Whose asking?" The woman seemed suspicious of Ona. Her graying hair was smoothed out and curled in tight ringlets. It was pinned back under a long straw bonnet, save for a few loose curls framing her face. Her burgundy dress flowed out from her waist, draping along the porch of the log home.

"Ona America Christie." She ventured a little closer to the porch, before curiosity got the better of her. "What is that? I've never seen anything like it before." Ona marveled. "It sounds lovely."

The woman cracked a smile. "You ain't never seen a guitar?"

"A guitar." Ona tested the word on her lips. "No. I seen a banjo before though."

The man laughed. "What you doing in this part of town, young lady?"

"I'm looking for my friend. His name is Enda. Enda Cambor."

"Never heard of him," The man frowned.

"She might try down at the church, Elias." The woman pointed out.

"Who do I need to talk to down there?" Ona asked.

"You'd be looking for Brother Solomon, the reverend." Elias said.

Ona followed Elias and Hannah's instructions down to the little cabin where the sign Freedman Church hung out front. She sat on the front porch of the church and Ona earned herself a look of shock from nearly everybody who was leaving. After some time, a man near Elias's age approached wearing black robes in contrast to his white hair.

"Can I help you, miss?" he asked, taking a seat on the step outside the church.

"Are you Brother Solomon?" Ona inquired, taking a seat on the porch beside him.

"Yes, ma'am."

"Elias and Hannah sent me here," Ona explained.

"Really now," Brother Solomon spoke with a welcoming voice.

"They said that you might be able to help me find someone." Ona toyed with a piece of her dress, wringing it between her hands.

"Well, I suppose that could be true," Brother Solomon nodded. "Who you looking for?"

"My friend. His name is Enda Cambor."

"Deepest apologies, Miss. I don't know that name," Brother Solomon said quietly.

Ona felt warm drops slide down her cheeks. She felt such an incredible tightness in her chest like her heart was breaking into tiny shards that might scatter to the wind at any moment. A woman wearing a soft pink dress appeared in the doorway, with a worried expression on her face. She sat down on the porch beside Ona, taking one of her hands away from fiddling with the dress to cup in her own. It reminded her of the sharp contrast between her own skin and Enda's. She stifled a sob with shuddering, short breaths.

"Shh. It's settle down now, young lady." The woman comforted, rocking slowly with Ona. "What happened to your friend? What could be so bad?" She soothed, rubbing Ona's back like a toddler. It had been so long since Ona had been comforted that way. She leaned into the stranger's embrace, shameless and hungry for a mother's affection.

"He was taken... By a man named Billy Titus. And now I can't find him, and I don't know where he is and," she began to hiccup. "It's already been four days! He could be anywhere by now!"

"Your friend was taken by Billy Titus? Or sold to him?" Brother Solomon asked seriously.

"I don't know. I think sold, maybe. But he was free! He's never been a slave a day in his life!"

"Did he have his papers?" The woman asked.

"No, we live in Calico. Hardly nobody keeps slaves for there to be a list of free ones. Enda was the only one, I think. Nobody gave him papers."

"If he don't have papers, he's for sale," the woman said quietly.

"Not necessarily, Ruth," Brother Solomon countered. "Even with papers, Billy Titus has been known to burn them and take a man regardless of who he is."

"Why did he do this?" Ona whispered. The sun was setting low in the horizon and twilight brought a series of new sounds to the streets. Women could be heard shrieking, giggling and men shouting heatedly at each other.

"People pay him to." Brother Solomon spoke with sadness.

"Where does he take all these people to? I have to go and at least look for him." Ona's tears were drying up with new resolution.

"Cheapside. That's where they all go. It's the market yard for goods... and for people." Ruth said darkly.

"What if he ain't there?" Ona dared to ask.

245

"Then he's already gone." Brother Solomon patted Ona on the shoulder.

"How are you going to get him back?" Ruth inquired.

"I don't know," Ona mumbled.

"Tell you what," Brother Solomon said. "If you manage to find your friend and need a place to stay, I'm preaching all weekend with the Methodists at a revival outside town. You bring your friend to Paris, I think you both might could learn a lot. We feed you a free meal, free place to sleep and best of all: safe."

He stood up on his feet, dusting his robes off. He picked them up over his head, draping them across the inside of the church pew before straightening out his suit coat.

"What your name again, Miss?" He asked, offering Ruth his arm.

"Ona. Ona America Christie." She responded, managing to smile a little.

"Well, Miss Christie, I expect it's time for you to get on home. I been a real pleasure getting to talk with you. Please come by any time you'd like to visit."

"Or if you're in trouble," Ruth added from the other side of her husband.

It was a short walk home comparatively; everything was close when accustomed to the distances Ona traveled back in Calico. She returned to the Francis Estate within the hour, just before the deep blue twilight had vanished into the night.

Ona stood at the front gate staring up at it, wondering if she should risk the climb to get back inside when a lantern bobbed towards her.

"Ona America!" Ezra McDaniel called loudly. He was apparently looking for her.

"Ezra! Over here!" Ona waved.

Ezra held up his lantern, squinting into the darkness. "Ona?"

"It's me!" She walked closer to him.

"Oh, thank God!" Ezra heaved a sigh of relief. He flung his arms around Ona and held her tight.

"She's safe!" He screamed into the night.

"What'd you say, lad?" Ona heard the stableman off in the distance. Suddenly she wondered how many twinkling lanterns were a part of her search party.

"I said she's safe!" Ezra shouted.

"She's safe!" Ona heard John Francis not far away, and saw his glowing lantern rushing their way.

Ezra pulled Ona back to look her squarely in the face.

"Are you hurt?" His deep brown eyes searched her face.

"No," Ona said, embarrassed for all the trouble she caused.

"Why, Ona? Why would you leave like that?" he demanded.

"I—" Ona was cut off by the front gate opening and Catherine swooping down on them.

"Miss Christie!" Catherine cried, exasperated.

"I dare say it's past time for you to come inside, young lady!" She marched Ona inside the estate to a room Ona had never seen before. She firmly directed Ona to sit on a golden floral couch. Actually, everything in the room was gold. The walls were lined with porcelain wares trimmed with delicate gold. The room was lit by candles and lamps in gold bases. Even the walls were decorated with a paper highlighting ornate little birds whose tail feathers were laced with a golden hue. Mrs. Lafayette's finest treasures couldn't compete with this. She wasn't even in the same social sphere as this.

"Are you the young Miss Christie whose name has been called so incessantly in the streets this evening?" Ona's blush turned into a deeper shade of red as she turned to face who she already knew to be the lady of the house.

"Hello, you must be Mrs. Francis. I am terribly sorry for the mix-up this evening." Ona spoke formally, deciding complete deference to be the tactic of least retaliation.

"Oh? Was it a mix-up, though? Darling, you lied to my poor stableman. You know he was beaten for his lapse in judgment? In less than two hours under my care at this household you managed to bring out every idiotic trait necessary of my son and our staff to aid your wild exploits." Mrs. Francis wore a black night dress concealed by a heavy silk covering, and a turban over her thin hair. Her nose was fine and pointed, like her overall frame.

"Well?" Mrs. Francis pressed.

Ona sighed, deliberating Mrs. Francis' words. Her shame could only extend so far. She did not lay a hand on the stableman. That was someone else's choice.

"Well is a deep subject," She smiled dryly. John Francis had joined Ezra and Ona for the better part of the show and his lips cracked into a wide smile at Ona's bold remark. Ezra, on the other side of Ona, drained of all color and stared at Ona in open horror.

Ona heard the slap before she felt it. Long fingernails left scratch marks and ring impressions on her cheek. Ona looked up at Mrs. Francis through bleary eyes.

"You wicked girl! You are our guest and I will not be disrespected in my own home!" Mrs. Francis stamped her foot. "Clearly only the Irish could produce such a disgraceful trollop!"

"Now, Molly, let's at least give the girl the chance to speak. Perhaps she can join you at confession tomorrow and we can make this right with the Father." A lean man still wearing his day clothes entered the room. He wore his hair in a fashionable pony tail, like the young Mr. Francis.

"William, don't patronize me. The girl is clearly too far gone for the church to save. Look, she hasn't a shoe on her black feet and trounces about with men's weapons."

"Catherine, fetch Molly some tea, would you?" Mr. Francis winked at Catherine. "Put a spot of the laudanum in it." He whispered as Catherine exited the room.

"Puts her right to bed," Mr. Francis smiled down at Ona.

"Now you know dear, it's not the way of the church to condemn a girl like this. We cannot know what she was doing. What were you doing, Ona?" Mr. Francis inquired politely.

"I was in the Freedman District," Ona began. "Well eventually. I wandered around a bit first, and saw some boys racing their horse."

Molly Francis turned her face away from Ona, mortified. "And the girl runs with gamblers. Street rats. Wonderful." She said out loud, although no one was paying attention to her.

"What were you doing in the Freedman District?" John Francis asked.

"I went to church. Sort of." Ona let a small smile tug at her lips.

"What sort of church?" Molly Francis demanded.

"Mother!"

"It's a fair question, John."

"Well, I'm not sure exactly. It was called Freedman Church. Methodist, maybe?" Ona recalled Brother Solomon mentioning the Methodist revival.

"Oh, William. This is simply terrible. We have a barefoot Methodist in the house!" Molly collapsed in a chair opposite of Ona. Grace, who had been hiding behind her lady, quickly took to fanning Mrs. Francis.

William Francis stroked his beard curiously. "Are you a Methodist, girl? Be honest."

"Honestly? I ain't got no clue what the Methodists do." Ona shook her head. This house was full of madmen.

250

"See, Molly? You were making assumptions!" William said cheerfully.

"Surely you're not a practicing Catholic, are you?" Molly said through closed eyes, leaning into the fanning.

"Mother, these are very personal ques—"

"What's a Catholic?"

Grace dropped the fan in her hand to the floor. William Francis sighed heavily, shaking his head. The stableman began tip toeing backwards towards the kitchen room.

"What? 'What's a Catholic' she asks?" Molly Francis sat forward in her seat. She gazed across at Ona, examining every inch of her navy-blue dress, plaid shawl, dirty bare feet and sword with the beaded belt. Ona's gun rested on its wooden stock. Molly Francis closed her hands together in the praying position, her eyebrows kneading into her fingers with furrowed concentration. She spoke calmly through closed eyes after several moments of silence.

"I understand now. Lord, forgive them as they know not what they do. Just like it is written and so it is in this house right now. It is not your fault, Miss Christie, that you are a heathen. Stay here, with us. We will teach you the Way."

Ona smiled nervously, nodding for the sake of staying close to Cheapside. When the family finally departed for upstairs, Grace followed behind Ona and closed the door.

"Is this your room?" Ona asked. "Sorry, thanks for sharing your bed." She smiled.

"What? Oh no, I never sleep in here. I sleep on the floor by Mama and Papa's pallet." Grace smiled, amused by Ona's naivety.

"I was sent to stay the night in your room, to make sure you did not, um..."

"Leave?"

"Just that," Grace giggled.

She showed Ona the porcelain chamber pot hidden underneath the raised bed. Now it was Ona's turn to giggle. Fannie would be irate if she saw such a waste of a good quality pot.

"You're not sleeping on the floor, are you?" Ona asked, furrowing her eyebrows while Grace sat down on the floor at the foot of Ona's bed.

"It's fine, I always do."

"This bed is enormous. You should just share with me." Ona suggested.

"I've never slept in a bed before," Grace hesitated only a moment before climbing in bed beside Ona, stretching slowly and yawning.

"This is a wonderful bed," Grace smiled.

"It most certainly is," Ona turned onto her side, and fell into a restless sleep where she dreamed of Billy Titus and cold floors to sleep on and a floating Molly Francis that followed Ona around the streets of Lexington.

Chapter 14.

Ona was up before sunlight the next morning, but Grace had already slipped out of the room for her daily work. Ona splashed cold water on her face from the bedside water pitcher before knocking persistently on Ezra McDaniel's door. Ona heard noise from inside the room and a loud thud as if he had fallen out of bed. Ona cracked the door open, peering inside to check on him.

"Ezra?" Ona whispered. "Are you alright?"

"Fine, fine, Ona." Ezra sat up on the floor, groggily trying to climb out of the pile of blankets that fell with him off the bed. He stood up yawning before meeting Ona at the door, his curly hair wild and unkempt from sleep.

"What brings you here so early in the morning before I've had my coffee?" Ezra smiled sleepily. When he was not trying to impress the Francis family, Ezra still had his Calico accent.

"Well, I have a lot of work to do today and after the stir last night, I wondered if perhaps, you might go with me and save John some headache?"

"I am supposed to meet John at three for a tour of Transylvania; but until then I suppose we could walk. When did you want to leave?" Ezra said through a big yawn.

Ona stared at him blankly.

Ezra sighed in defeat. "Let me get dressed."

"Thank you!" She beamed.

"Ona?" Ezra asked cautiously.

"Yes?"

"Would it be possible for you to leave your weapons at the house?" Ezra requested.

Ona deliberated for a moment. "I'll leave the gun."

Ezra rolled his eyes, slamming his door shut. He was changed into a black suit coat with black pants and a white shirt with a black tie underneath. He dawned a beaver fur topper hat and his curls had been smoothed attractively around his square jaw.

They stopped by the kitchen where Grace and Catherine loaded them up on pastries before they headed out the front gate toward downtown Lexington.

"Where are we going?"

"A law office. I need to speak with a lawyer."

Ezra raised his eyebrows but did not comment. "And after that?"

"I need to find a place called Cheapside. There's a chance that's where Enda is."

"Do you think you'll find him there?" Ezra asked.

"I ain't sure exactly, but I'm hoping so."

"Do you love him?" Ezra's voice was quiet.

Ona stopped to look at Ezra squarely. She sighed, frowning up at him.

"It is an egregious sin to commit. Be careful how loud, and to whom, you announce such unbecoming intent." Ezra spoke rather formally all of a sudden.

"As if it were any business of yours. Why are you even here in this cursed city?"

"I'm enrolling at the university this afternoon. I'm going to be a lawyer, Ona."

"Bully for you," Ona said sarcastically before stopping to consider his feelings. She paused before saying, "Really, Ezra, that's wonderful."

"It is not a crime," Ezra spoke to his defense, "To want to better your family. To want more than just hauling flour back and forth from the trading post on a wagon; to amount to more than the shop boy sweeping the floor and balancing books, and occasionally scuffling with the Indians."

"I know that," Ona said in a small voice.

"It is not a crime to want to live comfortably," He gestured at the rows of brick homes surrounding them. "Or to work hard in order to get those things. It is not a crime to desire an education." Ezra's voice shook as they walked quietly under the locust trees.

"I know," Ona whispered. She was ashamed for her behavior. Ezra did not deserve to be treated so poorly.

"You're admirable for reaching towards a life bigger than Calico." Ona said finally. "Just like your parents were brave to reach for a life past the poverty and starvation in Ulster. It's clear their blood runs through you." Ezra seemed to forgive her and began searching with great interest for law offices scattered in the business district.

There were four law offices in downtown Lexington. Ona marched past the first one that had a sign out front reading "PRACTICE FOR SALE." She entered another office and saw several runaway slave postings papering the walls, alongside bounty hunter advertisements. Ona grabbed Enda by the arm and quickly turned out of the building. In the third office Ona entered, the lawyer refused to wait on her without her husband present, which resulted in Ezra leading Ona outside the office as she spat a series of profanities at the lawyer.

Ona inhaled deeply, smoothing her skirts as she entered the fourth law office that was very well her last chance at helping Enda Cambor. A bell above the door chimed and a young man wearing a powdered wig scooted out from behind a desk. He was tall and lean and rushed to button his waist coat before extending his hand formally to both Ezra and Ona. Ona was impressed he offered her this much in greeting, compared to the last lawyer.

"Hello, welcome to Kegley Law." The young man smiled.

"Kegley huh," Ona nodded her head with approval. A sound Irish name. The young man was perhaps around John Francis' age in his mid-twenties. He smiled politely at Ona, eyes lingering on the sword and beaded belt resting on her hip, before turning to address Ezra.

"The Kegley Law office takes pride in representing the everyday person. How may I be of service?"

"Well, Mr. Kegley," Ezra began.

"Oh, begging pardon. My name is Mr. Meyers." The young man corrected. "Mr. Kegley is in his office." Mr. Meyers pointed to a closed door. "I am his junior attorney at law. Still studying at Transylvania." He smiled proudly.

"Mr. Meyers," Ona said sweetly. "Does the attorney have time to see me this morning?"

"With you?" Mr. Meyers stammered in surprise. "Well, perhaps. Mr. Kegley is very busy..." Mr. Meyers searched Ezra's eyes for permission to arrange a meeting.

"Mr. McDaniel is showing me around the city this morning." Ona said politely, gripping one hand on her sword to remain calm. "I am here on a matter of personal business."

"Ah— yes, right away, Miss. I mean Ma'am." Mr. Meyers appeared flustered from the encounter with Ona, not entirely sure on how to handle a woman in his law office. He knocked on the closed door three times before hastily entering and closing it tight behind him.

Ezra looked down at Ona and laughed. "You really have a way of bringing out the best or the worst in people. Trouble is, you never know which one it'll be until it's too late!"

Ona ignored Ezra's comment, forcing herself not to tap her fingers in nervousness. It was several minutes before a man, perhaps in his thirties, came out from behind the door with Mr. Meyers hovering anxiously behind. The man was dressed in formal morning attire, however his tie was crooked, and he wore no wig, although the collar of his coat showed signs of powder residue. His eyes dropped to Ona's bare toes on his wood flooring and her beaded belt and sword before settling to rest curiously on her face.

"Miss? May I help you?" Mr. Kegley asked.

"Well Mr. Kegley, it's a pleasure to meet you and I certainly hope you can help. My name is Ona, Ona America Christie," Ona chimed animatedly. Mr. Kegley walked slightly bent toward Ona, as if to hear her better. He nodded his head slowly at her words as Ona launched into her tale. Mr. Kegley ushered Ona into his office allowing Ezra to catch the door as it nearly closed on him. Ezra sat quietly beside Ona, listening in rapt attention as he heard for the first time in full, the story of Enda Cambor's trafficking. The further into the story Ona delved, the deeper Mr. Kegley's wrinkles furrowed, so that by the end of her account both Mr. Kegley and Ezra were leaned forward in their chairs with expressions of deepest interest set into their faces.

"Miss Christie, your testimony is highly compelling. The bondage of a free man is plainly put, illegal; however, the issue with your case comes into play with his parents. Was it his mother, or his father who was slave to your mayor?"

"His mother, Emmaline Cambor. She's dead going on six years, I believe."

Mr. Kegley pondered this information with his hand on his chin. "And did he live at the Mayor's house ever?"

"No, like I said. Enda's a free man who ain't never been a slave. He was raised by his parents, with the Cherokee. Axe? I think that was his father's name anyway. And after that he lived with a white man name Jeremiah Sunday. Always a-working for money or living off the land. He ain't never been a slave." Ona's passionate explanation gave way and her accent slipped.

Mr. Kegley sighed deeply. "Technically, according to the law, a man is a slave if his mother was a slave and a man is free if his mother was free. His mother was not lawfully free. She absconded. The question falls on whether or not her offspring is considered missing property that was simply never identified until recently. This is a special case."

Ona waved her hand dismissively. She leaned forward in her chair to face Mr. Kegley from across his desk. "Mr. Kegley, what will it take to draft his Freedman papers?"

"That is certainly a possibility," Mr. Kegley nodded. "If you could find someone willing to sell him to you. You would have trouble acquiring direct purchase, being a woman of your position." Ona crinkled her nose, pulling her head back in offense.

"Now hang on, Miss Christie," Mr. Kegley spoke evenly. "I'm on your side. I just want you to be prepared for every possible outcome in this situation. The fact of the matter is, even if this boy is still for sale, which it is entirely possible he won't be if as many days have passed as you say; even so, you being a woman complicates this matter. Legally, you are not allowed to own property. Do you have someone who will work on your behalf? A father or brother, perhaps?"

Ona lowered her head in defeat. "No, my father is dead. It's just me, and my godmother."

"Who controls the land you live on?" Mr. Kegley asked, trying to be helpful.

"What do you mean? My godmother Fannie and I do." Ona said, perplexed.

"Ah, actually..." Ezra, who had been silent the whole time, timidly spoke up. "My father handles their affairs." Ezra said awkwardly, not making eye contact with Ona.

"It was arranged several years ago, in case— in the event something were to happen to Ona's father who was actively involved in the military."

A distant conversation with Blanche Beaudin and the McDaniels somehow providing Ona with charity rang loudly in Ona's ears. Of course, Blanche's father, the presiding judge of Calico, would have been involved in organizing the affairs in an official capacity.

"I can't believe this," Ona muttered to herself. "Why are Fannie and I not in control of our own home?"

Ezra stammered, fumbling with his beaver fur topper hat in his hands. "There have been several studies Ona, discussing the capacity for a woman to... I mean it's nothing to be ashamed or embarrassed about, it's just for the best if... Well, at least until your life becomes more stable, perhaps once you're—"

"So help me God if you say 'married'," Ona spoke murderously. Ezra dropped his gaze and said no more. Mr. Kegley coughed politely, interrupting the feud. He rifled through drawers withdrawing a blank form.

"Ona, putting it plainly: You need a man. Someone you trust to help you find the negro boy, if he is even still in the area. Take this document. Once you acquire the boy, bring him to me, with the purchaser and we will draft the Freedman papers." Mr. Kegley looked at Ona squarely. "These forms are not valid until witnessed by a notary of the public. Without an official seal, you risk imprisonment and the slave in question faces execution. Understood?"

"I understand," Ona nodded, forgetting her argument with Ezra.

Mr. Kegley dismissed them and Mr. Meyers escorted them outside the office. Ona folded the documents inside the blouse of her dress. Ezra's eyes caught the clock on the wall above Mr. Meyer's desk.

"Is that clock correct?" Ezra asked.

"Yes sir, it's 2:20." Mr. Meyers confirmed.

"Ona, we should go. We need to meet John at Transylvania soon." Ezra said.

"Oh, the university is a short walk from here!" Mr. Meyers smiled, eager to be helpful. He provided them with directions and they were off toward the university to meet with John for a tour.

Outside the gates surrounding the university, Ona bade her goodbyes to Ezra. Women were not allowed inside the college. She watched him from the other side of the gate. Ezra had found a group of students gathered around the street and he was already chatting amicably with them.

"He's going to be brilliant here. You know that, right?" A voice spoke behind Ona. She turned to face John Francis, who was watching her and watching Ezra.

"Yes, of course," Ona agreed quickly. "With his wit, he will undoubtedly carve the way to success."

John Francis smiled cordially, bidding her farewell before joining Ezra among the group of young men in formal attire.

Ona stared down at her toes, for the first time since arriving in Lexington feeling embarrassed she had no shoes to wear. Ona wandered around the city, tracing her fingers against brick walls. The streets turned to dirt and she followed the rock fencing for a quarter of a mile before she finally stopped to ask directions to Cheapside.

It turns out, Cheapside was nestled right in between the business district and the university. Ona approached the crowded city block by the grand brick building surrounding her. She gazed upon the massive, three story courthouse. It had a brand new clock face and bell tower looking over the city.

On the street, she pushed through throngs of people, ducking under horses and carriages, stepping over piles of manure and scattered garbage. The whole block was chaotic. She edged her way closer to the center of the congestion. She passed vendors on the market, selling similar wares as a Trading Post alongside fruits, vegetables, breads and sweets.

Ona paused when a fine looking white stallion caught her eye, with his handler spouting off auction bids to a small cluster of men shouting at each other. All over the block by the courthouse smelled of food, smoke and feces. The volume of haggling shoppers shouting above the sounds of cooking instruments and crowds moving against the brick street were all drowned by the insufferable dong of the courthouse bell. Ona pushed herself closer to the center of the crowds.

When Ona found them, she was in such shock she forgot how to work her legs. It wasn't like the two Cherokee men selling the barefoot slaves in the snow this past winter at the Mondry Trade Post. On one side of the block there were perhaps twenty women huddled around each other, some clothed and some not. Some of the women were pregnant and some were old. Some of them had children clinging to them and others were calling back and forth to screaming children who were around the corner being sold away from their mothers. An image of little Mary flashed through her mind.

"Out of the way, girl!" A man shouted, leading his teenage son behind him.

"These is the house slaves, for the women. Ain't no good to us. Some might make for Fanciers," The man winked at his son before continuing.

"They keep the good ones round the corner: young, healthy men." Ona heard the man explaining to his son. She followed discreetly behind the pair, listening to the father give pointers to his son on how to haggle with a seller and what items they could trade to bring down their cost. They brought a lame mule but had weighted its shoe with lead to keep it from picking his hind leg up and pass it off as healthy.

Ona saw a few dozen men standing straight in a line side by side, still and quiet behind a rope. Like the women, some were with clothes and others without, but more often than not they were bare chested.

"That one's healthy as an ox. Look at his muscles. He's probably the most expensive one here." The father pointed, talking quietly with his son. "The trick is to get the best we can afford without spending too much. It's an all-day affair, really."

Ona split away from the father and son, weaving her way in and out of people to get as close to the rope line she could manage. She scanned the faces of every man on the platform. Enda Cambor was not among them.

The courthouse clock struck 5:00 in the afternoon and the crowds began to disperse. Ona saw an unfamiliar man tugging a rope that got the chain of men moving forward, leaving the market for the week. Enda Cambor was nowhere to be found.

Ona's thoughts muddied the direction her feet carried her. She took wrong turns and dead ends and walked smack into a small boy selling newspapers. Ona forced herself not to think about the Cheapside market so she could navigate her way back to the Francis Estate.

Some candles were already lit above shops while others had closed for the night. Ona passed a crowded tavern and paused out of curiosity at the raucous group that had gathered. They were celebrating, singing loud songs and clanking pewter tankards together. Ona had never been allowed to go inside the Calico tavern. She glanced sideways over her shoulder before slipping inside. Ona spotted the blonde teenage boy who was racing the dappled gray horse Sooty in the streets the day before.

"What's all the fuss?" She smiled, stepping beside him.

"It's a celebration!" He laughed. "It's amazing; the man has done it again!"

"What? Who's done what?" She asked eagerly hoping for some good news on such a wretched day.

"Billy Titus, of course!" the boy shouted, pointing at the man dressed in roughly patched clothing. His face was nearly hidden by his tangled beard and mess of black curls. "The man's a legend! Fifty-three negro runaways captured this year alone! And eleven rogue sales!"

"Rogue?"

"You know, like slaves with no papers. He catches them and brings them to sell. He's the hero of the Irish! Them loose running niggers steal away all our jobs!" the boy explained passionately.

Rogue. Is that what Enda was? One of eleven? Ona glowered at the filthy man before her with her hand hovering over her sword hilt. His hair could not have been that different from that of a bear. His skin was surely not more difficult to clean than a fox or bobcat. His life could not possibly be more resilient than any other wild animal Ona had claimed in the forest.

"You alright?" the boy asked her, cautious. He was eyeing her face and her sword.

"Billy Titus," Ona addressed him, but his back was turned to her and her voice was carried off by the echoes of loud conversation in the tavern. Ona took the boy's drink from his hand. She downed his half full tankard of sour ale and slammed it to the floor. The ringing of the metal quieted the tavern somewhat.

"Billy Titus!" Ona shouted, with her fists balled at her side.

His mop of greasy, tangled curls turned to face her. His shirt was stained with food and blood and beer and he stunk like sweat. Behind his bushy beard, his black eyes crinkled into an interested smile, revealing gray teeth.

"Which one of you sonsabitches bought me a night with this wild one?" Billy Titus bellowed in laughter.

"Come here, sugar. Who put you up to this? Be honest." He reached for Ona's hand, wrapping his thick, sticky fingers around her wrist.

Ona tried to yank her arm back, feeling for a moment that her resolve may have emptied with the boy's cup. Billy Titus' grip did not slacken.

"Ah, honey, don't be shy. She's shy. Let me buy you a drink." He winked at Ona and the men at the bar roared with laughter. Their sudden noise brought Ona to action.

Ona ripped her father's sword from its sheath using her free hand. She screamed, raising it high above her head with her free hand and swinging it powerfully down over his hand gripping her other wrist. Ona, after years of taking care of the property with Fannie, was no stranger to hard work, nor an axe.

Billy Titus' screams filled the room as he watched the sword slice into his arm. The men were out of their seats, shouting to subdue

Ona. There was so much commotion in tavern Ona managed to slip in and out of people's reach.

Billy Titus was blind with fury, holding his arm close to his body and fumbling for a short, broad blade that hung openly at his side. He swung wildly at Ona, bringing the blade closer and closer to her in quick, powerful motions as tavern patrons dived out of the way. Ona felt pressure slam against her arm and when she looked down, there was blood. A sharp pain took over her body, but after a moment her whole arm became numb.

Ona ducked underneath one man to get out the door. Billy Titus rushed after her, ignoring his maimed limb. He bowled down the man blocking the door and followed Ona into the streets, still hacking his blade into the air after her. He grabbed Ona by her skirts and yanked her to her knees. His eyes were unseeing. Billy Titus raised his blade above Ona's head and she screamed with terror, plunging her sword into his stomach until the hilt met flesh. Billy Titus dropped his blade and crimson spilled from his lips. Ona's breath was haggard, and she picked up her skirts, taking to the alleys as quickly as she could, carrying her father's sword with her.

There were men chasing after Ona, shouting that Billy Titus had been killed and his murderer was on the loose. Ona felt herself growing light-headed but managed to find a stretch of trees and shrubs planted alongside the rows of brick houses coming into her view. Ona took small steps through the foliage, hoping to hide in the greenery. The shouting voices became more distant and after a time, Ona could only hear her own footsteps crunching through leaves and her breath shallow from flight.

The sun set lower into the sky, and more homes lit up with candles in the windows and outside of each house. Ona crawled through the thick magnolia trees, recognizing a familiar wrought iron gate and the back of the Francis Estate. Ona finally remembered to sheath her sullied sword, just as she decided to avoid using the estate's main entrance.

Instead, she turned the corner round the brick mansion and entered through the kitchen house, running directly into Catherine. Catherine's typically neat hair was now untidy. Her smock was covered in flour and her cheeks burned bright pink from the intense heat rolling off the fire.

"Oh, thank goodness!" Catherine breathed. "Sweetheart, you're late. The guests will be here in an hour's time."

"What?" Ona asked, delirious.

"Didn't you go with your friends to the university? Young Ezra has been admitted at the law school and the Francis' have extended an invitation to host the lad while he studies. It's a celebration!" Catherine explained.

"What's that on your... Oh my goodness, girl! Are you alright? You're injured!" Catherine cried. "Oh, my dear girl, what happened? Let's get you upstairs, now. We will fix you right on up."

Catherine guided Ona up the staircase by the elbow, and there was already warm water in the metal bath beside her bed. Ona imagined it would have been hot if she were home sooner. Either way it was warmer than the chilly spring water this time of year. Ona was grateful to wash. Catherine had called in Grace to assist her. While Catherine worked on mending Ona's wound, Grace scrubbed away Ona's tears, the stench from the market and the dirt and blood that carried the weight of Billy Titus in its dust. Catherine wrapped a thick cloth around Ona's injury and the women left her to dress.

Ona climbed out of the brown water and sat dripping wet on her bed. She saw a beautiful dress laid out for her, one that Molly Francis set aside for her to wear to the party tonight. It was of simple design, yet elegant and ladylike. It was dyed a soft blue color that reminded Ona of summer chicory. The bust was cinched, and the shoulders marked with dainty silk puffs. There were minimal ruffles, to Ona's eternal relief; only a streak of silky white frill at the top of the bust, the base of the shoulder puffs, and around the wrists of the long-sleeved garment. A pair of white silk slippers rested on the bed beside the dress.

Ona admired the dress; however, she was too exhausted to imagine moving much more than to climb underneath the covers. Ona sat in silence on the bed until she her body was dry and her hair hung damp, still tangled. A gentle knock at the door preceded Grace's muffled voice from outside the room.

"Ona?" she asked, concerned. "The party's almost started. Are you ready?"

Ona could not bring herself to answer. The dress was beautiful and lovely and made for people who did not commit crimes against God, like murder and loving a colored person. Her eyes lingered on the sword, now sheathed and resting in the corner of her room by her father's gun. Ona remained frozen on the bed, quiet tears brimming over her gray eyes down her cheeks.

"Ona? I'm coming in now. Is that alright?" Grace asked more urgently.

Grace did not wait for Ona to answer her. She opened the door and rushed to Ona's side, picking up a throw blanket off a nearby chair and wrapping Ona with it.

"What's the matter?" Grace asked in a soothing voice. "What's wrong, Ona?"

Ona turned to look at her and her lips trembled like she wanted to speak, but she could not find any words. Grace picked up a brush and sat down behind Ona. Grace silently worked through the knots in Ona's hair. After some time, she pulled Ona to her feet, fastening complex underpinnings to Ona's frame that were laid out beside the dress.

"Here we go now, Ona." Grace said kindly, slipping the blue dress on. Grace narrated each step of the process to Ona in a patient, methodical voice.

"Now I am going to pull your arms through— mind the bandage now, that's it. Now I am going to fasten the buttons in the back."

Ona wasn't really listening to her, only flashing between images of Enda, wherever he might be, the blank gaze of the little man Thomas shot by Enda's arrow back in Ice Cave, and Billy Titus' face when her blade plunged through his middle.

"Where does your soul go?" Ona finally spoke in a rough voice.

"Huh?"

"When you die," Ona said quietly.

"Well, that depends, I suppose."

"On what?" Ona turned to face Grace. Grace sat down beside Ona, taking her hand and stroking it softly.

"On whether or not you believe in God. On whether or not you were a good person."

"How do you know? What if a bad person was a Christian? Or, what if a good person wasn't?" Ona asked.

"When they died, did they look at peace?"

Ona reflected on the visage of Billy Titus and the men back in Ice Cave. "No. They were not at peace."

"Then there's your answer."

"Good," Ona spoke bitterly. "I hope they never find heaven."

"It does not do well to speak ill of the dead, Ona." Ona looked sharply at Grace. Zelma McDaniel had once told her the very same thing. "Maybe you're right," Ona breathed deeply. Her body shuddered under her breath. "What about someone who has done unforgivable things?"

"God will forgive you, so long as ye believe in your heart that you're sorry," Grace said calmly.

"But what if they don't deserve to be forgiven? What if it's too late?" Ona whispered. The image of her sword inside Billy Titus could not be shaken. Grace rose from the bed and collected a thick book from Ona's dresser. She flipped through the pages silently for a moment before reading aloud:

"Ephesians tells us that, 'In Him we have redemption through blood, the forgiveness of sins, in accordance with the riches of God's grace.'"

"What blood?" Ona asked, afraid. She never wanted to see blood again.

"Jesus' blood. Jesus died and shed his blood for all people. Our sin is made clean because of his sacrifice. He loves us in spite of our nature. That's why He forgives when you ask."

"How could anyone forgive such sin as mine?" Ona played with her fingers in her lap.

"That's why they call it grace." She winked. Grace stood up, helping Ona off the bed.

"You look lovely." Grace complimented. She spun Ona to face a large mirror. Ona examined her reflection like she was a different person. Her wild curls were pinned obediently under her cap, only a few strategically arranged coils framed her face. After the blood loss, she looked paler than normal. Grace stooped to the floor; disguising Ona's calloused and cut feet with dainty white slippers.

"Please don't make me go to the party." Ona begged in a small voice. Thoughts of Billy Titus and Enda Cambor were at war with each other. Where was Enda Cambor right now?

"Ona, I'm sorry, but you must."

"I don't know if he's safe. I don't know where they took him!"

"Who?"

"Enda! Who else?" Ona cried, her body trembling. Her nerves had seen too much horror this day to suffer through a party.

"No sweetie, Ezra is just downstairs. You will see him soon enough." Grace smiled, thinking Ona had lapsed over his name.

Grace opened the door and steered Ona down the grand stair case. Ona looked back at Grace with pleading eyes and Grace smiled encouragingly at her.

Cheerful music filled the first level of the Francis Estate. A pair of fiddlers played fair melodies. Ona flashed back to a time when Rowland Christie played around the fire place in the McDaniel home with Ezra's father Wash. Anna McDaniel led the children in dances that lasted well into the night. Unlike tonight, it was a joyful time.

Ona's eyes first found the sophisticated Mrs. Francis, draped in golden silks with a low bust line and her hair combed fashionably underneath her matching turban. Ona did not make eye contact, instead avoiding Molly Francis altogether and moving straight into the papered room with the golden floral furniture. The room had been split with a wood carved divider and Ona could see wide skirts and silk muslins from underneath the divider on the opposite side of the room.

Ona found Ezra hovering beside John Francis, who was surrounded by important looking men smoking long wooden pipes. Ona directed herself to a piano bench where she examined the keys and resisted the temptation to touch them. Catherine smiled cordially at Ona, bringing her glasses of white wine.

"Miss Christie! It pains me to see one so lovely being so unsociable!" John Francis cried. He spoke just a little more loudly than he did naturally, and Ezra followed cheerfully behind him.

"Here, you must try this, you must!" John set down his cup of wine, selecting a small brown square from a tray of food sitting at a nearby table and offered it to Ona.

"What is it?" she asked doubtfully. It was the color of dirt.

"Just try it!"

Ona dared to break a piece of the square off, popping it into her mouth. The treat was sweet and melted on her tongue into robust flavors.

"It's chocolate!" Ezra said, laughing at Ona's expression.

"Isn't it perfect?" John smiled.

"I think John might be right about perfection." Ona forced a laugh. "By the way Ezra, congratulations!" Ezra blushed a shade of bright pink, muttering his thanks and passing Ona a fresh glass of wine.

"Oh dear, is she having chocolate for the first time? What a sweet girl." A woman nearby smiled.

"She's so adorable, look at her hair!" Another woman chimed in.

"Are you the girl from the mountains?" the first woman asked. She wore vibrant green silks with thick blonde hair piled on top of her head and took an immediate interest in Ona.

"Oh John has been telling us so much about you!" The second woman squealed. Her lavender muslin draped off her bare shoulder and her brown curls were pinned tightly up.

"Is it true you're a witch?" the blonde asked.

"I ain't a witch." Ona smiled awkwardly. "That's just a matter of saying."

"Oh, listen to her accent!" the brunette said excitedly. One of the men standing with Ezra and John earlier approached them, wrapping his arm around the brunette's side.

"Go on, say something for us!" he encouraged.

Ona stood up from the piano bench and grabbed a handful of chocolate before walking past the group, ignoring their teasing requests.

"Begging your pardon," she heard John Francis explain apologetically. "She might be shy in the presence of unfamiliar company."

"Poor thing!" The brunette woman gave a sympathetic nod.

Ona stalked into the kitchen area, kicking out of her slippers and picking at her chocolate. She managed to stuff several pieces into her mouth before she decided to go back out to the party. Ona's tongue was thick with chocolate and she found a barrel tapped with ale for the party. Ona selected one of the pewter tankards and filled her mug with sour ale. She downed the harsh beer before finding her shoes once more and returning to the lion's den. The night became surprisingly easier the more frequently she snuck into the kitchen to refill her mug. After a while, Catherine stopped bringing her wine.

"That's enough, young lady," Catherine reprimanded, catching Ona on her fourth trip to the kitchen house. "You need to eat something. You look ill." Catherine said. She sat Ona down in the kitchen, handing her a roll. Ona peeled apart the roll, stuffing bits into her mouth.

"How long is this going to last?" Ona asked.

"Several more hours, dear. You need to pace yourself." Catherine said, taking a seat beside Ona and patting her on the knee.

"I knows you don't want to be here, but this drink won't solve what's bothering you." Catherine spoke in a motherly voice.

Ona sniffled loudly, reaching for her tankard. Catherine took the mug from Ona's reach, instead handing her a glass of water.

"Why don't you rest in here a while and clear your head a bit, yes?" Catherine suggested.

"Alright." Ona mumbled. She seemed to consistently make a fool of herself at the Francis Estate. Ona couldn't help it though; she had been a mess ever since Enda was taken.

Ona ate two more rolls and realized she only wore one shoe. She looked down at her bare foot, wriggling her clean toes. There were fresh scratches and cuts layered upon old scars. Ona removed her remaining slipper, placing it on her stool. She'd rather be barefoot than look so silly with a single slipper.

Ona was feeling less queasy and found Ezra mingling in a group of men, hovering nearby him in hopes he could deflect the masses.

"Market gone mad," One man with an English accent muttered.

"Can you believe the price of coffee?" Another man shook his head, agreeing.

"My father says sales will improve now that the war is over," Ezra commented. "Resources will not be spread so thin."

"I certainly hope so!" Another man replied. "With the way things are now, I had to send four of my best workers down to Cheapside. Damn shame if you ask me."

"Did you at least get a fair price, Charles?" the Englishman asked curiously.

"More than double what I paid in the first place! Some English prick up from Louisville." Charles laughed heartily, jabbing the

Englishman in the side and winking. The Englishman rolled his eyes, dismissing the man.

"I think I'm about to be sick," Ona spoke all of a sudden.

"Too much to drink, girl?" Charles bantered.

Ona would not dignify his statement with an answer. She made her way up the stairs, fumbling over steps. The group of men watching her laughed riotously at her failure to walk steady. Ezra politely dismissed himself, catching Ona by the elbow and guiding her up the stairs.

"Jesus, Ona, how much have you had to drink?" Ezra shook his head.

"None of your business," she stammered.

"Honestly, what's gotten into you?"

"I looked for Enda today," Ona said suddenly. "At Cheapside. He wasn't there. They sell little children there. Right by the horses."

Ezra said nothing, but a frown registered on his face. "You should not be drinking like this," he caught Ona's hand as she fumbled up the final step. He opened the door to Ona's room, peeling back her covers and led her to the bed.

"Be serious. Did you hear what I said?" Ona pleaded.

"I am! You could have died walking up those stairs just now if I hadn't been there to help you!" He laughed.

"What kind of lawyer do you want to be, Enda? The kind that takes the most money from the biggest client or the kind that helps people?" Ona's room appeared to be spinning. She felt so nauseous and her head was beginning to ache.

"Ezra. I am Ezra."

"I'm sorry, Ezra. I'm sorry I'm like this."

"It's alright." Ezra sat down beside Ona, tucking her under the covers.

"It's just I'm very lost without my Enda." Ona's head hit the pillows and the spinning room slowed to a wobble.

"You will feel better, silly. Give it time." Ezra bent down to kiss Ona lightly on the forehead. Ezra stood up taking one last look at Ona before blowing out the candles on his way out of the room.

Chapter 15.

Sunlight blasted Ona into consciousness and her first thought bubbled to her lips in a croaky, unfamiliar voice.

"Water."

Grace's visage hovered above Ona wearing an expression of worry mingled with amusement.

"On the bedside, Ona." Grace pointed. She gasped when she saw Ona throw back the covers.

"You slept in that dress?" Grace was mortified.

"I'm sorry, I didn't realize." Ona said after downing the entire glass of water. Ona was taking great effort to pretend to care, but she was only focused on the pounding coming from inside her skull.

Grace unfastened the buttons, making a *tsk* sound when she realized one had been ripped off in the night. She peeled off the dress, and Ona obediently stepped away from the silk garment. Grace worked quickly; unpinning Ona from her burdensome under-clothes. Grace gasped again. Ona's body was covered in bruises from the restrictive clothing.

"Oh my," Ona managed to say.

"Oh my, indeed."

Grace handed Ona her green checkered dress, freshly laundered.

"Your other dress is in your bag. Catherine voted to burn it, but I saved it for you and mended the tear." Grace winked.

Ona slipped into her dress, inhaling freely as wide as her diaphragm would expand. It was truly remarkable to be free of those underpinnings. Ona poured herself another cup of water from the water pitcher, only just noticing her frenzied bed hair in the mirror, when a gentle knock at the door disturbed her.

Grace went to the door, but Ona beat her to the invite.

"Come in!"

Ezra McDaniel entered the room, dressed in a simple white frock and brown breeches. He wore no topper hat to conceal his black curls, only his well-loved leather boots.

"Ezra! You're back! I missed this Ezra!" Ona smiled approvingly.

"I thought you might desire a morning walk."

"Of course! I'm almost ready." Ona explained. She took one last look at her hopeless hair before shaking her head in defeat. Ona pushed Ezra back outside the door.

"Give me a minute," she instructed.

Ona sat on the end of her bed in front of the mirror. People would be looking for her today. Ona did not walk into the bar with the intention of killing anyone. Unlike in Ice Cave, when it was self-defense, Ona had chosen to pick a fight with Billy Titus. The crime for murder was hanging. Ona took strands of her thick, tangled hair and began weaving them into a braid that wrapped around the top of her head, framing her face. Unlike church, she left no rebellious loose strands dangling free. When she knocked on Ezra's door, it was his turn to be surprised.

"Why the sudden route for propriety?" Ezra joked.

"It's hot outside. Where's John?"

"Still sleeping off the party."

Catherine eyed Ona severely, handing them each a large hunk of cheese with bread as they made their way out of the kitchen house.

"She thinks I'm wild," Ona mused.

"You are. Like a feral cat. Lexington doesn't know how to handle you," Ezra teased.

They made their way through the business district, Ezra stopped to eye a particularly impressive horse, tall and lean and muscular. Ona rolled her eyes, crossing the street to examine a peddler selling his trinkets on the street corner. Ona watched Ezra look up to find her, but was so oblivious that he bumped right into a man dressed in a long black coat and a dome shaped black hat.

The man spoke with Ezra, giving him a paper and speaking hurriedly. Ezra's eyes glanced back at Ona briefly, before returning to the paper. Ona got an uneasy feeling in her stomach and decided to keep walking. She crossed over the street several blocks up, where she saw other watchmen patrolling in their black hats.

Ona ducked into the thick magnolia tree line that separated the alleys from the backside of the brick houses. She followed it just like the day before and used the familiar iron gate to slip back inside the Francis Estate. Ona nodded in greeting at Grace, who was working in the kitchen, but did not stop to chat. She made her way up the back set of stairs and closed the door to her room. It was perhaps half an hour before a loud knock rapping at her door spooked her nerves into pacing around the floor.

"Who is it?" Ona asked timidly.

"Ezra. Open up!"

"Are you alone?" Ona asked cautiously.

Ezra tried the doorknob, but Ona had locked it.

"Ona, of course I am!" he sounded irritated.

Ona let out a deep breath, opening the door for Ezra. He burst into her room with a wrinkled paper in his hands.

"What have you done?" He whispered, slamming her door shut.

"What do you mean?" She pretended ignorance.

"There is a constable out, with watchman. They are patrolling the streets, looking for a wild, red haired girl with no shoes who carries a sword. They're saying she just nearly killed that man Billy Titus in a tavern last night! Walked right up to him and sliced into his arm, then stabbed him through! Practically gutted him!"

"I—" Ona began.

"You're wanted for attempted murder!"

"It was an accident!" Ona cried.

"How could attacking a man in public possibly be any sort of accident, Ona?"

"I didn't plan on doing what I did. I wish I could take it back!"

"You need to get out of here! I'm sending you back to Calico as soon as the sun sets. Do you understand me? You cannot stay here! Is your heart even remorseful over this? Or are you still so affected by some half negro? They will hang you!" Ezra's voice rose.

Ezra paced around the bedroom, following the ornate carpet rugs and weaving around the fine wooden furniture until he had it all planned out. Ona was to pack her things and wait until dusk before riding back to Calico. Ezra gave her a map to follow, drawing out the way home with simple enough details.

"What will you do after?" Ona asked in a small voice.

Ezra shook his head. "I'll stay here, of course. I start school next week. You and the city, Ona, you're no good for each other. You belong back home in the mountains, with Fannie."

Ona bobbed her head slowly, agreeing.

"What about Enda?"

"He's gone, Ona. Let it go." Ezra's words echoed within Ona, resounded off of some hollow part of her soul that had not yet given up on Enda Cambor and finally allowing a painful realization to settle within her: Enda Cambor was gone.

Ona clung to Ezra's instructions. She felt very alone in the world and wanted to be home with Fannie all of a sudden. He gave her instructions not to leave her room. After a few hours had passed, Ezra returned wearing his formal attire, bringing Ona beef stew and warm bread from Catherine.

"I told them all you were feeling ill from last night. I'm going out with John Francis but will be back soon. I will fetch you when it is time to leave."

"Ezra, I'm not ready to leave yet." Ona said suddenly.

"Ona if you do not leave for Calico tonight, I can only assume that you have let your heart and soul steep into a sin that is concerned not for the life and health of others, only your own selfish passions. Go home once the sun is set, if for no one else than for Fannie. I will come back and tell you when it's time."

Ezra promptly closed the door behind him, leaving Ona to her thoughts. For a while, Ona lay in her bed staring up at the velvet fabric adorning the inside of her poster bed. She imagined coming home to Fannie alone, without Enda Cambor. Ona sat up on her bed and found the little wooden clock atop the fireplace mantle. It was 2:45 when she decided she was not ready to go back to Calico without Enda Cambor.

Ona tiptoed out of her room unarmed, down the narrow servant's stairs into the kitchen house. She smelled bread cooling, but the kitchen was low in its embers and she saw no one in her path. Ona delicately exited the kitchen house, quietly shutting the door behind her and winding her way around the back of the property towards the small wrought iron gate that led to the alley of Lexington. Ona wandered through the city, doing her best to blend into the crowded city's business block. She pulled out the map Ezra gave to her, pausing amid the bustling street to orient herself.

"Excuse me ma'am, are you lost?"

Ona looked up to find a watchman in black pausing to assist her while the crowds and wagons shuffled around them.

"Well, I suppose not. I just need a moment to orient—"

"Barefoot female with red hair, traveling alone. Look, that's her!" A rushed voice called out in the street and a man hurried towards them. The watchman's eyes narrowed. Ona took off running through the streets. She raced down muddied streets until brick and stone businesses turned into log dwellings reminiscent of the Freedman District. The sun hung blood orange in the sky slowly sinking behind the city, still alight and bustling with chimneys smoking.

Ona passed two young negro men on the street and nodding her head to the ground. The young men crossed the street, walking opposite of her and did not make speak or eye contact. Ona clicked her tongue, desperate to make her way out of the city, she turned around and called after the men.

"Excuse me! Do you know the quickest way out of the city?" The men did not speak, but one man pointed west before they turned on their heels, continuing silently on their way.

Ona breathed out slowly, eerily on edge from the silent men. She followed his guidance nonetheless, grateful for at least a direction to follow. The log houses disappeared, slowly replaced with wooden shops where Ona last saw the street boys racing Sooty the horse only a couple evenings prior.

"You are past curfew to be coming out of the negro district." Ona drew her head up sharply, spying the constable just in front of her.

"Who kept you hid? Tell me and I'll shorten your sentence." He spat chaw on Ona's bare feet.

Ona curled her toes back, "No one kept me."

"Bullshit. Your friends are honest people. You don't deserve to run with them. That boy has come to the courthouse and told it all; you're chasing some nigger that got himself sold off and you tried to murder a man for his honest day's work. That's two felonies I'm bringing you in for tonight, and don't be certain you won't hang for them. I'll say it once more, who kept you until dusk?"

Ona turned on her heels, darting toward the Freedman District. The constable followed her through the empty streets, finally tackling her in front of the church where Reverend Solomon preached at. His wife Ruth erupted from her rocking chair on the front porch, diving inside the church doors.

The constable kicked Ona until she would not squirm any longer. Ona focused on her breathing as ropes once more bound her hands for the second time in her life. He stood up from restraining Ona's wrists, pushing her face into the dirt street. He barged over to the church door, banging in outrage. From the corner of Ona's eye, she saw the silhouette of two figures fade from the door. One went further in the back of the church, and one crossed the threshold to meet the constable.

Reverend Solomon opened the door, "Constable." He said in feigned surprise.

"That negro woman sitting on the porch. She your wife?"

"Yes, sir." Reverend Solomon's face was unreadable, nodding only minutely in the direction of the constable.

"She was out past curfew. I'm taking her in. Get her out here, son." the constable spat.

"Ruth," The reverend spoke in a hollow sort of way. Ruth appeared moments later in the doorway, wearing the same lovely dress Ona saw her wear once before. Now, Ruth would not look at Ona. The constable took another rope from his pockets, tying just one of Ruth's hands to the cords, and connecting the long line to Ona. The women marched in front of the constable all the way back to the little jail beside the court house.

Ona was taken to one side of the little jail where she shared a cell with one other young woman, half-starved and blonde hair ratted with a wild look about her eye. Ruth was taken to one of many cells filled up each with four and five women, all different shades of brown.

Men teemed in and out of the crowded cells all night, slipping coins to the constable who yawned, bored, pocketing the money.

Ona could hear Ruth sobbing long into the night, more clearly even than the sounds of the men who forced themselves upon the other women. Ona prayed that no man would come to her cell. Her cellmate did not speak, but seemed friendly enough, babbling softly to herself.

The girl motioned excitedly when she saw a rat scurry across the floor. The girl dived, missing the creature and Ona wondered what would have happened if she caught it. Ona curled up on the dirtied linen piled into the corner of the cell, lying close to the wild eyed girl who could not speak, and waited for sunrise.

Through the window in front of the little jail house that sat just beside the courthouse, Ona watched the city slowly come to life. Curious children stared openly across the iron fenced yard of the courthouse, desperate for a peek inside the jail. Young men in fine morning attire did not look twice at the jail as they passed. Women walked dutifully besides their husbands, or somberly in groups with other women. Some of the men's faces Ona recognized to be visitors from the night before, strolling into coffee houses appearing ready to talk business.

Late in the afternoon, people began to gather around a lone pole that stood center in the courtyard. The constable unlocked Ona's cell, and her cellmate clung desperately to Ona. The constable peeled the girl away from her, dragging her outside to the pole. The girl stared up into the gleaming sun, and began to wail.

"Nancy Thomas, you have been found guilty of theft from the Wilson Bakery. You have elected not to pay the cost of the stolen goods." The constable kept having to raise his voice as Nancy Thomas' screaming overtook his words. She clawed at the constable, and watchmen wrestled her arms into a vice, tying her to the pole. She bit one of them and he swore, smacking her to the ground.

"Thereby," The constable continued, "The presiding judge of Lexington has deemed you a menace to our good city. This being your third offense of theft, you have been sentenced to five lashes. The court has deemed you unfit for trial and you have been directly sentenced with twelve months reform at the Virginia State Asylum. May God shed some of his light into your soul." Nancy's screams echoed in the courtyard when the first lash came. She writhed violently until the third lash, then she simply lay still on the ground, hiccupping and chest heaving in and out.

The crowd began to disperse shortly after the events, and Ona did not see Nancy again. That evening Ona was offered food for the first time since her arrest. She eyed the moldy bread between her hands, picking off the gray bits and swallowing the rest hurriedly in as few bites as possible. Again, the men came to the jail house after dark, and Ona tried not to listen. Were those the tears of Ruth? If not, then who? Was she next? The chilly April nights brought cold into her bones not known since the dead of winter. Ona forced herself to think about her happiest memories, mostly times spent with Enda, Fannie, and her father.

The next morning, Ona, Ruth and a few others were summoned to appear before the court. The women were marched in a line to the grand building just as the bell sung for 10:00. Ruth, with the barest of gestures, tugged Ona's checkered dress sleeve. Ona glanced back at Ruth. The reverend's wife spoke so low, Ona could barely hear.

"Solomon find your runaway. He staying at the Paris Camp Meeting."

"Be still, whores!" The watchman barked for silence and Ruth spoke no more. The watchman's voice deadened in the wake of Ona's thoughts, whirling around her and daring to reveal to her heart the most dangerous of thoughts: hope. Enda was at the Paris Camp Meeting.

Two women in front of Ona were sentenced lashes for trying to run away from their owner. Enda was safe. Another for stealing food. How would she get to him? Ruth, slave to the free negro Solomon Brown, was sentenced to seven lashes for being out past negro curfew. Ona looked up from her frenzied thoughts. Ruth took steps back from the defendant's podium, leaving room for the next person to be called.

"Ona America Christie."

Ona inhaled slowly, imagining herself and Enda catching fireflies at the creek behind the cabin on Calico Ridge. She approached the bench, recalling the soft texture of Enda's lips.

"Yes, sir," Ona breathed out, voice shaking.

"Speak when you are spoken to, girl." The judge harrumphed. Ona looked up to the judge, scanning the rows of black gowns and powdered wigs seated behind him. Most immediately the visages of the jury and lawmakers were wrinkled and severe. Behind them sat quiet, and eager students. Among them in the very back, not a wig for his brown curly head, was Ezra McDaniel.

"Ona America Christie, you are being charged with unlawful relations between an unmarried woman and a negro. You are being charged with aiding a negro slave escape from custody. You are being charged with attempted murder of Billy Titus, handler of the escaped negro in question. These accusations are most grievous. Miss Christie, how do you plead?"

"Your honor, before Miss Christie delivers an answer, I would like to consult with her. I volunteer to represent Miss Christie in this case." A voice shot up from the side of the court room and Ona was stunned to see Mr. Kegley rising from his seat, wig haphazardly falling to one side.

"Very well, Mr. Kegley. We shall recess and return at 2:00." The judge waived his hand dismissively.

Ona was led with the other women back to the jail house. Minutes later, Mr. Kegley was giving her instructions from her cell.

"Why are you doing this?" Ona asked.

"Because you're an interesting case, and I am bored of bonds and property disputes."

"The judge was not altogether lying." Ona persisted from the inside of her cell.

"Hush," Mr. Kegley glanced around him suspiciously. "The first two accusations are hearsay, completely based on character defamation antics. Who gave that information to the court? The boy who manages your affairs, who you will not marry, who sits within that courtroom? That issue will be easy enough to address." Ona raised her eyebrows, impressed with Mr. Kegley's deductions. Despite his messy appearance, the man was astute.

"Secondly," Mr. Kegley continued, "where were you on the night of the supposed escape of Enda Cambor?"

"I'm not sure," Ona furrowed her brow. "What day did he disappear?"

"That's perfect. Just answer honestly, like that. Have you been alone at all in the past three weeks?"

"Well, twice I suppose, this week." Ona nodded her head, thinking on the first time she met Ruth and the Reverend Solomon, as well as the day she went to Cheapside.

"The escaped negro in question disappeared over seven days ago." Mr. Kegley nodded optimistically.

"I was traveling with John Francis and Ezra McDaniel at that time."

"Traveling with respectable friends into town is a perfectly sound alibi. Now regarding the business with Mr. Titus." Mr. Kegley leaned against the outside of the cell, rubbing his fingers into his temples. "What can we say to at least land you on house arrest for the remainder of this trial?"

"He grabbed me first. It's true, I called out to him, angry; but he grabbed me and would not let go. He asked, 'who bought me for him for the evening?'" Ona kept her eyes on the floor, cheeks hot.

"Billy Titus grabbed you first," Mr. Kegley repeated, looking up. "Now, he has been severely wounded, mind you." He went on, beginning to pace back and forth at the front of Ona's cell. "Were you in fear for your life?"

"I thought he would do whatever he pleased. I was terrified." A few tears escaped down Ona's cheeks. Mr. Kegley's eyes were for a moment, deeply reaching towards Ona. He sighed, nodding his head and snapping his fingers loudly.

"Save those tears for trial, and say it exactly how we practiced. The Francis family will have you back in their care by nightfall before this can go any further."

When the judge called Ona back to testify, she gave her story exactly how Mr. Kegley instructed her to.

"This is a poor, uneducated woman from the far reaches of our state's most dangerous territories. She acted in haste, though in self-defense nonetheless." Mr. Kegley addressed the judge.

"In this year alone, Ona America Christie has lost half her town due to violence, and sickness. She herself lost her own father not yet one full year ago. She is young, and not fit to be held accountable for acts committed when she feared her life to be in mortal peril."

"I will dismiss the charge of intimacy with a negro due to lack of evidence, namely the negro in question, with special attention being noted to the aforementioned soured courtier being present in this courtroom today." Ezra wilted in his seat.

"While we wait on the testimony of Mayor Cambor of Calico to arrive by mail to continue the proceedings, Miss Christie is remanded to the estate of her caretakers, Mr. and Mrs. John Francis for the remainder of this trial." The judge dismissed the courtroom.

It was two hours before Mr. Francis was summoned to bring Ona back to the estate. In that time, she witnessed the women receive their due lashes. Unlike Nancy Thomas, the women sentenced that day did not falter, but accepted their punishment in total silence. Ruth's dress was shredded, and blood stained the peach fabric across her back. When Ruth was untied, she was allowed to hobble home. Ona could not see Solomon; there was no one around to help her back.

John Francis arrived in a carriage for Ona. He smiled warmly, his affectionate heart not one bit deterred from the presence of a criminal on trial for attempted murder.

"Well, you are welcome to stay as long as you need to Ona." John said kindly. "I would love more than anything for this to be sorted out. I am certain you will be back home, safe with Fannie, in no time." He spoke reassuringly, walking Ona up to her bedroom at the estate.

Ona lay on her bed for hours, contemplating the trial and the camp meeting. Surely one posed a more desirable outcome than the other; one might carry the death penalty, and the other held the promise of Enda Cambor. It was past supper when she heard the whispering outside her door.

"Just wait outside the door, Grace and ring the bell if she tries to leave. Do not engage contact, she is armed." William Francis spoke quietly in the hallway.

"Yes, sir." Grace's voice was shaking in a dreadful whisper.

Ona peered through the space between the floor and the door. Grace was seemingly assigned to a chair just outside Ona's room, busying herself in needlework that trailed in spools of thread to the floor. Ona swore, crossing the room to open the tall, glass pane window. She eyed the oak tree growing tall and thick alongside the house, wondering if she might leap to its safe embrace.

Ona slung the rifle over her shoulder but stuffed her sword inside her pack with her other belongings, including the blank freedman documents from Mr. Kegley hidden safely in her clothes. The sword stuck out nearly a foot, but Ona bundled the top with a small blanket, wrapping it around the hilt to disguise it safely.

Ona launched herself from the window, holding her breath while colliding with the thick branches of the tree, grappling for any hold while she tumbled to the earth. For a moment, she could not breath. Everything ached, but after a minute or so her lungs began to work properly and she was moving once more.

Ona followed the back of the property to the barn. The Francis's owned half a dozen horses and Ona craned her neck around the back side of the barn, looking for the stableman. She heard him talked sweetly to one of the horses, nearly finished with his work for the evening.

"Now girl, that's it. You're fine, come along," he soothed. He was sitting on a stool holding one of the horse's back hoof in between his legs. The barn dust irritated Ona's nose. She sneezed, tripping over a hay fork that clattered to the ground. The horse spooked, kicking the stableman and bolting. The man groaned in pain. His flat-topped straw hat fell to the ground as he crawled upright.

"Jesus Christ on a cross! Useless sack of meat eats better than I do!" James hobbled after the horse, muttering bitterly to himself.

As the stableman limped out of sight, Ona made her way inside the barn. She found the pair of bay gelding drafts that moved the carriage and selected the larger of the two to carry her. The horse would not be fast, but it would be able to travel a long time. Ona slipped a halter onto the horse's face, buckling it into place and tossing a blanket on its back. She eyed the saddles, but had never fixed one on a horse before and opted to save on time. Ona clambered up the massive horse, and squeezed her legs around its middle, guiding it out the back gate.

Ona rode atop the horse, forcing herself to present a false air of confidence, despite her inward terror. She navigated the streets between throngs of people flowing steadily in and out of shops and the university, crowding around making it difficult to move through.

Slowly, houses and shops became sparse between stretches of field and pasture line with split rail or dry stacked stone fencing. As the city fell away in the horizon, Ona followed the narrowing dirt road into the coming night. She waited until it was after dark before she hung her sword from her hip, daring to cross a large field in order to reach a small creek. She parted thick stands of river cane, dipping her hands into the water and drinking clear, cool spring water for the first time since traveling to the city.

Heavy breathing filled Ona's ears, from not one but dozens of pairs of lungs. The sounds were loud and cumbersome, making soft noises altogether foreign from cattle or horses. Ona crossed the creek, relishing the cool water running across her toes. She peered through the thick cane break, casting her eyes on enormous bison curled up in deep sleep. Half a dozen wooly faces hidden in the tall grasses, some chewing even while they slept. Ona trembled before them and wept.

Chapter 16.

Ona traveled the dirt road out of Lexington until daybreak before stopping alongside the cane lined creek to rest. She scanned the banks of the wide stream, past her grazing horse until she found a patch of wild strawberries that could be harvested. She feasted from the morning's offerings and focused on what to name the horse rather than reliving the events of the past week.

Ona traveled all day along the cane lined creek, pausing once in a while to observe what appeared to be the same group of peculiar bison roaming across the tall bluegrass. Eventually, the man-sized grasses were confined by stone fencing and tamed under foot of grazing cattle. As she progressed, cloth tents sprang into the horizon, all clustered together in little camps dotting the hillside. Ona squinted, examining a distant crowd of people that must have numbered into the thousands. She approached the group cautiously, pulling back on the horse's reins to study the scene for a long time before she saw someone she recognized.

"Brother Solomon!" she shouted, waving her hand in the air at him. Brother Solomon raised his eyebrows in surprise, but a welcoming smile encouraged Ona to dismount. She navigated through the crowd until she was able to hitch the horse outback of a rural cabin church.

"Who are all these people?" Ona wondered aloud. There were throngs of people, both black and white, mingling among each other. They explored the gathering, finding dozens of wagons, horses and carriages lined up off the road. Ona made her way inside the two story cabin church, reading the sign out front: "Bourbon County Methodist Church," Ona's curiosity peaked.

The Methodist church in Calico was so hated it had been burned down once in attempt to run the Methodists off. They stayed anyhow. According to Molly Francis, they weren't the most popular denomination in Lexington, either. Curiosity pricked the hairs on the back of Ona's neck. This was the church hiding Enda Cambor.

She followed Brother Solomon inside the two-story log church. A hunched over man with wispy white hair stood up in front of the podium to announce the beginning of the service. His voice was deep and booming for such a small frame, and hundreds upon thousands who could not pack themselves inside the building surrounded the church listening at the windows. Never in all her life had she seen such a gathering as this revival. Ona squeezed between congregants inside the cabin church. It was the oddest sight she had ever seen: White meeting goers crowded the lower pews of the cabin while black members lined the upper balcony from wall to wall.

The preacher continued addressing the crowd in his deep voice. "Today is a day to celebrate, brothers and sisters." Ona observed Ruth sitting in the front row of the balcony. There were no seats remaining, so Brother Solomon squeezed his way upstairs, to stand beside his wife. A familiar set of blue eyes and messy brown hair leaned over the balcony to watch the sermon. His eyes were intently focused on the preacher who orchestrated such an unusual gathering.

"Today we gather to honor the Father of each and every one of us. Today we are here to celebrate the love of God with our brothers and sisters in Christ. Whether your flesh resembles my flesh," the preacher gestured out into the room around him, "or the flesh of another, we are all His children, born of one blood."

The clapping of the crowd became deafening. Ona looked out the balcony window, seeing the throngs of people gathered outside, cheering for the preacher.

The preacher continued, "Whether you're Methodist," He paused between each word in his list, "Unitarian, Evangelical, Presbyterian, Quaker, or Shaker. We have all come together this day to celebrate our unity in the living Spirit of Christ. And let me tell you what, folks–" He took a breath, smiling into the crowd. "–If you ain't never been to a camp meeting before, y'all are in for something special." The crowd whooped and hollered, cheering him on.

Ona's brow furrowed, caught between laying eyes on Enda Cambor, and pausing to be swept up in the radical words of the Methodist preacher. Ona's feet carried her to the staircase, gliding her fingers over the smooth wooden banister of the balcony. She kept her ear turned towards the pulpit, and her eyes locked on Enda Cambor. Disgruntled whispers stirred among the balcony crowd and pews scraped loudly against the wooden floor, making room for her to pass through. Ruth looked up from her seat, locking eyes with Ona. Ruth sat gingerly on the pew, not leaning against its hard, wooden back. She nodded her head in acknowledgment ever so slightly, before tugging on Enda Cambor's shirt sleeve. His gaze followed her outstretched arm until his blue eyes locked with Ona's, clutching the balcony railing below.

The stairs to the balcony creaked once more, and a white man ushered at the staircase for Ona to follow. She drank in Enda's presence, before turning to face the man.

"We must not challenge the order of God, miss. Each belongs in their proper place. This seating belongs to negros. It's time to come away from the balcony now." He spoke low into her ear in a voice that was not chiding, but seemingly attempting to educate Ona in manners she was not familiar. Ona nodded slowly, following after him. Her feet dragged like dead weights beneath her.

Enda eased toward the stair case, choosing to watch the sermons from halfway up the balcony steps. Ona chose to hover near the base of the balcony steps, daring to brush his outstretched fingers along the backside of the railing. Enda eased down a step, ever so slightly nodding his head in the direction of the door. Ona exited first, and Enda quietly followed after. Twenty thousand eyes were turned towards the little cabin on the hill side, or grouped in little tent clusters with wooden stages carrying on dozens of sermons across the fields. No one paid attention to Enda Cambor and Ona Christie behind the mammoth bur oak stretching its wide limbs across the grassland.

"How did you get here?" Enda held both of Ona's hands in his.

"Ruth and Brother Solomon said you was here, so I came. How did you escape Billy Titus? I thought you been sold." Sounds of the jailed women across from her cell flooded her memory, colliding with each face at Cheapside Market replaced with an image of Enda's own visage. She broke down into sobs, almost mistrusting the Enda before her to be an illusion. Enda wrapped his arms around her, stroking her hair. "Let's not talk about this here. We are safe, so long as we are here to worship." He leaned in close, kissing Ona on her forehead, her mouth, her cheeks.

The sermons continued all day long and even past sunset. Different preachers from different denominations took turns speaking; even Brother Solomon stood up and delivered a sermon to the masses. There was a break for food, where folks gathered around at campfires to for supper. Dishes of hot ham and beans with cornbread and sorghum were passed around in the group where Ona and Enda ate with Ruth and Brother Solomon. Hundreds of groups dined together around fires scattered across the fields surrounding the rural church.

When the sermons quieted down after supper, the music began. Hymns of praise Ona had never known before filled her spirit with love. Ona had never seen instruments used in church before, except for Enda's family when they gathered around the fire to tell Bible stories. Banjos harmonized with guitars and fiddlers into raucous music that filled the fields with a joyful noise. The instruments lifted nearly twenty thousand voices from muddied fields up into the heavens where songs of God's love filled the space between every person standing, warming hearts and connecting souls underneath the stars of the chilly spring night.

For three weeks while the camp meeting carried on, Ona and Enda shared a tent with Ruth and Solomon. Ona slept on the cold earth with only the horse blanket for warmth. Enda curled up in borrowed sheets on the ground. They listened to the testimonies of lawyers, preachers, farmers and mid wives step forward to proclaim how God moved through them as instruments on this earth.

They were taught lessons of stewardship, to be neighborly, humble, and forgiving. During the moonlit sermons, some folks were so overcome with the Spirit they fell into fits of tears and hollering, begging for forgiveness and mercy. Others became electrified with the spirit of worship and music so that they spoke in unfamiliar tongues, delivering messages directly sent from God. They convulsed and shook, as if their bodies could not very well tolerate the Holy Spirit stirring within them.

Ona was among dozens to lift her hand up toward the heavens. She marched timidly toward the preachers praying over sinners who had not yet been dedicated to the Lord. Feelings of overwhelming compassion and acceptance flooded her heart. She joined the numbers of the baptized, being dipped under the same shallow creek water that the bison shared.

As time progressed, some wagons and carriages began to leave while others remained behind to continue worship. Each day more arrived to replace those that departed. On the eve of Ruth and Brother Solomon's departure, Ona spread the horse blanket over the dew-covered grass. She sat down beside Enda, letting the tent opening drape shut. It was a rare moment since arriving to the camp meeting that they were alone. Enda wrapped his arm around her, kissing the top of her head first, then her lips.

"Think we should stay one more night?" Ona asked.

"Let's head back to Fannie in the morning.

Chapter 17.

Enda and Ona spent an entire six days on the journey back to Calico. It could have been made in four, but the poor horse was weary to near exhaustion and they were drained from the events since Lexington. They bade farewell to the Bluegrass and traveled through knobs country camping out under the stars each night. As the hills transformed into steep, uncut mountainside they were soothed by the familiar forest chatter of colorful spring songbirds.

"Do you really think it's safe to go back? After what the mayor did and all." Ona asked.

"I'm not sure exactly if I will stay. But I would like to see my granny Trinity at least, to say goodbye," Enda mused.

"But where will you go? You're just a runaway without papers."

"What?" Enda seemed confused. It dawned on Ona that she had never mentioned her meeting with Mr. Kegley. She recounted the way that Enda could be safe as a free man through notarizing the freedman papers.

"I suppose the whole thing is dead useless now," Ona concluded dully. Enda was quiet for a long while.

They passed through North Hill Trade and the inn appeared warmly lit. Ona could smell delicious smoked meats coming from inside. She could see the enormous figure of Marcus Morgan, the owner of the inn at North Hill Trade, working bent over, chopping up great pieces of wood to burn. He squinted up into the light upon hearing the horse and waved in greeting when he recognized Ona.

"Well if it isn't the flower girl herself." Mr. Morgan admired, standing up straight from the wood pile and cracking his back. He was dripping with sweat under the morning sun.

"Mr. Morgan!" Ona smiled, reaching her arms around his broad shoulders for a sticky hug.

"You look terrible, young lady!" He laughed, scratching his head. "But you've got some light about you now. Is this the slave you went hunting after?" Enda stiffened up but did not say a word.

"This is Enda Cambor. He's a free man."

"Well boy, that's certainly some turnaround from the state I saw this here young lady leave in. And you're going back to Calico? Sure that's a good idea?"

"Just to say goodbye, sir." Enda Cambor kept his eyes on the ground.

"Very good." Mr. Morgan nodded. "And you'll go back to your family?" He shifted his gaze to Ona.

"I'm not sure," Ona spoke honesty. "I fled house arrest in Lexington. I think they will look for me in Calico." Enda shot her a glance shaking his head ever so slightly, warning her against speaking on the matter.

"You got arrested in Lexington?" Mr. Morgan boomed. A hearty laugh escaped him, and he gathered himself after clearing his throat.

"Would you two like a drink? That horse is dead on its feet, let's get some feed into it and sit down."

Enda sat at the edge of the tavern porch, silent and listening carefully to each word spoken. He observed Mr. Morgan cautiously from the corners of his eyes. Ona eased into a rocking chair, following Mr. Morgan's behavior, and his wife brought them all sour beers. Ona gaped openly at Mr. Marcus' wife. She was Indian and dressed well in western attire with a satin ribbon for her straw woven bonnet.

"Thank you, Mrs. Morgan," Enda said simply. Mrs. Morgan smiled politely before returning to the tavern interior.

"My wife cannot speak," Mr. Morgan said. "Her tongue was cut out when her village was raided back in Virginia. She's Shawnee, you know. When I met her, I had seen no other woman as beautiful, save for my own Portuguese born mother." Mr. Morgan sipped his drink.

"My wife did not want to marry me, but her father urged her to reconsider. I begged her for months. And finally, one day, she accepted. Quite possibly just to shut me up!" He chuckled. "That was fifteen years ago. But enough of memories. Miss Christie, tell me about this business in Lexington."

Ona haltingly came forward with her testimony once more, hesitating when directly questioned by Mr. Morgan if she actually committed the crime of stabbing Billy Titus and nearly killing him.

"It's alright young lady, I won't tell a soul. I get that code of honor from Mrs. Morgan." He winked. "Trust me, I am no friend of the law. They tried to sell me south once, claimed I was part colored. I had to prove my parents just to get out of jail. They're all crooked up there." He shook his head, disgusted.

"Speaking plainly, yes. He trafficked Enda, a free man. He caught hold of me and wouldn't let me go. I didn't know what would happen." Ona spoke slowly.

"And they put you on house arrest until they get his grandfather's testimony?" Mr. Morgan asked.

"Yes."

"And he's the one who sold the boy in the first place?" Mr. Morgan gestured towards Enda.

"That's right." Ona nodded.

"How did it come to pass that boy managed to get out from under the dealer in the first place?"

Ona lowered her gaze to her hands resting in her lap. Enda had not spoken of how he managed to flee from his trafficking. He tossed and mumbled and sweated in restless sleep most nights during the camp meeting, and it occurred to Ona that perhaps she should not ask.

Enda cleared his throat, lacing his fingers together to hold them steady. "Billy Titus picked up his partner while we was still at North Hill Trade. They shackled me with heavy chains and collected more people to be sold on the way back to Lexington. The two of them slept in shifts while we traveled to Lexington. One night Billy Titus' partner had drunk too much corn whiskey and fallen asleep.

"That's when I was able to knock his gun away and strangle him with our chains. When Billy Titus woke up, we attacked. We was beating on him with everything inside us. I used the butt of the gun. When Billy Titus surrendered the keys to the cuffs, he could scarcely move. We all scattered through the forest. Some stayed back at the camp site. They was fighting over his gun, his horses, and his money. I didn't want no part of it, I just wanted to be far away from that place."

Chills ran down Ona's spine, and she met his gaze with an unsteady voice. "How did you meet Brother Solomon?"

"I didn't, he found me. Two of us left one way, the man took me to the camp meeting in Paris on account of two Quakers inviting him a while back and he knew it to be a safe place. It wasn't safe to go back to Calico, and I didn't know where else to go, so I followed him. I met Brother Solomon that way, and he remembered my name from you. He said you was arrested for killing Billy Titus. I had no idea you was going to show up in Paris when you did. It must have been God himself bringing us to that meeting."

Mr. Morgan leaned forward with interest. "Well I'll be," He laughed. "And you took off from house arrest after they told you to stay? Well," Mr. Morgan sighed. "Honestly speaking young lady, I would not make plans to build a life in Calico." Ona's heart tightened, thinking of Fannie. She nodded, breathing slowly.

Mr. Morgan rubbed his fingers to his temples, thinking with his eyes closed for several minutes.

"Boy, you ever minded hogs before?" Mr. Morgan finally asked. Enda turned to face him, nodding slowly.

"I used to help my Uncle Elijah push hogs through the woods to graze on chestnuts every fall before slaughter. We worked with a local man, Jeremiah Sunday for about five years."

"And how many head did you keep after?"

"About twenty."

Mr. Morgan nodded slowly. "Think you could keep up with three times that?"

"Oh, sure enough."

"Our keeper quit on us, left for better farming west of here. He stayed up in a cabin by the hogs, oh about a mile or so from here inward the woods. We keep them far off because the guests don't like the stink. It's a lot to keep after."

312

"What all do you keep after besides hogs?"

"Well, the keeper lives in the cabin to tend the hogs. He rears the piglets and spends all summer and fall moving to keep them fed. We plant turnips and corn around the property to keep the sows fed through winter up in the pens. You'd be responsible for that, too."

"Is there pay?" Enda asked.

"Payment is board at the cabin, and meat to last the winter."

"When can I start?"

"My son has been out at the cabin for some two weeks now. Hasn't been to school a day since the last man quit. We'll have you as soon as you're able."

"I can start today," Enda concluded. Ona coughed, nodding to the horse and the road back to Calico.

"Or later this week." Enda corrected.

"Two days should give time to wrap up your affairs in Calico. I will see you then at sun rise." Mr. Morgan smiled.

The ride from North Hill Trade to Calico allowed just enough time for their weary bones to be jolted awake with nerves.

"Do you want to come with me to the cabin?" Ona asked as they neared town.

"I imagine I should." Enda responded. "At least for now until I get things sorted out."

The paths and trees she recognized as they came up on the town did little to welcome her. The poor old draft horse moved at a painfully slow rate, so that Enda wondered aloud if they were not better off to walk alongside it and relieve some of the burden in trying to get to the cabin sometime before winter came again. Enda led the horse through the muddy alleys of Calico. The horse flicked its tail, swatting at flies stirred up from moldy cabbage leaves on the ground. They passed the backside of Rue Royale but saw none of Enda's family outside.

"Likely better off this way. I should come back at night."

"How long will it be like this?" Ona asked. "Ducking heads, moving about from alley to alley."

"So far, this is no different than most other days," Enda shrugged his shoulders. He had no answer for her. Enda had grown increasingly irritable and quiet on the day's journey back to Calico. Ona relieved Enda of walking the horse some time ago and was just trying to make it back to Fannie. Ona paused at the track of land where she was first introduced to John Francis and performed her first water dowsing.

"Do you think it's wrong for a Christian to be a water witcher?" Ona furrowed her brow.

"The Bible says witchcraft is a sin," Enda reflected. "Granny Trinity calls it remedies. Fannie calls it tinctures. You helped all them kids when they got the fever. You help other folks find good water they can drink and build a house up on. How can it be a sin if in your heart all you do is helping others? Ain't that what Jesus commanded from us? 'Do unto others as you would have them do unto you. Love thy neighbor as thyself.'" Enda laced his fingers through Ona's, bringing her hand up to his lips and kissing it gently.

"It don't look like sin to me, Little America. It seem like God gave you a gift and you do wrong by Him not to use it to help others the way you've already been taught to."

"It is important to me to keep this life Fannie gave me. I always took pride in being apprenticed to the granny witch." Ona explained slowly, a smile tugging at her lips.

"You should. It's a special gift you have, Ona America, and you honor God when you use it to serve his people."

Both Enda and Ona breathed a little easier once they made it out of downtown Calico. The evening turned brighter with the sun warming their backs for the climb up the steep hill to reach Calico Ridge. They passed Ona's old school at the Methodist church and she smiled humorlessly. Upon setting eyes on the little log building, she could almost hear the booming voice of her former teacher.

Ona reflected upon men like Horace Wexler, who preach the religion of God without truly ever seeing the Spirit of God, or ever really experiencing the grace of God, or understanding the love of God. Men like Horace Wexler lacked any sense of compassion and so have not experienced firsthand the very nature of God on which they so often taught. And somehow Horace Wexler, a man so reviled in Ona's heart, became a creature of such sadness for whom she felt

315

great pity towards for having never known what it meant to experience such love.

It was dusk when they turned down the familiar dirt path leading up to the Christie cabin. Ona led the poor horse to the stream out behind the cabin, tying him to a tree near a thick patch of spring forbs. Ona breathed deeply, feeling herself relax a little for the first time since before Enda was taken. A few early fireflies flitted in and out among the forest, lighting their path through the trees. Ona pushed against the cabin door, registering the familiar scraping of heavy oak across the dusty dirt floor. A creaky rocking chair, well-loved and presently occupied, became suddenly still and silent.

"I was just a-wondering when y'all were going to come home," Fannie spoke in between puffs of her pipe tobacco. Tears brimmed over Ona's eyes and she flung her arms around the old woman. Fannie stood up slowly, stretching with her hands on her back when she spied Enda Cambor.

"Glad you made it back in one piece as well," Fannie breathed, easing back into her rocking chair and resuming her pipe. "Where have you been?" Ona recounted the tale from her account, including her arrest and the attack on Billy Titus.

"You come back to me wanted for arrest in Lexington?" Fannie whistled lowly, chuckling to herself. "You found the boy though, Cricket. That's real good, even if he managed to make it out from under Billy Titus on his own accord."

"And you? What's your say in all this?" Fannie focused her attention onto Enda Cambor, who answered her honestly.

"It was the worst experience I ever gone through," he spoke haltingly. "And I ain't much better for being out of it."

"What you mean you're not any better off now than working as a slave?" Fannie inquired.

"I don't got no papers, Fannie. I ain't free. And now they will be looking for me, as one who run away."

Fannie clicked her tongue, mulling over his words. "You ought to just go ahead and fill the things out," Fannie suggested.

"We can't, Fannie!" Ona exclaimed. "If we get caught without that seal, we all be in jail and Enda could be hung!"

"Cricket, we'll get that seal easy enough. There are three notaries in Calico and we see two of them on a regular basis." Fannie countered.

"Oh yes, because the mayor himself will certainly sign Enda's papers after the dirty deal he done." Ona rolled her eyes.

"He don't have to know a thing. We just need his seal is all. And a little luck— which, I might add," Fannie met Enda's eyes. "You must be chock-full of it to come round back this far."

Fannie's words gave Ona reason to pause. Fannie, when is Virginia Cambor's next medication due?"

"Whenever I decide to make the trip down. My knees is getting so bad anymore." Fannie rubbed her bones gingerly from the rocking chair.

Fannie, Enda and Ona took to the dusty dirt road, traveling down the steep mountainside into town. Ona touted her father's gun and sword while Enda kept the freedman papers tucked into his shirt. Enda and Ona parted ways with Fannie when the alleys opened up. Fannie walked down the brick streets of Rue Royale while Enda and Ona crept around back, toward Granny Trinity's.

Ona removed her weapons, leaving them leaned up against the back of the house while Enda breathed slowly, easing open a back door into the home's scullery. Ona tiptoed behind him, fearing to breathe too loudly lest the voices of Fannie and Virginia Cambor give way to an unnatural pause.

They followed after each other, and Ona pointed at the little door she knew led up the stairs from the back end of the house. Their fingers brushed in the narrow stairwell and a chill ran down Ona's spine, giving her an involuntary tremor. Enda took his time traveling up the steps, working to make little more sound than a mouse. Once upstairs, it was a matter of trying every door knob and peering into every room.

Most of the rooms were filled with four poster beds, fine carpets and ornate storage trunks. Ona tried a door at the end of a hallway, frowning when she discovered it was locked. She peered through the skeleton key, spying a handsome study on the other side of the door. Ona gestured toward the door helplessly, and Enda examined it carefully, removing a jack knife from his pocket. He squinted one eye through the lock, feeling with his blade and relying the same precision used to skin a perfect pelt. Ona heard a faint click before Enda tried his hand on the doorknob, exhaling slowly and wiping the sweat from his brow.

The study was decorated in carpets with elaborate patterns and deep maroon and gold upholstery. The room was centered with an imposing desk made of dark cherry wood. Enda slipped his fingers over the drawer handles, sliding them open one by one to examine the contents. Ona's eyes scanned the top of the desk carefully. Enda opened a small wooden box containing a wealth greater than all the timber on the mountain and more valuable than all the salt underneath it.

It was a simple seal of two men clasping arms and the words "United We Stand Divided We Fall" placed along the border and "Kentucky Notary of the Public" on the opposing border. Enda carefully drew out his freedman papers from his shirt, laying them out on the table. Ona dipped a feathered quill into a small vial of ink, carefully examining the papers before her. The top of the document read, "Deed of Manumission." Ona took great care writing methodically, relating her words in a hushed voice to Enda who leaned rigid over her shoulder, watching each stroke of her hand.

"Enda Cambor, negro grandson of Maxwell Cambor, mayor of the village Calico in Clay County, Kentucky issues on this day of May 29, 1806 that Enda Cambor is a freed man under God." Ona exhaled slowly, proud that her script was passively attractive. Perhaps Horace Wexler had taught her after all. Her eyes scanned the text at the bottom of the deed and she read aloud the already-written words. "I serve this affidavit that the slave in question carry on a freed man." There were lines at the bottom of the document, identifying where there should be signatures of the slave to be emancipated, the slave owner, the notary, and for a witness.

Ona considered the names that could fill inside the blank. The first line was easy enough. Enda Cambor left a nearly legible mark in his uncoordinated scrawl. Below that Ona signed on behalf of the Mayor Cambor, smiling that he was at least legally acknowledging his grandson, even if he didn't know it. She signed again for Mr. Kegley, the lawyer from Lexington, and finally for the witness none other than John Francis, who had become a dear and unlikely friend.

In between the forged signatures of Mr. Kegley and the Mayor, she melted a drop of hot red sealing wax with which she used the Mayor's seal of the notary of the public to finalize the deed into a living document. Ona's fingers shook as she returned the quill, replacing the seal inside its little wooden box and gently closing the study drawer.

"That's it," Enda whispered. He held the paper in his hand, watching the wax dry before folding it back into his shirt. He turned to face Ona, brushing a loose lock of her wild curls out of her eyes before kissing her gently on the forehead.

"We ought to get back," Ona whispered.

They crept silently down the back set of stairs before peering around the corner. All was quiet in the Cambor home. Ona supposed Fannie must have gone on home. She exited out the back door, turning at the sound of shattering porcelain crashing against the wooden floor. Enda was frozen in the doorway, with little Mary staring wide eyed up at them. They must have nearly scared her to death.

"You idiot! If I find out you broke my china, girl, you are going to get it!" The shrill voice of Virginia Cambor echoed from the front rooms. Mary's little knobby legs began to shake underneath her as Ona pulled Enda out of the home, closing the door behind her. Ona pretended she did not hear the small girl's screams ringing from inside the house when they opened the door to Granny Trinity's dwelling.

"Well?" Fannie asked impatiently. She sat at the little wooden table across from Granny Trinity, with two cups of sassafras tea steeping in front of them.

Enda withdrew his papers, showing them to Fannie and Granny Trinity. Ona read aloud once more the contents of the document.

"I can't hardly fathom this." Granny Trinity's voice shook, and she held the paper in her hands for several minutes in silence, gripping Enda's hand tightly.

"Boy, you must fly from here with this opportunity God has blessed you with."

"She's right," Fannie nodded in agreement.

"I'm set to start working tomorrow." Enda smiled. "About ten miles away from this place."

"Does it pay you money?" Granny Trinity asked. "Real money for real work."

"It pays in board and food." Enda commented. "It's far away from towns, too. I'd rather it be like this."

"Where will you stay, Miss Christie?" Granny Trinity asked.

"I'm not certain. I can't stay in Calico for very long." Ona frowned.

"If you go with Enda, you must be something cautious. It's a serious crime for a white and a negro to be affiliated. But if you live out of town a ways, you might could keep it secret," Fannie spoke thoughtfully.

"Use your water witching just like down here." Granny Trinity encouraged. "Make tinctures, find water. Towns need folk like you. Think on it."

"But who would stay with you, Fannie?" Ona asked.

"You know them McDaniels keep us close. And that old scoundrel, the Reverend Johnson, huh." Fannie spat chaw on the floor. "He won't let me die so long as he has breath in his lungs to argue with."

"You best get on now. It'll get harder to leave once the mayor comes back into town." Granny Trinity clucked. She stood barely to his chest and he had to bend down for her to kiss his cheek.

Ona wrapped her arms around Fannie and was returned with a tight embrace.

"I love you, Fannie."

"Be good, Cricket."

It was not more than an hour later when Ona and Enda found themselves scrambling across the creek that ran past Jeremiah Sunday's place where Enda collected his bow and arrows, and animal pelt blankets stored in the shack.

They stopped and prayed to God once they made it out of well out of town. They prayed for the health of Fannie and Granny Trinity. They prayed for the McDaniels and Iris and Elijah and little Mary. They prayed for Awenasa, hopefully safely tucked away deep in Carolina. They prayed for themselves, and for what the future may hold as they marched toward North Hill Trade and the little cabin behind the inn bursting with possibility.

About the Author:

R.R. Roberts works outdoors in the field of environmental and agriculture education. When not writing, she enjoys going to see live music, scoping out yard sales, and taking day trips to different natural and historical sites around the state. R.R. Roberts lives in Kentucky with her two cats, hound mutt, and house rabbit.

14395712R00204

Made in the USA
Lexington, KY
06 November 2018